Broken Parts Included

Alyson Root

J&M Books

For permission requests, write to a.rootauthor@alysonroot.com

Published by J&M Books

Lytchett House, 13 Freeland Park, Wareham Road, Poole, Dorset, BH16 6FA

Print ISBN: 978-1-917785-04-4

Ebook ISBN: 978-1-917785-19-8

Developmental Edit & Cover design by:

Tara Sullivan, The Write Gal Co.

www.thewritegal.com

Line & Copy Edit By:

Linda Slate

To all the perfectly imperfect.

Broken Parts Included is written in British English.

<u>1</u>

Lydia smiled to herself. Now wasn't a time to smile, but she couldn't help it. She had correctly guessed Tim's motivations, and even if those motivations sucked, there was still the satisfaction of being right.

Well, he'd lasted longer than her last partner. What was it, four months? Not bad.

"So, you're not mad?" Tim fiddled with the napkin lying to the right of his dinner plate. Lydia gazed at him for a second, taking in his features and his sweaty brow. At least he looked sorry for inviting her to a fancy restaurant to dump her.

"No point in being mad. Thank you for being honest."

"Wow, this is the easiest break-up ever." He smiled.

That's because I'm so used to it.

"Shall we split the check?" Lydia was done with the evening. They may have only eaten the starter, but she was in no mood to wade through the rest of dinner.

"No, I'll get it. I think it's the least I can do." Tim raised his hand, signalling the server. Lydia didn't even wait for the bill to arrive before she donned her coat, gave Tim a pat on the shoulder, and left.

The high street was busy, which was to be expected on a Friday night. Popping into a bar to drown her sorrows flitted across Lydia's mind, but she dismissed the idea. No, she needed to get home, have a long hot shower, curl up under her weighted blanket on the sofa, and binge watch *Sex Education*.

Twenty minutes later, Lydia dropped her keys in the bowl on the sideboard next to her front door. A wide smile spread across her face as soon as Monty's paws echoed through the small flat. The waddling ball of fur skittered as fast as his legs would take him, until his front paws were planted firmly on Lydia's thighs.

Monty was a mutt, through and through. The rescue centre thought he was part Kerry Blue and part Irish Wheaten, with some sort of terrier thrown in for good measure. Lydia didn't care if he was part unicorn. Monty was true, loyal, and loved her for exactly who she was.

"Come on, Monty." Making their way down the small hall, Lydia opened the back door. Monty slipped out and began his nightly routine of checking the perimeter of his tiny kingdom. The garden was the size of a postage stamp, but at least they had some greenery. *Advantage of a ground-floor flat.*

Knowing her bestie was happy outside, Lydia shed her coat, hanging it on the back of her solitary kitchen chair. Flipping the kettle switch, Lydia prepared her teacup. As the water boiled, she dug her phone from her coat pocket, navigated to her contacts, and deleted Tim's number. How many was that now? Six, maybe seven people that couldn't deal with Lydia and her "issue." Scoffing to herself, Lydia couldn't believe she'd even bothered to date again, not after Mary. Maybe she was a glutton for punishment.

"Monty, come on lad, it's sofa time." Monty's yip told Lydia he was on his way. They loved nothing more than snuggling on the couch together. Her hot shower could wait for a little while. Lydia needed to feel love, instead of rejection. That was her general feeling most days, and she was sick of it.

"That's it, Monty, I'm done." Monty cocked his head, clearly listening. "No more men, no more women, no more! Just you, me, and occasionally, your Aunt Fe."

Fe, Lydia's older sister, was the closest thing she had to a best friend. Over the years, Lydia's social life had shrivelled to nothing. Pain and bloating were a real mood killer for most people.

"Speak of the devil," she muttered as the buzzing from her phone cut through the silence. "Hey, sis."

"Hey, sorry, I didn't know if you'd still be out with Tim."

"Nope."

"Oh fuck. It happened again, didn't it?"

What could Lydia say? Of course it happened again. They always left.

"Yeah. But it's whatever. I'm over it and I'm done."

"Done?"

"Yeah, done with dating. I've got enough on my plate."

"Oh, sweetie, don't say that. You'll find the one."

"Nope. And that's fine. I have you and Monty. That's more than some people have."

"Lyds—"

"Don't, Fe. Really...don't."

"Fine. Do you want me to come over?"

"No, I'm jumping in the shower and then Monty and I are watching the new series of *Sex Education.*"

"Oh, it's so good. Eric—"

"No spoilers!"

"Blurgh, fine, I'll call you tomorrow. Love you, baby sis."

"Night. Love you too."

Setting her phone down, Lydia pushed her rising emotions back down. She'd cried enough tears to fill the local pool. They solved nothing, so why bother? Tim was a nice guy, but Lydia knew he wasn't the one. She also knew he wouldn't put up with her "issue" for long.

"Stay there, boy. I'll be back soon." Dropping several kisses on Monty's head, Lydia left him curled up while she took that well-needed shower. The bathroom was the size of a broom cupboard, but the water temperature was above freezing and the pressure was good, so things could be worse.

Stripping off her dress and underwear, Lydia took in a deep breath before lifting her gaze to the full-length mirror hung on the back of the door.

Standing at five foot three inches, Lydia was far from tall. Her long chestnut hair hung down her back. Large breasts sat high on her chest. At least she had those going for her, not that they were much good when her hormones were playing, silly buggers. Sighing, Lydia continued her observations: Creamy skin adorned with beauty spots. Wide hips and thick thighs. A small waist that led up to wide shoulders; not as wide as a swimmer, but enough they completed Lydia's hourglass figure.

Gently caressing her face, Lydia felt the first prick of tears. Her skin was clear except for the area near her chin where she suffered with hormonal blemishes. No amount of expensive creams or facial masks got rid of them. Thank God for makeup.

Wiping her eyes, Lydia did her level best to shake off the black cloud that was trying with all its might to descend on her. No. She wouldn't let it. She wouldn't let the sight of extra weight, blemishes, or anything else imperfect on her body, bring her down. If she did, Lydia feared she'd never get out from under it.

Smoothing shower gel over her body, she finally felt her mood mellow. Steam filled every inch of the bathroom, fogging the mirror.

At least I don't have to look at myself again.

Clean and dry, Lydia trundled back to the living room. Monty hadn't moved an inch. His little body curled in an almost perfect ball.

"Move up, let me squeeze on." Monty shifted slightly, allowing Lydia to curl up next to him. The television came to life and Lydia let herself drift off, her mind filled with nothing more than fictional characters and funny storylines.

In the past, Lydia would have obsessed about a breakup, spending hours analysing what she could have done differently. But now, she didn't waste the energy. It was time to see the forest for the trees. Lydia wouldn't find love and that, was that.

Eyes drooping, she finally gave in to sleep. It wasn't unusual for the duo to sleep on the couch. There were countless times she'd woken with a stiff back and cricked neck, courtesy of her sofa.

This time, however, it was Monty's soggy kisses that stirred her from slumber. It was still dark out, but the microwave timer told Lydia it was almost seven. Bloody winter.

"Morning," she mumbled to her pooch, who was eager to carry out his morning business.

Rolling off the sofa in a less than graceful manner, Lydia set about her morning routine. She liked routine; it gave her a sense of stability. And the one thing Lydia craved was stability, ideally in her hormone levels, but that was just laughable at this point.

Checking the time again, she cursed herself for taking so long to get ready. Ramming a piece of whole-wheat toast in her mouth, she ruffled Monty's head and headed out the door.

Working a Saturday shift wasn't so bad. This way, she wasn't forced to spend the day in her own company. Yeah, Fe would come over if called, but that would only lead to emotional conversations that Lydia wanted to avoid.

"Morning, sunshine," Cathy shouted from further down the street. Slowing her stride, Lydia waited for the older woman to catch up. "You on shift as well?"

"Yup, nine 'til four. You?"

"Same, love. Oh, I'm glad it's you with me today. I worked with Harrison yesterday. My God, that kid is dumber than a bag of rocks."

Lydia tittered. "He's working today too. He's an interesting character."

"No, he's not. That's the problem."

"He's just shy, Cathy. The poor lad has to work with us. I was shy when I first started too, if you remember."

"I do," Cathy laughed. "You were so quiet. Now look at you!"

To most people, Lydia was a fun, outgoing woman. For the most part, that was a correct assessment. What her colleagues didn't see were the tears, frustration, and pain. Lydia kept that to herself. Fe, their mum, and Halle—Fe's best friend—were the only ones who knew the full extent of Lydia's misery.

"We'll coax him out of his shell. Don't give up on him yet, Cathy."

They'd just rounded the corner when Cathy spotted the bus pulling up to their stop. "Bugger, come on. We need to make a dash for it."

Planting a hand across her chest, Lydia set off at a jog. Her bra was *not* made for running. The ladies would be all over the place if she didn't keep them locked down with her arm.

"Made it," Cathy huffed, her face red. The morning air was chilly and a light frost covered the ground. "Thanks for waiting," she directed to the bus driver, who was stealing—not so subtle—glances at Lydia's chest.

Cathy paid both their fares and ushered Lydia to the back of the bus, away from the driver's wandering eyes. "Ugh, men."

Lydia barked out a laugh. Cathy was a known man-eater. "Yeah, men," she giggled.

"The saying's true, you know: Can't live with them; can't live without them."

"No hunk on the horizon, then?"

"I didn't say that." Cathy winked, dramatically tossing her golden hair over one shoulder. At one time, Lydia had a slight crush on Cathy. She was extremely good looking, and even though she was ten years-plus Lydia's senior, she was captivating. The crush fizzled as fast as it started, though.

"So, how did the date with Tim go?"

Great.

"He dumped me." No point in lying, Lydia reasoned.

"Twat," Cathy huffed. "I swear, men are all the same. See a stunning body and that's it. As soon as things get serious, they cut and run."

Lydia wasn't going to disagree. Most of her ex-partners were honest enough to admit Lydia's body was the first thing they saw. But in the end, her curves weren't enough.

"I'm over it. Time to focus on me." And it was true. Lydia had to focus on herself now. She had another doctor's appointment on Monday, and she was determined to get him to listen.

"Good for you, honey. Do you want to have lunch together? I'm in the blue zone today."

"Green zone for me," Lydia replied.

"Want to swap? I know you like the dinosaurs."

Grinning, Lydia bumped Cathy's shoulder. "Yeah, thanks."

Lydia had worked for The Natural History Museum in London for six years. As a visitor assistant, Lydia spent her days chatting with the public, directing them to parts of the museum and answering questions. The salary wasn't great, but it was enough, especially with the money willed to her by her grandad. Technically, she didn't need to work, but that wasn't an option. Lydia needed a regular job, with regular hours, and people to socialise with.

Fe, on the other hand, took full advantage of her large inheritance and became a stay-at-home mother of three. Triplets on the first try. Fe's husband was a computer nerd and earned a very tidy sum. They were set for life. Their house was enormous and their car was flashy. It baffled Fe that her sister still lived in a tiny, rundown flat, but as Lydia explained, it was her home. It had been for nearly fifteen years.

What Lydia didn't tell Fe was that her heart was set on buying a house with a partner, creating a family, and settling down. A flash of hurt seized Lydia's lungs, making her gasp slightly.

"You alright, love?" Cathy placed a hand gently on Lydia's thigh, bringing her back to their conversation.

"Yeah, fine. Sorry, zoned out. Anyway, I'd love to have lunch. Harrison is in the red zone today. We should invite him, too."

"Didn't we just have a conversation about how boring he is?"

"Yes, and we also said we would coax him out of his shell."

"Fine, but if I fall asleep when he talks, that's on you."

The pair nattered for the rest of the journey. Cathy filled Lydia in on her latest piece of ass—her words, not Lydia's. Lydia told Cathy she needed to stop watching so much American TV. Cathy was from Wales, where nobody was referred to as a 'piece of ass'. It wasn't the British way. Cathy invited Lydia over for a girls' night on the following weekend, which Lydia happily accepted. Truth be told, Cathy just wanted to see Monty, but that was fine.

Before long, the bus stopped. Lydia and Cathy began the five-minute walk to the museum. The sun peeked out from behind menacing-looking clouds. Lydia prayed the heavens would remain closed until they were safely inside.

"Tea?" Cathy shouted from the breakroom. Lydia stuffed her coat and bag in her locker, popping her phone in her pocket—on silent, of course. She didn't want another reaming from Norris, the world's most unreasonable boss. Lydia loved everything and everyone at the museum, aside from him, and that was because he was constantly on her case. And not just hers; everyone's. Nobody did their job well enough for Norris. He was just an impossible man to please, miserable with his life, and on a mission to bring everyone down with him.

"Just a small one. We haven't got much time."

"Hobnob?"

Lydia glanced down at her belly. She'd been eating healthy for months, cutting out sugar and processed food, and still, her weight fluctuated. She may as well enjoy a bloody biscuit.

"Sure. Are they chocolate?"

"Don't insult me," Cathy tutted.

The break room door squeaked open. Harrison shuffled in, his gaze averted to the floor. "Morning."

His mumbling was an issue. Especially when he had to communicate clearly to the masses as a day job.

"Harrison, good morning. Ready for a fun day?" Lydia spoke clearly, hoping her upbeat tone would rub off on him.

"Sure, I like the red zone. Full of cool stuff."

"Indeed, it is," Lydia replied enthusiastically. "So, how're you finding it? Enjoying the work so far?"

"Yeah."

"And getting on with people?"

"Yeah."

Good grief, he was hard work. Lydia disagreed with Cathy's assessment of the young man. He wasn't boring, just painfully shy. Possibly even suffering from a form of social anxiety. Lydia noticed the way he fisted his shirt as they conversed.

"Well, we're happy to have you. Do you want to have lunch with Cathy and me today?"

Harrison's eyes flitted to Cathy, and Lydia had to suppress a grin. His eyes made a beeline for Cathy's very shapely arse. No wonder the kid was a nervous wreck. He had a crush.

"Um...really?"

"Yeah, we'd love to get to know you better, Harrison. Isn't that right, Cathy?"

Cathy twirled around from the kettle, with a large and very fake grin plastered on her face. "Absolutely!"

"Um... Okay then. See you at half twelve. I have sandwiches."

"Great." Lydia waited for Harrison to leave before letting out a little chuckle. "He's got a crush."

"Really? On who? How the hell did you find that out?"

"I found out the moment he checked out your derriere."

Cathy grinned. "Well, you can hardly blame him."

"You're incorrigible."

The morning slipped by in a blur of screaming children, lost tourists, and Norris lurking around every corner. By the time Lydia sat down to eat her grilled chicken salad, she was dead on her feet.

"Is it me, or has today been completely nuts?"

"Bonkers," Cathy answered, slipping into the chair opposite Lydia.

"Hi," Harrison muttered a few seconds later.

"Take a seat, sweetie," Cathy cooed. Lydia rolled her eyes.

"Um, there's two women outside, with three kids, looking for you, Lydia."

The only women who would come to the museum with kids were Fe and Halle.

"I'll be right back." Chewing as fast as she could, Lydia made her way out to the entrance hall.

"Aunty Lydia, look, I have a dinosaur pencil case!" Jack screamed, bouncing up and down.

"I've got a new rubber," Joey blurted just as loud.

"Mummy bought me a sword," Jenny chimed, her eyes sparkling with mischievous excitement.

"And I've got a headache," Fe retorted, making Halle and Lydia chuckle.

Dropping to her knees, Lydia scooped her three niblings into her arms. "Give me a kiss."

After a sufficient amount of time inhaling their soft smell, Lydia let them go. All three shot off in different directions.

"They'll be fine," Fe said, not looking the least concerned her children were running wild. "We wanted to invite you to book club tonight. It's a good one."

"Hey, Halle." Lydia leaned in and gave Halle a kiss on each cheek. "And no thanks. You know I don't like your book club."

"Fine, what about a drink, then?"

"Where?"

"Passion," Halle interjected. "They're having a ladies' night."

Lydia cocked her eyebrow. She could see what was going on here. Fe was meddling and using her best friend to help.

"No, thanks."

"Why not?" Fe tried to give her an intimidating 'mum' stare. It failed.

"Because you're trying to hook me up. I told you last night I'm done."

"I promise I will do no such thing. Lyds, it's like the law to go out and have a drink after a breakup."

"Come on Lydia, I could do with a hand keeping this one in line," Halle pleaded.

Looking from Halle to Fe, Lydia gave in. How could she compete with those two giving her puppy eyes?

"Ugh, fine, but I'm bringing Cathy."

"Deal," Fe grinned triumphantly.

Lydia knew better than to believe Fe was going to butt out of her business—she wasn't that daft. But she went along with things, anyhow, partly because sometimes it was just easier to relent to her sister, and because some part of her still believed she might have stamina for one last go at dating. Who knows, maybe it wouldn't end in heartache.

Yeah, right!

2

Nerves jangled around Lydia's stomach. It was ridiculous; she was only going to a bar, for God's sake. There would be a few drinks consumed, possibly some light flirting, but that was it. Lydia would not let Fe and Halle bully her into finding a date. It's a shame Cathy couldn't come. She was the perfect buffer.

The little voice in the back of her head still urged her to try one more time. It was sad, really. Why couldn't she just be happy alone?

Because you want love.

Was that really too much to ask for? A person who would love Lydia exactly the way she was made, broken parts included.

The shrieking of the doorbell pulled her back from the brink of gloom. Smoothing down her modest dress, Lydia grabbed her purse, kissed Monty, and opened the door. To her surprise, it wasn't Fe, but Halle.

"Oh hey, I was expecting Fe."

"Yeah, she's going to meet us there. Jack and Jenny got into it over which dinosaur is the best. Apparently, it got kinda heated."

"Oh, dear," Lydia chuckled. "Who won?"

"Who do you think?" Halle grinned.

"Jenny kicked his little arse, didn't she?"

"Oh, yeah!"

Laughing, Lydia shuffled out, closing the door behind her. Halle smelled great. Was that a new perfume? In all honesty, it was rare for Halle and Lydia to spend time alone together. Halle was Fe's best friend growing up, and on a few occasions, Fe made it clear to her annoying little sister that she wasn't to get too cosy. No one liked a third wheel. To Lydia's thirteen-year-old self, those words had cut deeply, and made her take a step back from interfering.

As they grew into adults, Lydia and Fe grew much closer, but Lydia never tried to cosy up to Halle. Fe's stern warning all those years ago still lingered at the back of her mind.

"The taxi should be here any minute," Halle commented.

Lydia smiled, taking a second to cast her gaze over Halle. At nearly 5'9", she towered over Lydia, just like Fe. Somehow Lydia had inherited all the shortcomings in her family: squat, on the heavier side, reproductively and hormonally challenged. Fe got the height, the slim build, same colour hair, and creamy skin sans imperfections.

Halle inherited her height and beauty from her mum. Lydia had met Mrs Cartwright once, a few years ago. Halle and her mum were freakishly similar in nearly all aspects of their lives. They both worked in physiotherapy. Both had shortish black hair and clear copper skin. Halle had a tighter body because of all the swimming she did, but even then, Mrs Cartwright wasn't too far behind. Yoga paid off.

Had Lydia spent a little too much time thinking about Halle and Mrs Cartwright? Yes, and she wasn't going to overanalyse it. Halle was hot, and her mum was too.

"You look nice." It wasn't a fib. Halle looked great, in tight black jeans and a red tank top.

"Thanks, I was going for uber lesbian. Did I get it right?"

"Spot on. Oh, the taxi's here. Shall we?"

"After you."

They sat in comfortable silence the entire journey. Lydia felt a pang of envy that her sister had a friend like Halle. Lydia had Fe, but it wasn't the same as having a real best friend. It's a shame Fe was so weird about sharing Halle. Lydia had a feeling they would get on pretty well.

"Twenty-five pounds please, ladies."

Jesus, how much?

"I've got it," Halle murmured, already handing the driver his fare. "Let's get a drink."

Halle's hand wrapping around Lydia's, pulling her along, came as a surprise, but she let it happen. Halle didn't let go until they were both at the bar.

"Wow, there's a lot of ladies here tonight!"

"All of the sapphic persuasion, too." Halle wiggled her eyebrows playfully. Another thing they had in common; Halle identified as a lesbian, and Lydia as pan.

"Are you on the prowl?" Lydia half joked.

"Nah, not tonight. I just want to have a drink and enjoy the company of two beautiful women. One of them is already here. I wonder if the other will turn up?"

Blushing slightly, Lydia brushed off Halle's compliment.

Has she always been such a sweet talker?

"She'll turn up. Fe never misses the chance to let her hair down."

Halle nodded. "I don't blame her with the triple terrors she has to deal with."

Lydia chuckled. "Triple terrors. That's brilliant. And so true!"

"I watched Joey bury Jack's head in a bucket of sand last week. Jenny stood by, laughing maniacally. They're only five. What the hell will they be like as teens? Jesus, I shudder to think."

"Oh shit, I think that's my fault. I told Joey about the time Fe buried me alive on holiday."

"Ha, don't tell Fe that."

"Don't tell me what?" Fe said from behind them.

"You made it, finally." Lydia was an expert at redirecting a conversation. "I hear it was bedlam at home."

"There were tears, tantrums, more tears and then a glass of wine for me. But it's all sorted and I'm ready to have another drink. What are we having?"

After a short debate, Fe ordered a bottle of champagne and a tray of shots. The trio drank liberally and danced with abandon. Lydia had to admit she was pleased Fe and Halle made her come out.

"Hey li'l sis, you've got an admirer," Fe slurred.

Lydia followed Fe's gaze to a table at the edge of the dance floor. A very pretty blond sat staring at her, making no bones about the fact she was checking out Lydia's ample breasts.

"No thanks," Lydia answered, continuing to dance.

"Oh, come on. She could be the one," Fe pushed.

"Fe, leave her be," Halle interjected. "Lyds told you she doesn't want to date."

Fe shot Halle a look before returning her attention back to Lydia. "Sis, you can't just swear off people. This woman might surprise you."

"Do you know her?" It was becoming crystal clear now. This *was* a set-up. "Fe, did you invite her here tonight to meet me?" Lydia's anger was rising rapidly.

"Just go and talk to her."

Seething, Lydia stormed off the dance floor towards the woman. "Hi, I'm Lydia, but you already know that, right?" Not giving the blonde a chance to talk, Lydia forged on. "Okay, let's see if you're still interested after this. If you date me, you will have to go weeks, sometimes months, without sex and deal with mood swings and an overall depressive-like state at least two weeks out of every month. There will be times I won't want to leave my flat, not even to visit you. How does that sound? Still want to go on a date?"

"Um..." Lydia quirked her eyebrow at the stunned blonde. "I..."

"I didn't think so. Sorry you came all the way here for nothing. Have a drink on me." With that, Lydia slipped a ten-pound note on the table and left. Walking in the opposite direction of her sister, Lydia headed for the outside terrace. If Fe tried to speak to her, they'd get into it, and it wouldn't be pretty.

"Hey, hey, what happened?"

Lydia whirled round to face Halle, who had a hand on Lydia's shoulder. "Did you know she was bringing someone?"

"No, I swear. You know what she's like. I would have told her not to if I'd known."

"Why is 'no' not in her fucking vocabulary?" Lydia was breathing heavily. "Out of everyone, she knows the crap I go through. How could she not understand? I don't have the emotional bandwidth to deal with dating anymore. I have enough pain in my life. I told her no, Halle!"

"I know, I know." Lydia felt Halle's arms engulf her petite frame. "She doesn't mean to upset you, Lyds. Fe just wants you to be happy."

"I don't need a partner to be happy. I need the doctor to listen to me. I need to have a life without pain. Of course I want to find love, who doesn't, but it's not going to happen until I get my health sorted out."

"It's okay, Lyds. I'll talk to her. Sit here. I'm going to grab us a drink and tell your meddling sister to stay clear of you for a little while."

The cold air felt good on Lydia's heated skin. A sliver of guilt wormed its way through her chest. She shouldn't have spoken to the woman like that. It wasn't her fault Fe had gone against Lydia's wishes. Crap, should she go back inside and apologise? Surely that would make everything way more awkward. No, it was done. Hopefully, Halle could get through to her pig-headed sister.

"Here, drink this." Halle's voice made Lydia jump. "Sorry, didn't mean to scare you."

"I zoned out. Did you speak to Fe?"

"Yeah, that went as expected. I put her drunk arse in a taxi."

Lydia huffed. "Thanks, and sorry I spoiled your night."

Halle sat next to Lydia, her legs straddling the bench seat. "You didn't ruin a thing. Fe was out of order. That's on her."

"You don't have to stay with me, Halle."

"I want to. Come on, have a drink."

Running a hand through her hair, Lydia took a cleansing breath. "Thanks."

Sitting in silence, Lydia knocked back the champagne. Fatigue set in. Halle was looking at her.

"You have a doctor's appointment on Monday, right?"

Nodding, Lydia massaged her temples. "Yeah, all the good it will do."

"He's still not listening?"

"Nope." Lydia had pleaded with Dr Watson for over three years to be taken seriously. Every time, he downplayed Lydia's symptoms and offered her another birth control pill, each time insisting Lydia stick at it for at least six months. Surely, he was running out of pills to try by now. None of them worked. They simply extended her period, which was the last thing Lydia needed.

"I have a suggestion. How about I come with you on Monday? I'd say take Fe, but I think the two of you could do with some space. Maybe if you have someone with you, he'll be less quick to dismiss you."

Lydia sat back, studying Halle. No one had ever offered to go along with her to an appointment.

"You'd come to a doctor's appointment with me?"

"Of course. I should have offered sooner. I know you've been having troubles. I just didn't want to overstep, but...well, now I think the good doctor is taking the piss. No one should suffer the way you are."

"I don't know what to say."

"Say yes."

"Okay, thank you."

"I don't understand why the doctor is being so...dickish. I could kind of understand if you were under the NHS."

"I sometimes wish I was. I think I would have got somewhere by now."

"Still no luck finding another GP?"

"Nope, even private doctors aren't taking on new patients."

"Want another?" Halle pointed to Lydia's empty glass. As tempting as it was, Lydia knew too much alcohol would exacerbate the pain. She only had three days until the worst of her symptoms would kick into high gear.

"No, I think I'll call it a night."

"No worries. Let's grab a ride home."

"You can stay, Halle. There were plenty of ladies giving you the eye in there."

"Nah, not tonight. Let's go."

A dull thud hovered at the back of Lydia's head. She should have drunk more water when she got back last night, but tiredness had won out and she'd collapsed in bed after only half a glass of H_2O.

Monty lay half under the covers, his back legs stretched out onto the pillow next to Lydia. He'd always slept like that in her bed. When he was a pup, Lydia worried he would suffocate, or overheat, but no matter how many times she moved him, Monty crawled his top half back under the duvet, leaving his hindquarters outside.

Giving Monty a quick bum scratch, Lydia rolled over, grabbing her phone. Predictably, Fe messaged her first thing. An apology that Lydia wasn't quite ready to accept. Dropping the phone back on her bedside table, Lydia's mind wandered back to Halle's offer to accompany her to the doctor's tomorrow. A lump formed in her throat, threatening to choke her up. Why was such a paltry offer making her so emotional?

Lydia didn't have time to overthink. The thudding on her front door put a stop to any meandering thoughts. Rolling her eyes, Lydia checked her phone. Fe hadn't messaged again, but considering she'd sent Lydia a message three hours ago without a response, it didn't take a rocket scientist to know who she'd find standing on the other side of the door.

Grabbing her fluffy robe, Lydia padded to the door, unlatched it, and turned to go to the kitchen. Fe walked in, looking a little worse for wear.

"Tea?" Lydia called over her shoulder.

"Please."

"Buttery toast?"

"Thanks."

Lydia busied herself with breakfast, needing a few minutes to gather her thoughts.

"I'm sorry, Lyds."

"Hmmm."

"Don't 'hmm' at me. I *am* sorry. Fuck, Halle tore me a new arsehole first thing this morning. I didn't realise it had upset you that much."

Placing the freshly brewed tea on the table, Lydia sat down. "That's because you don't listen. I'm not being melodramatic when I say I'm done with dating. I need to focus on me, and it hurts every time I get dumped. It hurts every time I see the disappointment on my partner's face when they get their advances rejected, time and time again, because I'm in pain, or bloated, or bleeding. I'm already fighting an uphill battle with my arsehole doctor, just to be taken seriously. I don't need to be fighting you, too."

Reaching over, Fe grabbed Lydia's hand. "I'm sorry, sweetie, I didn't think. I hate that you have to go through this alone."

"I'm not alone, am I? I thought I had you and Mum. Even Halle, who offered to come to the doctor with me tomorrow."

Fe fidgeted in her chair. "That was nice of her." A pregnant pause descended. Fe looked uncomfortable. "I should have offered, shouldn't I? You've struggled with this for so long, plus the arse that's your doctor, and I haven't even offered to go with you for support."

Lydia was taken aback at Fe's sudden outpour of emotion. They generally ribbed each other when things got serious.

"It's okay, I could have asked."

"No, Halle was right. I need to support you more."

Halle had said that?

"Fe, you have three tearaway munchkins. You're busy, and rightly so. I'm a big girl. I promise in the future, I'll ask you to come along with me if I need some support."

"I can come with you tomorrow, if you'd like."

"Stop fretting. Halle will be with me tomorrow, although I'm not convinced having someone else there will help."

"He's really that bad? The doctor?"

"He mansplains everything. I don't understand why he won't refer me to have other tests. The birth control pills aren't cutting it, but he just won't listen."

"Do you want me to kick his arse? I will, you know."

Lydia burst out laughing, Fe following suit. "Calm down, sis. I don't think I'm quite there yet."

"Why don't you come over for dinner tonight? We can talk about it, or not. Clark's taking the kids to his mum's for their tea."

"Sure. What time is he leaving, though? I want to see them before they go."

"Usually around half four. I tell you what; get dressed, and we'll head over to Mum's for a coffee. Then we can go straight to mine so you can entertain the brood."

"Ah, I see what this is," Lydia chuckled. "Your apology was to make sure I was still up for triplet distraction duty, right?"

"No, of course not," Fe scoffed. "Although, you are the best aunt in the world, and they would be devastated if we fell out."

"Wow, you went full Mum then. Emotional manipulation is normally her jam."

"Rude! I'm not like Mum."

"You so are. Anyway, it's a plan. Let me grab a shower. Can you sort Monty out? He'll need his winter coat put on and his toy bag packed."

"Christ, Lyds, you spoil that mutt way too much."

Monty barked in displeasure. "Don't call him a mutt. And I'll spoil him all I want. Look at those beautiful brown eyes," Lydia cooed, grabbing Monty by the face and squishing her lips to his muzzle.

"Good Lord," Fe mumbled. "Go on, I'll sort out King Monty."

Entering her bedroom, grabbing clothes to put on after her shower, Lydia paused. Halle had told off Fe. A small frisson of something flitted in Lydia's stomach. Dropping the clothes bundled in her arms, Lydia scooped up her phone and navigated to the last message thread between herself and Halle. It was almost three months since they'd communicated separately from Fe.

Sucking in a breath, Lydia composed a message thanking Halle for her support last night and for talking to Fe. Why was she feeling so weird about messaging her? It's not like they were strangers. They'd known each other for years; nearly twenty, by Lydia's calculations.

The ping of her phone caused a little squeak of surprise to slip past Lydia's lips. Darting her gaze to the bedroom door, she listened for Fe. Stupid, really; she wasn't doing anything wrong.

That funny feeling was back again. Lydia read the message, a smile creeping on her face. What a difference having someone by her side would make. What a shame Halle was off-limits.

Hang about. Where the hell did that come from?

Throwing the phone onto her bed as if the plastic device had physically scolded her, Lydia shook her head, ridding herself of such silly thoughts. There was no situation where thinking of Halle as anything but Fe's bestie was allowed.

None.

3

Lydia nervously bounced her leg as she sat waiting for Halle to pick her up. Daft, really, that a doctor's appointment should get her so worked up. But she'd been fighting with Dr Watson for so long, and as soon as an appointment loomed, Lydia felt her anxiety skyrocket.

There was still plenty of time. Halle messaged again last night, asking if Lydia wanted Halle to pick her up a little earlier so they could grab a coffee before the appointment. It would be a first for them. Café trips always involved Fe. Lydia wondered if it meant something, that Halle wanted them to go without her sister. Then she felt silly for thinking such a thing. Halle was just being supportive, as a good friend would. Although Lydia wasn't used to Halle being *her* good friend.

Three rapid horn blasts signalled Halle's arrival. Wrapping the warmest coat she owned around her body, Lydia kissed Monty and headed out the door. Lydia tittered as she walked across to a waiting Halle. Considering how tall Halle was, it defied physics, in Lydia's opinion, how she managed to fit herself in the small vintage Mini called Nora.

"Hurry up, it's brass monkeys out here," Halle called from her open window.

Picking up the pace, Lydia scuttled around the car, finally dropping into the low passenger seat. "You know, if you had a modern car, you'd be able to keep yourself warm," Lydia grumbled, rubbing her hands together, desperately trying to heat up her fingers.

"Shh, don't listen, Nora. I'll never dump you for a younger model." Halle flashed Lydia a grin. "Ready to get some caffeine in your system?"

"Oh, yes. I'm craving a mocha."

"Onwards, then," Halle called, putting her foot to the floor. Nora zipped off faster than Lydia was expecting. She couldn't help but grip the sides of the seat as Halle manoeuvred them through traffic. 'Terrifying' was one word to describe the experience. Every single car on the road was twice the size of Nora, and equipped with much better safety features.

Letting out a sigh of relief the moment Halle put on the parking brake, Lydia did her best not to show Halle how nervous she was—not just because of their death-defying journey to Starbucks, but because the doctor's appointment was steadily creeping closer.

The café was busy with office workers ordering their horrendously complicated coffees. A few mothers gathered with prams, yapping about their weekend. Lydia spotted a small table at the back of the coffee shop. Without thinking, she made a beeline for it, leaving Halle in the queue.

"Sorry," she mouthed to an amused-looking Halle. Lydia would give her the money for the coffee later. Unbuttoning her coat, Lydia did her best to relax. The buzz of the shop was nice, and the smell of pastries was making her salivate. Lydia almost launched herself at Halle when she placed a tray of coffee and Danish on the table.

"Here, I thought we could treat ourselves." Halle picked up a Danish and took a huge bite. As usual, Lydia looked down at her belly and then at the sugary treat. "Hey, you don't have to eat it if you don't want. Sorry, I should have asked."

"No, no. I... I've just been trying to watch what I eat. It was thoughtful of you, really."

"No, it was thoughtless. Shit, sorry, Lyds, you've mentioned before about cutting down on sugar."

"It's to help with the bloating and blemishes," Lydia mumbled, her face heating.

"I'll take it back." Halle went to stand, but Lydia stopped her before she took a step.

"No, it's okay. I'll have half and then you can take the other half with you for a snack later."

Frankly, Lydia was getting sick to the back teeth of watching what she ate. Until her hormones were balanced, nothing would stop the bloating or blemishes.

Halle carefully cut the Danish in half, wrapped one part in a napkin and slid the other over to Lydia. Not wanting to make the situation any more embarrassing, Lydia nibbled on the sweet treat. Halle continued to devour her Danish. Oh, how Lydia wished she could be that carefree.

"So..." Halle began, "I think you should ask for a copy of your medical records."

"Why?" Lydia wiped her mouth and took a sip of coffee.

"I think you should know what Dr Watson has been noting. I…I spoke to Mum about it. I hope you don't mind?"

"No, that's fine."

"Phew, good. Well, anyway, she was shocked, too, that you've been fighting this for as long as you have, especially going private."

"Um, I suppose I can ask."

Halle nodded. "Are you working later?"

"Yeah, I took this morning off, but I need to go in after lunch."

"We could have lunch together if you like, depending how you feel. I could drop you off at work."

Was Halle nervous? Lydia had never seen her like this before.

"Sure, that would be nice. Could we eat at the museum?"

"Only if we eat at the T.rex Restaurant."

Lydia rolled her eyes. "You big kid. Sure, if that's what you want."

"Awesome. Right, shall we get this over and done with?"

Swallowing thickly, Lydia nodded. The drive from Starbucks to Watson Medical Practice flew by in the same heart-stopping manner as the drive to the café. Lydia wrangled her way out of the tiny car with immense difficulty, only to witness Halle rise out gracefully, her tall body towering over the tiny toy of a car.

Dr Watson's medical practice was state-of-the-art. Lydia signed in via an iPad as soon as she entered the reception. The receptionist, a buxom redhead, smiled sweetly. Mellow music played softly over hidden speakers.

"Jesus, is this a doctor's or a spa?" Halle mumbled.

Sitting down, Lydia nodded, "Yeah, it's a bit much."

"Lydia Archer," the receptionist called. "Dr Watson will see you now."

Drawing in a deep breath, Lydia prepared herself. Halle's hand on her shoulder gave her a shot of confidence. Rising, Lydia made her way to the doctor's examination room. No need for her to check if Halle was following. She could feel the support radiating off her in waves as they walked down the corridor.

"Lydia," Dr Watson said, without taking his eyes off the computer screen on his desk.

"Dr Watson. Um…I have a friend with me today." That got the doctor's attention.

"Oh, okay." Clearing his throat, Dr Watson gave her his full attention. Lydia saw Halle pull out a small notepad out of her bag. Flipping it open, she then popped a pen from her coat pocket. She looked at Lydia and winked. Dr Watson took several seconds to compose himself. Halle's presence had unnerved him for some reason.

"So, what can I do for you today?"

Lydia had to stop herself from scoffing. He knew damn well what she was there for. "I've come to ask you for a referral. The pill you gave me isn't working. Just as the others before."

"Now, Lydia," Dr Watson replied in a condescending tone, causing Lydia to grit her teeth, "we've discussed this. I know you have a bit of pain and bloating, but we can manage that with pain pills until we find the correct birth control for you."

"Wow," Halle muttered, loud enough to be heard. Dr Watson's gaze shot down to the pad Halle was feverishly writing on.

"I've told you how bad things get, Doctor. I can't keep going through this. It's ruining my life." Lydia felt the first tear fall. Dr Watson looked, wide-eyed, from Lydia to Halle, who was shaking her head gently, taking more notes.

"Now, don't cry." The doctor fumbled with a box of tissues, poking it towards Lydia. "Let's just try one more pill. I don't want to refer you unnecessarily."

"Unnecessarily?" Halle echoed, her gaze firmly on the doctor. "Are you kidding?"

"I'd like a copy of my medical records please," Lydia stuttered. "I think it's time I got a second opinion."

It was an idle threat. There were no other doctors to talk to, no one was taking on new patients.

"That's your prerogative, Lydia, but it's unlikely you'll find another doctor close by, taking on—"

"Dr Elise Maynard will take her on." Halle's eyes were locked on the doctor, with fire burning in them.

Who the hell was Dr Elise Maynard?

"Dr Maynard, really?" Dr Watson was taken aback.

Lydia wanted to scream out, "Who the fuck is Dr Maynard?" but she didn't. Instead, she watched the unfolding scene play out.

Halle tucked the notepad back in her bag. Hoisted it over her shoulder and stood. "Lyds. I think you're done here."

"Um...okay." Did Lydia enjoy being told what to do? No, not normally, but, hell, she'd be lying if she didn't admit watching Halle get all defensive and sassy, turned her the hell on. "Please let me know when I can collect my records."

Lydia threw a quick wave over her shoulder at the perky receptionist before exiting the surgery behind Halle. "Halle, wait up!"

Approaching Nora, Halle began pacing bonnet-to-boot, over and over. Lydia stopped a few feet away, unsure what was happening. After a few more moments of frantic pacing, Halle stopped, turning to Lydia with wide eyes.

"Shit. Oh crap, I'm sorry, Lydia. I just full-on hijacked your doctor's appointment. I swear that wasn't my intention. I just got so worked up with how he spoke to you. I know I overstepped. Shit, I *really* overstepped. I'm so sorry."

"I just have one question." Lydia took a couple of steps forward, placing her hand on Halle's forearm, hoping to convey calm. "Who the bloody hell is Dr Maynard?"

Halle blew out a big breath. "Okay, that's another line I may have overstepped. Um...so I dated Elise for all of two weeks, but we stayed friends. She's an excellent gynaecologist, and after I saw how upset you were in the club the other night, I sort of called her."

"Sort of called?"

"Okay, not sort of. I definitely called her. Um, I gave her a brief rundown of your symptoms and told her your doctor was blatantly refusing to do anything…"

"Okay. And she's agreed to take me on?"

"Not quite. I said that to piss off Dr Useless. But I can give her a call. If she can't see you, she might know another doctor who can."

Lydia took a second to digest the last few minutes. She was disappointed Halle's announcement wasn't quite true, but maybe there was still a chance this Dr Maynard could help her.

"Sure, give her a call."

Halle wasted no time pulling out her phone. Lydia's mind wandered as Halle spoke to her friend. "That's great, Elise, thanks. Yeah, see you soon." Halle finished her sentence with a wide smile. "Success. If we can get there in the next thirty minutes, she can fit you in."

Lunging forward, Lydia took Halle into her arms. This wonderful human had done the impossible: She'd given Lydia hope.

"Whoa, okay, so you're not mad I took over your appointment and told a little lie?"

"Not right now. I'm just so thankful, Halle." Letting go of the strong hold she had over the taller woman, Lydia blushed. "Sorry," she chuckled when Halle took in a deep breath, happy to have access to air again.

"Great, now I don't fear for my life," Halle grinned, making Lydia blush harder. What the bloody hell was happening to her? "Shall we head over to her clinic at the hospital?"

"Sure, okay. I haven't got my records though."

"No worries. I'm sure Elise will want to start from scratch."

Lydia climbed back into Nora with a bit more enthusiasm, closed her eyes, and prayed for Dr Maynard to be the one who would listen at last.

Traffic was light. They made it to the hospital within twenty minutes; a minor miracle in itself. Butterflies fluttered in Lydia's tummy as they rode the elevator up to Dr Maynard's office. The aesthetic of the space was much nicer than Dr Watson's. That was Lydia's opinion, anyway. Comfy chairs, real plants, and a calming shade of blue greeted them. Oh—and a very sweet receptionist who looked like she wanted to bake everyone biscuits, while making the best hot chocolate in the world.

"Hello, I'm Lydia Archer to see Dr Maynard."

"Of course, love. Take a seat and I'll call you when she's ready. There's a tea and coffee machine just round the corner. Help yourself to a digestive too."

Lydia spied the receptionist's name plate. "Thank you, Jean."

"I'll grab us a coffee. Get comfy." Halle was already walking off before Lydia had time to comment.

Giving the only other patient in the waiting room a small smile, Lydia let her gaze wander to all the informational literature and posters stuck up around the room. Was any of it relevant to her? Would she finally get some answers? God, she hoped so.

"Ms Archer, Dr Maynard is ready."

"Oh...thanks." Halle wasn't back from the coffee machine, but Lydia didn't want to keep the doctor waiting. "Would you mind telling my friend I've gone in?"

"Of course, dear."

Running a hand through her hair, Lydia entered Dr Maynard's office. Unlike Dr Watson, Elise Maynard sat straight, her full attention on Lydia the moment she entered.

"Ms Archer, good morning." Elise Maynard was gorgeous. Close to fifteen years older, Lydia would guess. She had short platinum-blonde hair in a stylish pixie cut, friendly blue eyes, and laugh lines. Even sitting down, Lydia could tell she was tall; probably as tall as Halle.

"G-good morning, Dr Maynard. Thank you for seeing me. And please, call me Lydia."

"Then call me Elise. I didn't have an option, not after what Halle told me. You've been struggling for nearly three years, I'm led to believe?"

"Yes, that's right."

"Let's go back to the beginning, then. Tell me what's happening."

Lydia bit her tongue to stop tears welling in her eyes. She already felt a thousand times better just from this brief interaction with Elise.

"I've always had heavy periods and bad cramping. Roughly three years ago, it all got worse. The pain was, and still is, so bad, I usually vomit."

"Is that throughout the entire time you bleed?"

"No, just the first three or four days, usually. But even before the pain, I know when I'm going to begin my period. I can set my watch by my hormones. A week before, I gain an insatiable appetite. No matter what I eat, it's never enough. Then my mood sours. I feel so low, like nothing in my life is good." Lydia couldn't hold back the waterworks any longer. "I-I'm sorry," she spluttered. Just what the doctor wanted, a snotty, hysterical woman in her chair.

Lydia heard the scraping of chair legs on the carpet. A warm arm slid over her shoulders. "It's alright, Lydia, let it out."

Five minutes later, Lydia finally ran out of tears. "Sorry, I'm okay now," she mumbled, her head dipped in embarrassment.

"Please don't apologise. You've had a lot to contend with." Elise gave Lydia's shoulder a quick squeeze before returning to her desk chair.

"As soon as I bleed, it's like the clouds part and my mood gets better," Lydia continued. "But then I have the heavy flow and the pain. My face erupts with spots, too."

"Do you remember the medication your previous doctor prescribed?" Lydia listed them off easily. "And did any of them have a significant impact on your symptoms?"

"They only gave me side effects. Headaches, more nausea and prolonged bleeding."

"And you relayed this to your GP?"

"Absolutely."

"Hmm." Lydia noted the furrowed eyebrows. What did it mean? "I'm utterly shocked you haven't been referred to a specialist. No person should have gone through this for so long. I want to get an ultrasound done today and schedule you to have your hormone levels tested. Is that okay?"

"Yes!" Lydia could have done a jaunty dance right there and then. It was happening. She was getting help!

"Excellent. Pop behind the curtain and slip into the gown. I'll get the machine ready."

Not wasting a second, Lydia skittered around the medical curtain, stripping herself off. "I'm ready," she called.

Elise stepped around the curtain. "Great, hop onto the exam table and open your legs, letting your knees fall to the sides."

Usually, this sort of thing would feel mortifying, but not today. Lydia would show her hoo-ha to the entire clinic if it meant she got some answers.

"Oh, that's cold." The gel Elise spread on her abdomen sent chills up her spine.

"Sorry. Now, once I've done an external ultrasound, I'll do an internal one, too. Is that okay?" Lydia nodded. The room fell silent except for the odd clicking of buttons on the ultrasound machine.

"Can you see anything out of the ordinary?"

"Not conclusively. Lydia, I want to schedule you for an endometriosis test. The only way to diagnose endometriosis with confidence is through laparoscopic surgery."

"Okay, yes, let's do that."

"Halle told me you are a private patient."

"Yes, that's correct."

"Okay, in that case, I can schedule an appointment relatively quickly. I'll need to check my calendar, but I think we should be able to get the test done within the month."

"Really? That quick?"

"Yes, really. You will need to meet with an anaesthesiologist a week prior. And as long as your blood work is good, we will proceed."

"Oh, Dr Maynard, thank you." If she wasn't in such a compromising position, Lydia would have hugged her.

"It's Elise, remember. Halle is a good friend, and she cares a lot about you."

That was news to Lydia. Sure, Halle was caring, but did she care *for* Lydia?

"We'll sort this out," Elise continued. "In the meantime, you'll need to stick to painkillers and hot water bottles."

"That's fine. I can deal with that, knowing I'm finally going to get some answers."

"Why don't you get dressed and I'll look at my schedule."

When Lydia exited Elise's office ten minutes later, she felt as if she were floating.

"Hey, how'd it go?" Halle sipped on her coffee, eyeing Lydia. Could she tell how happy she was? Surely, the stupid grin across her face gave it away.

"Elise is wonderful. Oh Halle, how can I ever repay you?"

"For what? Sticking my beak into your private business?" she laughed.

"Yes, that!" Lydia pointed. "Exactly that."

"You can buy me a T.rex burger."

"Deal. I'll even throw in a milkshake."

"Now you're talking," Halle laughed.

4

"There you go, one large T.rex burger with extra gherkins, cheese, and bacon. And a large chocolate milkshake." Lydia slid the behemoth burger towards Halle.

"Oh, come to mamma," Halle whispered, licking her lips. Shaking her head and laughing, Lydia picked up her fork and began picking at the chicken Caesar salad she'd opted for, even though her mind was screaming at her to dive into a big, juicy burger with fries and onion rings, then follow with a big wedge of chocolate molten volcano cake.

By Lydia's calculations, her period would start within the next two days. That left her just another forty-eight hours of insatiable hunger to endure. She'd done well this month, hardly giving in to her cravings.

As disappointed as Lydia was not having a delicious T.rex burger, she knew it was the right choice. Junk food made the pain so much worse, plus her skin just couldn't cope. And nothing made Lydia feel shittier about herself than a face full of craters.

Fe often scoffed when Lydia tried to explain that food played a big part in pain and bloating. Her sister couldn't wrap her head around the fact sugar made cramps worse.

As supporting as Fe was in so many aspects of Lydia's life, she just didn't understand. Lydia spent hours upon hours scouring the internet, looking for things that could make her life a little better.

The truth of the matter was, Lydia had to sculpt her diet, even if that meant pissing off family members because she needed to eat something different.

"How're you feeling about everything?" Halle's question was almost unintelligible through a mouth full of food.

"Good, really good. Like, for the first time in years, I can see the end of the tunnel, if that makes sense."

"Totally. It should never have gone on this long." Halle looked deep in thought. Lydia continued to munch on her lettuce, observing her friend. They could call each other friends now, right? "Can I ask how much you paid to see the dickwad?"

"Oh, um…each appointment was quite expensive."

"Okay, like, what are we talking? Fifty quid a session?"

"More like three hundred."

Lydia bolted from the chair when Halle choked on the half-masticated burger still rolling around her mouth. Coughing and spluttering, Halle finally got herself under control after a few well-aimed smacks to the back from Lydia.

"Lyds, you paid three hundred quid each time?"

"Yeah, I know it's expensive, but that's how it is going private. Dr Watson is supposed to be a fantastic doctor, so I didn't mind paying it."

"But he's a terrible doctor!"

"Well, I know that now, obviously. In the beginning, I just presumed he knew what he was doing. He's the one with a medical degree."

"And now?"

"Well…"

"He was scamming you, Lyds. Keeping you on the hook for the money. Jesus, I wonder how many other women are trying to get help and getting sweet fuck all, but still paying his obnoxious prices?"

"I-I didn't think a doctor would do that." But it was clear Halle was on to something. The only thing Dr Watson got out of stringing Lydia along, was more money.

"You could sue him."

"I just want to feel better, Halle, that's all."

Halle was visibly annoyed. Lydia noticed Halle's knee bouncing up and down and watched her run a hand through her shaggy hair. "He shouldn't get away with what he's doing, Lyds."

"I know, and I agree, but one battle at a time."

"Shit, yeah, of course. We'll get through this."

Lydia's brain stumbled over the *we* part of Halle's sentence. Where was this sudden support coming from?

"Halle, why are you doing this? I mean, why now?"

Wiping a French fry through a glob of burger sauce, Halle chewed on her lip. "We should have been there for you more: Fe and me. I've known you just as long as I have Fe, and there is nothing I wouldn't do for either of you. I know Fe's my best friend, but you're just as important."

"Really?" Lydia couldn't help the surprise laced around that one word. Halle's shoulders deflated a smidge. Shit, had she offended her with that comment? "Sorry, that sounded bad. It's just we've never been particularly close. We only hang out with Fe, so I'm a little surprised to hear you say that."

"It's fine. You're right. The truth is, I always wanted you to be friends with me, it's just—"

"Fe went all possessive."

"Kinda. But we're not kids anymore, and Fe has a life outside our friendship. Why can't I? Sometimes I think we have more in common, anyway."

Lydia could see where Halle was coming from. Even though they weren't allowed to spend a lot of time together as kids, Lydia remembered a few conversations that revealed they had music, movies, and books, in common.

"Alright then. Friends?"

"Friends. And as a friend, it's my job to help you through this, Lyds. Fuck all those arseholes who left. You don't need them."

"I can't exactly blame them," Lydia sighed. It was true. Her ex-partners hadn't signed up for any of her baggage. "A new relationship should be exciting and sexy. I couldn't give that to them."

"I disagree, but whatever. Their loss. I want to help you concentrate on getting better."

"That's very sweet, Halle."

"I'm a sweet kinda gal," Halle winked.

"Who's a sweet kinda gal?" Fe's voice broke through the atmosphere like a knife.

"Hey, sis, what're you doing here?" Had Lydia done a good job masking her disappointment at being interrupted?

"I knew you were on shift this afternoon, so I stopped by to see how the appointment went. Like I said, I plan to be there for you more than I have. Hey, Halle."

"Hey, sweetie." Did Halle look just as disappointed?

"So, the doctor?"

"Well…" Lydia chuckled. "It went slightly off the rails at one point."

"Oh?" Fe was tucking into Halle's fries like she'd not eaten all day.

"So, we go in, and he's being—"

"Rude, that's what he was. He didn't even have the courtesy to look at you."

"Oh, you went in with her?" Fe asked. The chip she was about to eat, frozen halfway to her mouth.

What was that about? Why did Fe look so surprised? Irritated even.

"Of course I did. I wanted to see what this clown was going to say."

"He looked like he was going to piss his trousers when you started scribbling in your notepad. What was *that* about?"

Halle smiled brightly, causing something odd to happen in Lydia's chest. "I wanted to throw him off. I had a feeling he was going to dismiss you. So I thought if he believed I was taking notes of the conversation, he might pay a bit more attention."

"And did he?" Fe asked, taking the milkshake Halle was holding, drinking it liberally.

"Fe, do you want some food? You're eating and drinking all of Halle's." Lydia couldn't explain why she was so pissed at her sister's actions.

That meal was my way of saying thank you to Halle.

"She doesn't mind," Fe commented, still chugging on the milkshake. Lydia dared a glance at Halle, who shrugged.

"Anyway, he was a little more attentive but still—"

"Condescending as hell," Halle finished.

"The next thing I know, Halle is barking at the doctor about some other doctor and I'm asking for my medical records. It was a bit nuts, to be honest."

"What doctor?" Fe asked Halle.

"Elise Maynard."

"Oh yeah, your older lover," Fe teased.

"We went out a couple of times." Halle rolled her eyes playfully. The thought of Halle with Elise felt uncomfortable, but Lydia buried that down. Elise was going to be her saviour, and nothing would impact that; not even thoughts of Elise doing things to Halle, and those thoughts causing Lydia to cringe inside.

"The next thing I know, I'm being whisked off to see Elise," Lydia continued, hoping her feelings would settle down.

"You got her an appointment with Elise?" Once again, Fe was talking to Halle with a weird look on her face.

"Yes, I did."

After a pause, Fe turned to Lydia. "How did that go?"

"Great," Lydia burst. "She did tests there and then. And I'm scheduled to have a minor procedure in three weeks to get a definitive diagnosis of endometriosis."

"A procedure? What procedure?"

"It's just a minor surgery, done laparoscopically."

"Surgery?" Fe's voice was high pitched.

"Yes, surgery, but it's no big deal."

"I think you should take some time to think about this, Lyds."

Lydia could feel her frustration mount. She should have known Fe would have something to say. "I've had three painful years to think about it."

"I know but—"

"I don't think you do know," Halle butted in. "I don't think any of us know what she's been through, sweetie. This is her decision, and we are going to be there for her."

Wow, Lydia was stunned. There weren't many people in her life who stood up for her the way Halle did. Of course, Fe was one of those people, but Lydia never had a person help her battle Fe and her—sometimes overbearing—opinions.

"Of course I'll be there for her." Fe's tone shifted to something softer. "Always, Lyds, you know that. Sorry, I just heard surgery and freaked."

Reaching over, Lydia grabbed Fe's hand. "This is long overdue, Fe. I need to get my life back."

"And you will. Send me over the details and I'll make sure I'm with you at the hospital."

Another pang of disappointment. Halle hadn't offered to be with Lydia for the surgery, but she'd hoped that would be the case.

With details handed over, Lydia reluctantly left Fe and Halle to finish lunch. Dashing through the museum, Lydia made it with a few minutes to spare. As expected, Norris was hanging around, hoping he'd get the chance to tell her off for tardiness.

Not today, Norris, you old windbag.

***

"I can't believe you dragged me out on a school night." Lydia groaned.

In reality it had taken little for Cathy to convince Lydia she needed to go to the pub after work.

"Oh pish. It was a long day, and we deserve a glass of wine," Cathy replied, taking a long draw of her drink. She was already on her second of the night.

"And we have another long day tomorrow—starting early."

"Bloody hell, Lyds. You know you're the younger one here, right?"

"Doesn't mean I'm irresponsible."

"No, but it does mean you're being a stick in the mud. Relax and have another drink. Norris is off tomorrow, so we can skive off a little."

One glass of wine was more than enough. The tell-tale signs of Lydia's impending misery were upon her. Halfway through her shift, a dull ache formed at the base of her spine. Lower back pain was horrendous, and also a warning of what was to come. Lydia wouldn't be surprised to find herself in the bathroom this evening, feeling rotten.

As if back pain wasn't bad enough, Lydia's body liked to throw cramps at her in the middle of the night, usually meaning she got little sleep.

"One is enough, Cathy."

Knocking Lydia's shoulder, Cathy scoffed playfully. "You never let yourself go. Just once, I'd like to see you let your hair down."

Cathy was letting her hair down enough for the both of them.

"I don't need alcohol to enjoy myself."

Not a complete lie.

"I just think—"

Lydia had enough. Why did she always have to explain herself?

Maybe if I opened up a little more, Cathy would understand.

"Look, I don't drink for medical reasons." Lydia reeled off the vast list of problems she faced every month.

Cathy sat, looking shocked at Lydia's sudden need to unload on her. Usually a response like Cathy's would have Lydia's guilt-o-meter spiking, but since she'd felt the comfort of having support from Halle, Lydia wanted more.

"Christ, why didn't you ever tell me?" Cathy looked affronted at being kept in the dark.

"I didn't want to dump my issues on you."

"But we're friends. Well, I thought we were."

"Of course we are."

"Friends lean on each other, Lydia. I tell you everything about me."

That was true. Cathy wasn't shy about airing her dirty laundry, in the slightest.

"You know, now. Please don't be mad at me, Cath."

"Those times I thought you were hungover. You weren't, were you?"

Several times Lydia had dragged herself to work, even though all she wanted to do was curl up in a ball with Monty and a pile of pain meds. When Cathy had seen her in that state, she'd assumed Lydia had been out partying. The pale skin, sunken and bloodshot eyes. Sometimes sweating; it added up to a monstrous hangover, and Lydia hadn't corrected Cathy's assessment.

"No, I wasn't hungover."

"Jesus, is that what it's like every month?" Lydia nodded and took a sip of her wine. "But you're getting help now?"

"Hopefully."

"I'm still a little miffed you didn't tell me."

"Sometimes, Cathy, I just want to forget about it. Working with you, even Harrison, helps take my mind off it. I feel like all I do is worry and think about the next month and how bad it's going to be. I've not had a break from it for three years."

"Okay; we don't need to talk about it, only when you want to, okay? But hun, if you're suffering at work, let me know. We've got each other's back, right?"

"Right."

"Okay, drink up. I'll call a taxi. Like you said, early start tomorrow."

Being a weeknight, Cathy found a taxi quickly. Thank God, because Lydia's nipples were going to freeze off if she had to stand outside much longer.

Monty greeted Lydia with an excited zoom around the sofa. After five minutes of roughhousing, Lydia let him outside to do his nightly business. Her work attire for the next day was ready, and all she had to do before falling into bed was make a quick whole wheat pasta salad. Eating at the museum hiked up her monthly outgoings, unnecessarily.

With Monty snoring in his basket at the bottom of the bed, Lydia showered and got ready to sleep. Just as she settled under the duvet, a wave of heat rolled over her body.

"No, not tonight, please!" she begged. A change in body temperature meant only one thing. Lydia would definitely start her period this evening.

At least my mood will improve soon.

Yes, her melancholy would disappear, but the rest was still going to be shit. Popping out of bed, Lydia took her pain meds from the bathroom cabinet and placed them on her bedside table. She wandered back into the kitchen, switching on the kettle, ready to make herself a hot water bottle. Preparation was key.

Sleep came quickly. The excitement of the day finally caught up to her. However, it didn't last long. Lydia was stirred from a very pleasant dream, about a tall copper-skinned beauty, by dull pain radiating from her abdomen. Groaning, she rolled over, popped two extra-strength painkillers from their packets, and grabbed the water bottle patiently waiting at the side of her bed. Curling into the foetal position, Lydia pressed the bottle hard to her body.

I'm okay, I'm okay, I'm okay.

The saliva swarming her mouth indicated she was, in fact, not okay. Running to the bathroom, Lydia positioned herself on the toilet with her head in her trusty sick bucket. A violent cramp surged through her body, causing her stomach contents to rise in her throat. Sweat beaded above her lip and brow.

The painkillers will kick in soon. I'm okay.

Twenty long minutes later, Lydia felt her abdomen relax. She still felt nauseous, but she hadn't wretched in a while. Monty lay in the bathroom doorway, his caring eyes never leaving Lydia.

"I'm good, buddy." When she could finally leave the loo, Lydia hopped in the shower, trying to cool her fevered body.

With a pad in place, the only thing Lydia needed now was some sleep. Monty had made the executive decision to comfort Lydia for the rest of the night. Snuggling up to his warm little body, Lydia inhaled his scent. Even though the cramps were still there, the pain was manageable. Maybe she could go back to that lovely dream she was having before she woke to a living nightmare?

Lydia must have fallen asleep again at some point, because the blaring of her alarm violently ripped her from slumber. She hated it when that happened. There was nothing worse than feeling discombobulated first thing in the morning.

Without thinking, she reached over and popped another two pills, throwing the rest of the packet in her handbag for later. Her clothes would need to be swapped out for something looser. Lydia thought she had a couple of days still, so had opted for a form-fitting skirt. That wouldn't be happening now, not when Lydia could physically see how swollen she was. Loose slacks and an oversized jumper it was!

With her bowl of oats consumed, Lydia kissed Monty and slowly made her way to the street. Nothing on this earth would get her to move any faster today. Norris could moan all he wanted. Lydia had to take it easy. And then she remembered the old curmudgeon was off today, so that was a silver lining.

"Lyds, wait up, love." Cathy called from behind.

Lydia stopped and unconsciously massaged her abdomen, hoping to give a little relief. She'd read that palpating just below the belly button was supposed to help with cramps.

Cathy eyed her closely. "Bloody hell, you look like shit."

"Gee Cathy, thanks."

"Sorry, but you do. Didn't you sleep?"

"Not much."

"Oh shit, it's happening, isn't it?"

Lydia couldn't help but laugh at Cathy's dramatics. "Yes, it's happening."

"Right, we have a good ten minutes before the bus turns up. Let's nip into the corner shop and get some supplies."

"What supplies?"

"We can get you small packets of nuts and some fruit for the breakroom. I read last night about eating things that will help with inflammation."

"You read things?"

"Yeah. There are loads on the internet. Do you take Omega-3? What about magnesium supplements? It's okay, we'll make a list."

Lydia let Cathy drag her to the corner shop, her friend jabbering away the entire time.

<u>5</u>

Today could take a running jump as far as Lydia was concerned. Crippling fatigue had washed over her within the first two hours of her shift. Thank God Cathy was aware of the situation and swapped places with Lydia. It took everything she had to just sit at the information desk and talk to enquiring visitors.

When lunch time rolled around, Cathy became so concerned about Lydia's pallor, she marched straight over to Norris—who had volunteered, unnecessarily, to work an extra shift, just because he enjoyed torturing his employees—and demanded he send Lydia home.

So, here she was curled up on her sofa with a surprised Monty by her feet. Embarrassment burned deep in her stomach. Lydia had always powered through. She'd never taken time off work, even though she probably should have. What must Norris think? Obviously, he didn't know the true reason Lydia was incapable of functioning today. He probably thought what Cathy used to think: Lydia had come in after a night out on the lash. Groaning, Lydia buried her head deep into the sofa cushion.

The sun had disappeared a while ago, not that Lydia had taken advantage of it. Monty had nipped outside a couple of times, but even then, Lydia simply opened the door and shuffled back to the couch. Day one was always the worst, but this month was kicking her arse.

Surprisingly, the doorbell rang at seven. It couldn't be Fe; she was at a parents' evening. The thought brought a smile to Lydia's face. Fe had been dreading it. Her terror triplets seemed hellbent on causing mayhem wherever they were, including school.

Had Cathy decided to pop round after work? That was a possibility. She was taking her "friend" status seriously. Since learning about Lydia's condition, Cathy had been a pillar of support, sometimes invasively so. At one point in the morning, Lydia had to physically remove Cathy from the toilet stall she was trying to use. No moral support was needed to pee!

Rolling off the sofa, Lydia shuffled once more. "Hang on."

Whoever was on the other side had to be patient. Lydia was currently operating at whatever was the opposite of warp speed.

And whoever had come to visit had to be okay with Lydia looking like a bridge troll. She wore the baggiest jogging bottoms and largest T-shirt in her wardrobe, with fluffy slipper booties and a topknot that screamed, *"I've been dragged backwards through a hedge."* No doubt her makeup was smudged too.

Ah, well, *c'est la vie*, right?

"Halle?"

What the chuffing hell was Halle doing here? And how dare she look so good when Lydia looked like a trash fire?

"Hey, Lyds, up for a movie night?"

"Um..."

"I stopped in to see you this afternoon. Cathy told me they'd sent you home. I'm guessing the Red Devil has appeared."

Well, this was mortifying. Did everyone know she'd started her friggin' period?

"Yeah, it's not been a super fun day for me."

"Would watching lesbian films help?"

Halle wanted to spend the evening with her watching films? What in the world was happening?

"You don't have to babysit me, Halle, I'm fine. There has to be something better you could be doing?"

Lydia watched Halle's excitement ebb away. "Sorry, I should have called first. But for the record, I didn't come here to babysit you, Lydia. I just thought it would be nice to chill together."

Now Lydia felt like an arsehole. "Shit, yeah, of course it would be. I'm just a little out of it. If you're okay with me falling asleep during the first hour, then I'd be happy to chill with you."

"You can even dribble if you want." Halle smiled, squeezing past Lydia and through the door. "I brought popcorn, but not buttered. It's supposed to be healthy. Oh, and these crisps are made from lentils or something."

Lydia followed Halle to the kitchen. Monty launched himself at the back door, demanding to be let in, so Halle could shower him with the love he deserved from every human.

"That's sweet of you, thanks. Monty, get down!"

"He's alright," Halle laughed as Monty bounced around, trying his damndest to reach Halle's outstretched arms. "Come here, you nutter."

Leaving Monty and Halle to their love fest, Lydia excused herself to the bathroom. Christ on a bike. She looked bad. Ideally, she'd jump in the shower, because her hair was not going to cooperate. The brush Lydia tried to run through it got stuck several times. In the end, she tied it back into a less frantic topknot.

At least her makeup was easy to remove, although Lydia wasn't sure she looked any better for having a fresh face. Her chin displayed several angry looking blemishes and her eyes looked tired.

"Do you want a sugar-free hot chocolate?" Halle called busying herself in the kitchen, leaving Lydia a few uninterrupted seconds to observe. Halle looked great in athletic wear. She'd probably come over straight from work.

Realising those few seconds were stretching out too long, Lydia cleared her throat. "Love some, please. Can I do anything?"

"Nope, go get comfy on the sofa. I'll be in soon."

A lightness seeped through Lydia's heavy mood. How could it not? Halle was here, taking care of her. There had been a couple of previous partners who had adopted the role, but after a few days, they got irritated with it all. Would Halle feel the same in the end?

Surely it was inevitable. Halle was only a couple of years older than Lydia's thirty-four years. She had a great job, good health, and some fine looks. As soon as the shine wore off, Halle, like everyone else, would disappear; not entirely, they were still friends, but Lydia knew she'd end up alone again, every month, until Dr Maynard worked her magic.

"Grub's up." Halle announced balancing two hot chocolates and a bowl of popcorn on a tray far too small for everything to sit safely.

"I would have helped, if you'd called." Lydia made a move to take one mug off the tray.

"Ah, ah, ah, I got it. Sit your bum down." Halle skilfully set the tray down, spilling nothing, much to the chagrin of Monty, who was eagerly awaiting to snap up any fallen popcorn kernels. "For tonight's entertainment, we have three classics. *Imagine Me & You, Kiss Me,* and *Elena Undone.*"

Lydia groaned comically. "*Elena Undone* is not a classic. It's painfully cheesy. Who names their kid Payton?"

"That rules out *Elena Undone,* then."

"I've never even heard of *Kiss Me,* so that can't be a classic either!"

"Hold the phone. You've never heard of *Kiss Me,* or its original *Kyss Mig.*"

"Nope."

"Lydia, Lydia, Lydia. How is this even possible? It's a gorgeous film. Swedish, but don't fret, it has subtitles."

"I'm gathering you'd like to watch that one."

"We have to, now. You're gonna love it, just you wait and see." Halle bent over putting the DVD in, causing Lydia to avert her eyes from Halle's toned backside.

Chuckling, Lydia curled herself in the corner of the sofa. Monty took his usual spot at the other end, leaving Halle no choice but to sit next to Lydia. The sofa was only a small two-seater, so the space between them was minimal.

"Comfy?" Halle asked, already throwing popcorn in her mouth.

"Yeah, let's do this. I've never watched a Swedish film before."

"You're in for a treat."

Even though Lydia had struggled with fatigue all day, she was wide awake now. The film—true to Halle's word—was wonderful. It was heart-warming, and no lesbians died. What a treat!

Lydia's face heated when Mia and Freda got hot and heavy on the screen. She almost strained her eyeballs, making sure she didn't look in Halle's direction.

As the credits rolled, Lydia inhaled deeply. "That was gorgeous. I can't believe I'd never heard of it before today."

"I told you so," Halle answered, her attention on her buzzing phone. Lydia gathered the mugs and bowl, leaving Halle to message whoever had contacted her. When she returned, there was a frown on Halle's face.

"Everything okay?"

"Absolutely. Do you want to watch some TV, or do you want to call it a night?"

"We can see what's on."

They were twenty minutes into a *Dr Who* episode when the doorbell went off. It was nine in the evening, and Lydia was less than impressed she had to drag her arse from her comfy spot.

Ready to give whoever it was a piece of her mind, Lydia was surprised to see Fe. "Is everything okay?"

"Yeah, why wouldn't it be?" Fe answered, pushing herself past Lydia.

"Well, because it's a bit late for a social visit."

"Halle, you're still here?"

Lydia watched the odd exchange between Fe and Halle. Had she missed something?

"Do you want a drink, Fe, or some food?"

"A cuppa would be great. I'll tell you... parents' evenings are rough."

And just like that, Lydia's night alone with Halle came to an abrupt end.

❧

"You're looking brighter today." Cathy said, smushing Lydia's face with affection.

It was day three into Aunt Flo's visit, and Lydia had woken to the sun shining and birds chirping. Her sullen mood had finally buggered off, and life was looking up, even if she was still cramping and bleeding profusely. It all seemed a little easier to cope with when the black clouds had cleared.

"I'm feeling better. You, however, look..." Lydia let her comment trail off. Cathy, who usually had an immaculate appearance, was looking rather dishevelled.

"I'm never having kids. They're monsters."

Lydia rolled her lips in, trying not to laugh at Cathy's misery. "Oh my, what happened?"

"A school trip, that's what happened."

"Hang on, you have something…" Lydia peeled what looked like Silly String off Cathy's left shoulder.

"That's just perfect. I've been walking around with cheese string on me. Wonderful."

"Why have you got cheese string on you?" Lydia made them both a cup of tea. First, because Cathy looked as if she were going to murder someone. Second, because Lydia couldn't hide her laugh any longer.

"I swear to God they were feral, the lot of them. And I can state, categorically, I detest *Night at The Museum*!"

"Um… Okay, care to elaborate?"

"The entire group was convinced the models were going to come alive. One little boy, who looked like he was jacked up on sugar, started running round the exhibits and hitting them with his cheese string, which he pretended was a sword. The teachers did bugger all!"

"Oh shit," Lydia sniggered.

"Of course, I intervened before someone got hurt or the display got damaged. Can you imagine what Norris would've said? Anyway, the little shit with the cheese string turned it on me."

"Cathy, what the hell?" Both Lydia and Cathy jumped at Harrison's voice, booming through the breakroom. "You abandoned me with a bunch of devil kids!"

"I did no such thing!"

"Yes, you did. You radioed me and asked me to help with something and then scampered the moment I arrived. I got poked in the eye with a Chupa Chups!"

"Oh, Cathy, that's mean!" Lydia interjected playfully.

"They attacked me with cheese, Harrison!"

"Have the kids left yet?" Lydia asked, breaking the glaring contest between Harrison and Cathy.

Harrison cradled his left eye dramatically. "Yeah, the teachers herded them out."

"Oh, give over, you're not blind," Cathy huffed. The whole thing was highly entertaining for Lydia.

"How about we go for a drink after work? You two deserve a pint. You're heroes!" Lydia exclaimed dramatically.

"Cathy's buying," Harrison grumbled, however, there was a glint of humour in his "good" eye. Lydia knew they would laugh their arses off about it this evening.

"Lydia should buy the drinks. She's the only one not injured."

"How are you injured? Cheese string isn't exactly a solid weapon, Cath."

"Emotionally. I'm emotionally injured."

"Good grief, fine, I will buy the drinks. Can I invite Fe and Halle?"

"Sure. The more the merrier."

Shooting off a quick text to her sister, Lydia paused momentarily. She could message Halle separately, right? That's what friends did. Christ, how long was it going to take for the friendship with Halle to stop feeling weird? Choosing to ignore her overanalysing brain, Lydia sent the invitation to Halle.

The Royal Oak Pub was bursting at the seams when Lydia pushed through the doors; later than expected, due to Norris chewing her ear off about something completely out of Lydia's job description. She'd only had enough time to change her clothes before heading back out.

Cathy and Harrison had snagged a table near the open fire, much to Lydia's delight.

"How did you get this hot piece of real estate? It's usually the first table to go."

"Cathy is magic." Harrison was deadly serious as he spoke. "There were two blokes sitting here. I went to the bar to order us some drinks. I turned around, only to find

Cathy saying something to the blokes, and then they just upped and gave her their table."

"Gotcha." There really wasn't any need for Harrison to say anymore. Lydia had witnessed Cathy's "magic" dozens of times. "I thought I was buying the drinks?"

"You're not off the hook. You can get the next round."

Slipping off her thick coat, Lydia basked in the delicious heat radiating from the fireplace.

"Oh, I'm ready for this." The first taste of a good pint of ale was always the best. Smooth and satisfying. Yum!

"There's Fe and Halle." Cathy waved them over. Lydia noticed instantly something wasn't quite right. Halle and Fe were thick as thieves; they always had been, but tonight there was an obvious tension simmering between them.

Standing from her seat, Lydia hugged Fe, then moved to Halle. "Take a seat. Harrison will get you a drink."

"Charming," Harrison mumbled, but headed to the bar.

"Everything alright?" Lydia directed the question to Fe, but her eyes strayed to Halle, who was sitting rather rigidly.

"Everything's great." Fe's overly enthusiastic reply was anything but convincing.

"How are you feeling?" Halle's voice was tense, as was her body. What the bloody hell had happened? It was unusual for Fe and Halle to fight. At the back of Lydia's mind, she wondered if their obvious spat had anything to do with Halle spending time with her.

"Much better, thanks. I have my blood tests on Friday afternoon."

"Oh, do you—"

"I'm coming with you, right?" Fe interrupted. "We can pop out for dinner after. Or spend some time with the triplets. It's been a few days."

"Um...sure. It would be nice to see them."

Harrison sat down with a pint of ale for Halle and a white wine for Fe. "I got some nuts and stuff too."

The table fell silent, and Lydia was beginning to feel uncomfortable. "How was your day, Halle?"

"Fine, thanks. I had a tough session with Ben today."

Halle'd told Lydia about Ben during their film night. He was a thirteen-year-old who was the victim of a hit and run. The incident left the young boy with only one leg.

"Oh no. What happened?"

"Who's Ben?" Cathy asked. Halle filled the rest of the table in.

"My heart just aches for him. He's the hardest working patient I think I've ever had. He's so determined to get back to a normal life. Well, as normal as possible. I see him wince every time I have to push him a little. Usually, I can handle it. It's for the patient's benefit, but with Ben... Ah, I hate it."

"He's a brave boy. And I'm sure he knows you're there to help him," Lydia said softly.

"Oh, he does. He gives it his all, every session. Today, he had to walk on his new prosthetic. He fell halfway, but he wasn't put off. He got right back up and tried again. That kid is an inspiration. I say it was a tough session, but more for me, emotionally, than it was about Ben, struggling."

Lydia gave Halle a small smile. "Hey, if you ever need to talk. You know where I live."

"That's what her bestie is for, sis. Don't worry, I've got her covered."

"I know, I was—"

"Oh, Halle, I got you a date." Fe's change of subject completely threw Lydia.

"Why?" Halle shot.

"Why not? You don't usually mind. Plus, Sally is lovely."

"No, thanks."

"What do you mean? Why wouldn't you want to go out with an available, appropriate woman?"

"Guys, what's going on?"

"Nothing's going on, Lyds," Fe replied sweetly.

"Nope, everything's fine, Lyds," Halle added.

"Uh-huh, sure." Sinking the rest of her pint, Lydia left to place another order. If it was going to be like this for the rest of the evening, she'd rather just go home.

"What's happening?" Cathy's voice was low in Lydia's ear.

"They're clearly fighting. I've no idea what *that* was about."

"It's getting worse," Harrison said, joining them at the bar. Lydia turned back to the table, only to find Halle and Fe in what seemed a heated discussion. Suddenly, Halle stood, grabbed her jacket that was hanging on the back of her chair, and walked out of the pub.

Casting a quick look at Fe, Lydia followed Halle. Foolishly, she did so without thinking of how fucking cold it was outside.

"Jesus Christ," Lydia hissed, as icy air pelted her right in the mush. "H-Halle, hang on." Bloody hell, Halle was already halfway up the street. "Halle!"

"Lydia, go back inside before you freeze."

"Not until you tell me what that shit show was about."

"It's nothing, just Fe being Fe."

"Well, that hardly narrows it down. Come on, we're friends now, right?"

"Really, Lyds, leave it alone. We'll work it out. We always do. Seriously, you need to go and sit back by the fire. You're going blue."

Lydia made another decision that she wasn't sure was a good idea. "Will you wait here for me?"

"I'm going home, Lydia. It's been a day."

"I know, and I think you could do with a chat. Away from noise and crowds. Will you wait, so I can grab my coat? The chippy is open. Let's grab a bite. Please?"

Fe was going to be pissed!

<u>6</u>

The smell of freshly fried chips made Lydia's mouth water. Battered cod was on the menu tonight, and she was going to enjoy every greasy morsel of it! Blemishes be damned.

"What can I get ya, love?" a short woman who barely reached the top of the counter asked. Lydia reeled off her order and then looked to Halle.

"I'll have the same, please."

Whatever was going on between Fe and Halle, Lydia did *not* like seeing Halle look so forlorn. They waited in silence for their food, Lydia casting a watchful eye over Halle every few seconds.

"Let's sit." Halle followed Lydia without a word. Unravelling her meal from its paper, Lydia busied herself adding salt and vinegar, hoping Halle would start talking. When it was clear Halle was going to keep schtum, Lydia pressed on. "Will you please tell me what's wrong?"

Puffing out a breath, Halle finally looked at Lydia. "Fe's just being Fe. Normally I can handle it, you know. She's always been the same. Right now, though, I'm struggling." Halle dragged a chip through a blob of ketchup, seemingly lost in thought.

"What exactly do you mean, it's 'Fe just being Fe?'" That really could mean anything.

"She's getting pissy I'm not spending enough time with her."

"Bloody hell, you practically live with her. She can't be serious. Has she had an argument with Clark? You know she gets clingy when they fight."

Fe and Clark were a brilliant match, but Clark's work schedule often led to disagreements. Although Lydia had pointed out several times, that if Fe wanted that kind of lifestyle, with the big houses and nice car, Clark had to work long hours. Fe's inheritance would only stretch so far with the way they lived.

"Maybe," Halle sighed.

"And what was with the arranged date? You didn't seem elated by that."

"Far from it. It's just…"

"Halle, you can talk to me. I know she's my sister, but I also know how much of a pain in the arse she can be."

Finally, Lydia cracked Halle's glum expression. She only showed a hint of a smirk, but it was there.

"I just wish everything I did or do, wouldn't have to be run by her. Fe's always been a control freak, and I love her for it. That's who she is. But not everyone needs their life controlled. I can find my own dates; I can have different friends. *I* can organise my life."

Chewing quickly, Lydia swallowed her fish. "How long have you felt like this?"

"A little while. I'm not the type of person to rock the boat. And Fe's had a lot going on with Clark working so much and the triple terrors."

"Yeah, she has, but that doesn't mean you should make yourself smaller to accommodate her every need. Look, Fe is a grown woman. She has support around her; that doesn't just fall on you."

"I think we've just relied on each other for so long. She finds it hard to accept change."

"Fe hates change. She always has. But again, Halle, that's her problem. Look, I adore my sister. She's my best friend, but she's not perfect. Fe can be self-centred. And most of the time, that's okay. We should all be a little selfish at times. That means you too, Halle. If you need a change, tell her. Your friendship will be fine. Fe will need a few weeks to sulk, and then she'll get over it."

"How did she take it when you left?" Halle was back to avoiding eye contact, which was strange.

"Oh, yeah, she was pissed. I knew she would be. But like I told her: You've had an emotional day and needed a chat, more than she did. Plus, Cathy and Harrison would've stayed. Cathy can get anyone talking. I guarantee, five minutes after we left, Fe had already forgotten she was mad."

"Thanks, Lyds."

"No worries. Now, how about we polish off these chips and then take a walk? It's not too late. We can talk about Ben if you want, or not?"

"I'd like that."

"Sweetie, it's lovely to see you."

Lydia's mum wrapped her up in a tight hug. Bonnie Archer was almost sixty, but she had the complexion of someone half her age. Tall, slim, and gorgeous. Well, Lydia thought so. She was also the best mum in the world. Bonnie raised Fe and Lydia by herself after their dad up and left, never once letting her heartache win. Bonnie turned her grief into love, doling it out generously, and Lydia admired her so much for it.

"Hey, Mum, you look great."

"Thanks, love. How're you feeling?"

"I'm great. I have my blood test tomorrow."

"Yes, Fe said she was going with you. You could have called, flower. I'm happy to go along with you whenever you need me to."

Chuckling, Lydia shed her coat, hanging it on the peg next to the front door. "It seems I have a whole gang of people supporting me at the moment."

"Good, so you should. Fe was upset the other day. She told me she felt as if she'd let you down."

Shaking her head, Lydia followed her mum into the kitchen. "I've never thought that."

"Tea?"

"Please." Sitting at the kitchen table, Lydia deliberated asking her mum about Fe. What could it hurt? "Mum, is Fe okay?"

"Why do you ask, love?"

"She's fighting with Halle, for one. They never fall out."

"Really? She hasn't said." Bonnie placed two cups of tea on the table. "Biscuit?"

"No thanks. Anyway, they had a blowup at the pub the other night. Halle left, so I went after her. Fe was pissed at me, but Halle seemed really upset."

"Are you and Halle friends now?"

Why was her mum looking at her like that?

"Yeah, I suppose so. She's been great with everything going on with me. I couldn't believe she got me an appointment with Dr Maynard."

"That's Halle for you." Bonnie sipped her tea, keeping an eye on Lydia, which was a little disconcerting.

"We've got a lot in common. It's been nice spending time with her."

"There's your answer then."

"What answer?"

"To what's bugging Fe."

"You've got to be kidding me. She's upset Halle and I are spending time together?"

"It's only a guess, but I'd say that would be about right."

Lydia scoffed. "That's ridiculous and childish. Halle has every right to have more than Fe as a friend, for God's sake."

"I agree, and I don't think Fe cares if Halle has other friends."

"So, you think it's me she has an issue with?"

"Talk to her, sweetie."

"Why should I?" Lydia was being stubborn. She knew it, and it was silly, but sometimes Fe really riled her up.

"Because she's your sister."

"Mum, she's the one being ridiculous."

"Maybe so, but Fe's obviously having a tough time with something."

Lydia wanted to stomp and scream. This is what Fe classed as a *tough time*? Being stupidly jealous of her friend and sister? How utterly... Argh!

"Sure, I'll talk to her. It must be really hard having to share a friend. How ever must she be coping?" Lydia's tone dripped with sarcasm.

"Lydia Marie Archer, that was mean. All because it seems insignificant or silly to you, doesn't mean it's any less upsetting for your sister."

Feeling suitably chastised, Lydia drank her tea in silence. "Sorry, Mum."

"Just talk to her, okay? Now, do you want some lunch? I'm making chicken pesto salad."

When Lydia said goodbye to her mum, she did so with the promise of heading over to Fe's that evening. It would be nice to see the kids, and to clear the air, although Lydia wasn't sure how that was going to play out. Would Fe expect Lydia to stay away from Halle?

Sending her sister a message letting her know she was stopping by this evening, Lydia tried to put the issue with Fe to the back of her mind. Norris was on her shift today, meaning Lydia needed to summon every ounce of patience to get through the day without beating herself to death with a dinosaur bone to escape his whining.

Pete, the security guard, gave her a warm smile as she entered the museum. There were kids running wild, parents looking harassed, and groups of tourists taking pictures. It was mayhem, and Lydia loved it.

"Afternoon, Pete. Everything good?"

"Aye, lass. You're gonna be busy today."

"Just how we like it. Catch you later."

A busy shift was just what the doctor ordered. Lydia had far too much zinging around in her head this afternoon. The upcoming blood tests were at the forefront of those thoughts. Excitement and trepidation bubbled low in her tummy. She'd waited so long to move in a positive direction, it was difficult to believe, in less than twenty-four hours, she might have some answers. Then, it was only two weeks until the exploratory surgery. What would happen? What would the doctor find?

"Norris is on the warpath," Gillian, another visitor assistant, mumbled as she scooted past.

Great.

Fe's house was lit up like Blackpool Tower. Paying the cab driver, Lydia took a deep breath. "Here goes nothing."

The door was unlocked, as expected. What wasn't expected—or maybe it should have been—was the three screaming children sprawled out on the floor in the foyer. Fe was nowhere to be found. Clearing her throat, Lydia tried to catch the triplets' attention, to no avail. The screaming continued, with a fist thump on the floor, thrown in for good measure.

Tiptoeing her way around the kids, Lydia set off in search of Fe, who she found sipping on a rather large glass of red wine in the kitchen.

"Oh hey, sis," Fe shouted over the din.

"Um?" Lydia jabbed her thumb over her shoulder towards the chaos.

"They're all taking some time out to think about their actions."

"I doubt there is a lot of thinking happening." Lydia's ears were ringing.

Sighing, Fe stood from the stool, held her index finger up to Lydia, silently asking her to wait a second. Lydia's eyes followed Fe into the foyer, where she laid in the middle of her children and let out an ear-piercing scream. The children immediately stopped their tantrums and stared wide-eyed at their mother, just as Lydia did. Fe was still screaming. It was almost primal.

Fe finally fell quiet, presumably after she ran out of air. That woman had a set of pipes on her. Sheesh!

Standing, Fe returned to the kitchen and her glass of wine. Lydia stood dumbstruck, not knowing what to do or say. Finally, she addressed the kids first, who looked disturbed by their mum's performance.

"Kids, why don't we head upstairs and get your pj's on?" They nodded simultaneously.

Upstairs, the triplets were still silent. What in the heavens above was going on in this house?

"Jenny, why were you all screaming on the floor?" Jenny shrugged. "Jack?"

"Daddy was supposed to be home by now. He promised he would read to us."

"He's says that every day, Jack," Joey huffed.

"Daddy called Mummy and said he would be home later. Mummy got mad and then told us we had to go to bed without a story." Jack sniffed.

Jenny's voice was quiet, almost a whisper. "Mummy could read to us, but she doesn't want to anymore."

"Oh, my little darlings, come here." Doing her best to stretch her arms around all three, Lydia squeezed the children tightly. "Mummy is probably really tired. Of course she wants to read to you. But sometimes she might not be able to, and if that happens, you can't throw yourselves on the floor like that. You scared me when I walked in."

"Sorry, Aunt Lydia. We just wanted to see Daddy," Joey said, his voice muffled in Lydia's top.

"And we wanted a story," Jenny added.

"Well, I can help with that. Go and brush your teeth and then I'll read to you, okay?"

"Yes," they collectively chimed. The triplets shared a room. Eventually, Jenny would get her own bedroom, but for now, they were still young enough they needed to stay together. They each had a single bed, all three lined up against the wall. When Fe first showed the room to Lydia, she'd laughed, because it reminded her of the seven dwarves from Snow White. The kids' beds even had their names, carved intricately into the foot of each bed frame.

Minty fresh, the kids hopped into their respective beds and settled down. Jenny had already pointed to the story they wanted. Three renditions later, Lydia kissed each goodnight and flicked off the light. Only the soft glow of a night lamp illuminated the room.

Padding downstairs, Lydia wasn't surprised to see Fe still perched on the kitchen stool with what looked like a fresh glass of wine.

"Can I have one of those?" Lydia asked, already reaching for a glass.

"Go for it."

"Want to tell me what the bloody hell that was? You sounded like a banshee. Scared the piss out of me for a second."

Fe chuckled. "Sometimes I just need to vent. They weren't listening to me, and by the time you arrived, they'd been at it for fifteen minutes."

"Jenny said Clark was supposed to read to them."

Fe gave a mirthless laugh. "Clark promises them, every time. And every time, he lets them down. Guess who gets the brunt of their ire?"

"Oh, Fe, I'm sorry, sweetie."

"Me too." Swallowing two thirds of her glass, Fe reached over and topped it right back up again. "I think we're in trouble, Lyds."

"It's that bad?" Lydia slid onto the stool next to Fe.

"Yeah. All we do is argue. The kids need to see their dad more than one hour a week."

"What about weekends?"

"He works in his home office or is out with clients."

"And you've told him how you're feeling?"

"Of course, Lydia. Bloody hell."

Holding her hands up in surrender, Lydia leaned back, giving her sister some space. "I meant nothing by that, Fe. Just trying to figure out where you're at."

A sob wracked Fe's body. "I-I'm sorry, Lyds. Shit. It's such a mess. I think Clark is having an affair."

"An affair?" The last person in this world Lydia thought would be unfaithful, was Clark.

"It's that, or he's just tired of being a family man. The kids are testing us daily. If he's not shagging someone, he's purposefully working too much so he doesn't have to deal with me or the kids."

"Christ." Lydia held her sister until Fe stopped crying.

"I have to have it out with him, Lyds. This is driving me nuts. I'd rather know than carry on like this."

"Of course. You need to talk, sweetie. I can have the kids if you want? I can take them to the museum. They always have fun there."

"On your own? Did you forget about the carnage you witnessed earlier? They're bloody monsters at the minute."

Rubbing soothing circles on Fe's back, Lydia tried to keep her voice low and calm. "I think they can sense something is going on. They probably don't understand it and are acting out."

"Great," Fe choked, "we're ruining their childhoods."

"Calm down, no one said that. The sooner you talk to Clark, the sooner you can help them understand."

"*I* need help to understand. I don't get why he's disappearing from us. Nothing has changed."

"Something has, for him, obviously. Why don't I come over Saturday afternoon? I'm not working."

"You're going to take the kids to work on your day off?"

"Hey, I love the museum, too. I can ask Halle to come along. The kids love her as much as me."

"Mmm, not sure Halle is a good choice right now."

"Are you still fighting?"

"We're not fighting," Fe huffed.

"Something's going on between you two."

"Shouldn't you already know? You ran after her the other night, after all."

"Christ, are you still sour about that? Fe, she needed to talk, and you obviously weren't in the right place to listen."

"What did she say?"

"Nope, I'm not doing that. What you tell me is confidential, and that goes for Halle, too. If you want to know, talk to her."

"I've not done anything wrong!" Fe reached for the wine bottle. Lydia intercepted it, earning a scowl.

"Getting tanked isn't going to help."

"It makes me feel better."

"Not tomorrow, it won't. You're supposed to be coming with me to my blood test."

"Shit, that's tomorrow. I haven't got anyone to look after the kids."

"Fe, you offered!"

"I'm sorry, okay. I've got my own shit going on, Lydia."

"I never said you hadn't."

"Sometimes I think *you* forget everything isn't about you and your broken fucking uterus!"

Lydia sucked in a breath. Fe should have just punched her in the chest. It would have hurt less. Grabbing her bag, she ripped her coat from the back of the stool and stormed out.

Fe's voice trailed behind her, but Lydia didn't hear what she said. Blood pulsed in her ears as she tried to keep her tears at bay. This is why she didn't ask for help and support, because some fucker always found a way to throw her condition back in her face. Lydia just couldn't believe, this time, it was Fe who'd done it.

Tears finally escaped as Lydia turned the corner, running smack into something taller than her. Christ, had she run into a phone pole? Stumbling, Lydia thrust her hand out, grabbing on to whatever it was she'd careened into.

But it wasn't a what, but a who. "Whoa, Lyds, careful."

Looking up through tear-clogged eyes, Lydia could just make out Halle's face. "S-sorry."

"Are you okay?"

Shaking her head, Lydia tried to sidestep Halle. All she wanted was to be alone. It was better that way. No doubt Halle would turn out like Fe and everyone else: tired of Lydia and her problems.

"Lydia, stop." Strong hands gripped her shoulders as Lydia tried again, in vain, to leave.

"Please, Halle, I just want to go home."

"Okay, we can do that. I parked Nora just over there. I'll drive you home."

"No, it's fine I—"

"I'm not taking 'no' for an answer."

Overcome with fatigue and hurt, Lydia let Halle steer her towards the little Mini. This was the last time she would let Halle, or anyone else, help.

<u>7</u>

Lydia jabbed the 'reject' button on her phone for the third time. Fe was persistent, but Lydia was pissed. Fe could stew for a while longer. Halle's silence for the entire journey to Lydia's place was wholly unpleasant.

"Just drop me off, thanks." Lydia wanted to be alone, and knowing Halle, she would try to walk her to the door. As sweet as that was, Lydia didn't need it right now.

"I'll walk you to—"

"No, really, it's fine. You should go back to Fe's and talk to her."

"Aren't you going to tell me what upset you so much?"

"No, not tonight. I'd just like to be alone."

Lydia saw Halle fighting herself, wanting to argue. Thankfully, she didn't push any farther. Giving a tight smile, Lydia bid her a good night and left the car. Monty was by her side the moment she stepped through the door.

"Hey, buddy." God, she wished he could talk. Lydia wouldn't need another living soul, then. No one to make her feel bad. No one to care about. "It would be great, Monty. Don't you think? Just me and you, against the world."

The little pooch cocked his head to one side, listening to Lydia ramble on. Lydia's phone buzzed again. Scoffing as she read the name, there was little choice but to answer.

"Hi, Mum." That was a low blow on Fe's part. Using their mother to get Lydia to talk. Another red mark against her sister.

"Fe called, love."

"I'm truly shocked," Lydia deadpanned. This was Fe, all over. Say something hurtful, and then when Lydia needed space to cool off, Fe would push to be forgiven, and if that didn't work, call in the big guns. Lydia could never ignore her mum.

"No need to be like that. I'm just ringing to check up on you."

"Sorry, Mum. I'm fine, just tired, so I plan to have an early night."

"Fe told me what she said." Well, that was a surprise. Fe didn't normally admit any fault. "She knows what she said was wrong, love. Can you call her?"

"I appreciate she's sorry, Mum, but I just need a little space? We're both going through something and clearly need to deal with those things in our own way."

"Lydia—"

"Mum, please."

"All right, all right. I'll leave it. But, honey, please don't leave it too long."

Gritting her teeth, Lydia took a silent breath. There was no point arguing. Fe would always get the benefit of the doubt where their mum was concerned. "Thanks for calling, Mum. I'll talk to you tomorrow."

Throwing the phone down, Lydia headed for the kitchen and the bottle of wine in the cupboard. Screw it. She needed a drink. Sure, the alcohol might exacerbate her cramps and pain, but so what? Lydia was already hurting.

The bottle of Merlot disappeared, leaving Lydia hungover the next morning and regretting every decision she ever made. Dragging herself to the bus stop was the icing on the cake. It was freezing cold and icy underfoot.

Well, I'm going to the doctor's, so at least I'll be in the right place if I fall.

Lydia took a cursory glance at her phone. She was solely relying on Google Maps to get her to the appointment on time. Dr Maynard had contacted a good friend of hers and got Lydia registered at his practice. She really had a lot to thank Halle for.

Stepping off the bus, Lydia cursed her stupidity. A bottle of wine on an almost empty stomach was a rookie move. Quelling her nausea the best she could, Lydia forced herself to walk. In reality, she would give her left boob for a bed and a weighted blanket right now.

The building which housed her new doctor was set in a Victorian townhouse. The setting imparted a sense of homey comfort; a stark contrast to the sterility of Dr Watson's.

The waiting room was relatively busy. Heading to the reception desk, Lydia felt that usual pang of nerves. "Hi. Lydia Archer, here for a blood test."

"Good morning," the young receptionist replied. His hair was gelled within an inch of its life. "Take a seat and the nurse will be with you soon."

Her bum had only just touched the padded fabric of the waiting room chair, when a gorgeous woman in blue scrubs stepped out of a door next to the reception desk. "Lydia Archer?"

If it had been appropriate, Lydia would have given the nurse a low whistle. Holy cow, she was stunning: long dark hair tied up in a high ponytail and golden eyes that sparkled. Okay, they didn't really sparkle, but Lydia was in that place between reality and fantasy as she looked on.

"Ms Archer?"

Clearing her throat and blushing profusely, Lydia scrambled from the seat. Keeping her head down, she followed the very shapely bottom of Nurse Hottie.

"Take a seat. I'm Nurse Bell. We're going to draw some blood today. Is that correct?"

"Y-yes, that's right."

"Excellent. Can you roll your sleeve up?" Following Nurse Bell's request, Lydia let her eyes wander again. It had been a while since someone had grabbed her attention like this. "How are you with needles?"

"No problems."

"Lovely. Okay, ready?" Lydia nodded. Nurse Bell efficiently extracted three vials of blood. "All done. We'll get these sent off today. You should receive results within a few days. A copy of the results will be sent to Dr Maynard."

"Great, thanks." Lydia rolled her sleeve down and fumbled to pick up her bag. She was a bumbling idiot around this woman.

For all her nerves, the appointment lasted less than ten minutes. Deciding a hot cup of coffee was in order, Lydia left the surgery and headed into the local town. On the corner of the high street stood a quaint little café. It was quite unbelievable; she was only a bus ride away from the centre of London. The town seemed lost in time, which Lydia appreciated.

The inside of the coffeehouse was warm and cosy. Soft sofas and armchairs took up most of the room. The counter area was small and crammed with optional extras. Lydia eyed the salted caramel slice until finally winning the internal war against her hunger monster.

"A black coffee, please."

"Anything else?"

Did the barista know how badly she wanted that caramel slice?

"No thanks, that's everything."

"Take a seat, love, and I'll bring it over."

Settling on an overstuffed armchair in the corner of the room, Lydia scanned the sitting area. There were several other customers, all of whom seemed relaxed.

They must be regulars.

Lydia could imagine coming here every morning for a coffee, watching the world go by without a care in the world.

"Here y'are. One coffee."

"Lovely, thank you." Watching the barista leave, Lydia scanned the café again and then let her gaze drift outside. The little high street was busy. People scuttled by, trying to get on with their day. Lydia's mind wandered to the blood test. Would it reveal anything? Would the results stop her from having the exploratory surgery?

Two coffees later, Lydia was getting ready to head home. "Ms Archer?" Lydia snapped her head up, only to find two golden eyes staring back. Nurse Hottie stood next to Lydia's table with a smile on her face.

"Nurse Hot...Bell, hello."

"Are you leaving?"

She obviously wants the table.

"Oh, yes, here, take the table." A warm sensation crept up Lydia's arm. Looking down, she saw Nurse Bell's hand on her forearm.

"Would you like to join me?"

Um, was that ethical? Nurse Hottie was, after all, Lydia's nurse. Or was she? It's not like they'd be running into each other soon. Lydia didn't plan to have blood extracted regularly. No, it was fine.

If Lydia had any more coffee, she'd be vibrating off the chair. "Sure, I'll—"

"Do you like hot chocolate?"

"Love it."

"I'll be right back."

Oh my God! I'm going to have hot chocolate with Nurse Hottie. Shit, don't call her that to her face, you numpty.

So much for Lydia's vow to focus solely on herself. Well, what choice did she have? Nurse Bell was simply lovely. Plus, the nurse hadn't indicated this was anything more than a friendly meetup. It would be quite nice to make a new friend.

"This is the best hot chocolate in the UK." Nurse Bell stated, sitting opposite Lydia, sipping on her own gargantuan mug of chocolatey goodness.

"That's quite the statement, Nurse Bell," Lydia laughed.

"Zoe. Nurse Bell sounds weird when I'm not at work."

"Then call me Lydia."

"So, Lydia, do you admit this is the best hot chocolate in all the UK?"

Laughing, Lydia took a hearty gulp. The chocolate assaulted her taste buds in the most delicious way. "Holy cow! That's yummy!"

"I told you so. It's a secret family recipe."

"Are you a local here?"

"My family owns it. That's my sister." Zoe tilted her head to the barista, who wasn't even trying to hide the fact she was eavesdropping.

"Oh, wow. So could you tell me what the secret ingredient is?"

"I could, but that's reserved for very special people. We'd have to go out on a few dates first."

❦

"A date, Monty. Can you believe it?"

Monty clearly didn't believe it either. How had Lydia left the house for a blood test and returned with a date? So much for swearing off people. That lasted all of a couple of weeks.

"She's super-hot, though, Monty. If you saw her, you'd totally understand. Nurse Bell, that's her name. Well, Zoe is her actual name, but I enjoy calling her Nurse Bell.

Maybe we can roleplay?" Monty yipped. "You're right, I shouldn't be thinking like that. We need to have dinner before any sexy times." Lydia had finally stopped bleeding, so she was ready for action if it came to that.

Wow, it was good to feel that side of herself again. Like a normal, sexual adult. Halle's face flashed across Lydia's mind. Nurse Zoe wasn't the only one who made her feel that way, but Halle was off limits. Shaking her head, Lydia busied herself by rifling through her wardrobe. Jogging bottoms and baggy T-shirts wouldn't do.

Lydia would usually call Fe with any type of wardrobe emergency. Picking up her mobile, she scrolled to Fe's contact. Huffing out a breath, she hit the green call button. If Lydia didn't make an effort, she would have her mum harassing her until she gave in anyway. Add on to the fact that Lydia was worried about her sister, she knew there was no point sulking. Fe's words cut deep, and Lydia would need a little time to forget, but her sister was struggling. If anyone could understand what it felt like to be out of control, it was Lydia.

"Lyds, oh God, I'm so sorry!"

"Jesus, were you waiting with the phone already to your ear?" The speed at which Fe answered the call was shockingly fast.

"Yes. I was just deciding whether to call again. If you didn't pick up, I was going to come to your apartment with a boombox."

Lydia chuckled. "That's a tad romantic, Fe. You can just buy me a drink sometime."

"Do you forgive me? I shouldn't have taken my frustration out on you, Lyds."

"It's okay. Let's just forget about it, yeah?"

"Alright. But I will definitely buy you that drink, and a takeaway, too."

"Deal. Now, how are you? Did you speak to Clark?"

Fe's sob told Lydia everything she needed to know. "He moved out this morning."

"Shit! Fe, what happened?"

"He's been sleeping with Janey."

"His fucking secretary. Oh, for God's sake."

Could you be any more cliché, Clark? Arsehole.

"What do I do now?" Fe wasn't looking for an answer. Her sobs grew heavier, and Lydia's heart broke for her sister.

"Right, I'll be over in half an hour. Where are the kids?"

"Halle took them to the park."

"Good. I'll be there soon, sweetie. Don't worry. We've got you."

Grabbing her duffle bag from the bottom of the wardrobe, Lydia crammed as many clothes in as possible.

"Come on, Monty, we need to see Aunty Fe."

The cab arrived just as Lydia locked the front door. Hopefully, the driver wouldn't have an issue with Monty riding along. Throwing everything into the backseat, including herself, Lydia wrapped the seatbelt around herself and Monty.

"He's a little cutie." The driver remarked.

Ah, Monty's charm wins over another unsuspecting human.

"I've never seen a dog with such pretty eyes. Is that weird to say?" The driver was a big burly guy with a heavy London accent.

"Not at all. Everyone always comments on them."

"Where to then, love?"

Supplying the driver with Fe's address, Lydia blew some hair out of her face. She was feeling all hot and bothered after rushing around like her arse was on fire. Monty wasn't as flustered. He sat silently, looking out the window as the world rushed by.

Twenty minutes later, Lydia paid and thanked the cabbie. Monty shot off towards Fe, who was already at the door waiting. Lydia watched on as her sister made cooing noises at her little man.

Setting her bag on the floor, Lydia scooped Fe into her arms. "I'm here. Let it out."

Fe didn't need telling twice. Lydia felt her top become damp with tears. Only the triplets' screams pulled them from their embrace. Lydia looked over her shoulder to see what the ruckus was about. Halle had Jack and Jenny hanging off her belt buckle, pleading for ice cream. Joey simply stomped his protest at the door.

"Kids," Fe barked. "Knock it off."

"How was the park, niblets?" Giving Halle a quick smile, Lydia wrangled the children away from Fe and into their playroom. "Did you have fun?"

"Yeah, but we wanted ice cream. Aunty Halle said we had to wait until after dinner."

"Those are the rules, you know that," Halle called from the hallway.

"Rules are stupid," Jenny protested.

"That might be so, but you guys need to stop throwing strops every time you don't like what you're told." Lydia understood they were reacting to the tension and stress in the house. That's why she was determined to stay as long as possible to help them all get through the tough times ahead. "How about you watch TV for a while? If you're good from now until dinnertime, I'll order Chinese."

"Yes!" Jack shouted, pumping his fist. The three terrors ran as fast as their little legs could take them.

One crisis down.

"You can't keep bribing them," Fe said from the kitchen island, deflated. Halle had the kettle boiling, ready to make everyone a cup of tea.

"I can and will," Lydia stated. "They're happy for now, which gives us time to talk and come up with a plan. Oh, and I'm staying with you for a while."

"Lydia, you don't nee—"

"It's happening, Fe. Now, tell me exactly what was said."

Lydia listened intently as Fe recalled her conversation. Clark was sleeping with his secretary, who was almost twenty years his junior. He'd told Fe this 'Janey' was in love with him. Apparently, he still loved Fe, but felt he had to give a relationship with Janey a real chance. He was happy for the kids to stay with Fe in the family home.

How chivalrous of him.

"I think he's having a midlife crisis," Halle chimed in. "Clark's forty this year and is suddenly feeling it. I'm telling you: Give it a few months and he'll come crawling back."

"I don't want him to come crawling back," Fe hiccupped.

"What do you want?" Lydia could see the conflict in her sister's eyes. She was sad and hurt, but Fe was also livid.

"I'm going to file for a divorce."

"Wow, really?" Halle's eyebrows were almost in her hair.

"Yes. I'm not hanging around while he decides if he wants this family. If Clark wants to shack up with this Janey, then she can have him. The kids need structure and safety."

"Are you sure you don't want to think about it a little more?" The last thing Fe should do—in Lydia's opinion—was make decisions based on how she was feeling at this moment.

"I'm positive. I've known for a while something was seriously wrong. I think I just needed him to tell me. I deserve better. The kids do too."

"I'll support whatever you want to do."

"For now, I want to have a glass of wine, eat too much food, and try to enjoy an evening with my kids and two best friends."

"Now that we can do," Halle piped up. "I'll order the food. Fe, go give the kids a kiss. They're freaking out, and Lyds, do you want to pour the drinks? I don't think tea is going to cut it."

"On it," Lydia chirped. She'd just finished pouring the second glass of wine when it hit her. Lydia had a date with Nurse Hottie tonight! Shit, she'd completely spaced. "Crap, crap, crap."

"That's an awful amount of craps," Halle laughed. "Did you spill?"

"No, I forgot I had a date tonight," Lydia replied. "Where's my bloody phone?"

"Here." Halle handed Lydia the mobile. "I thought you weren't dating."

Glancing up from the screen, Lydia saw it plain as day on Halle's face: Anger. What the hell?

"I wasn't, but it just sort of happened."

"How does it 'just sort of' happen?"

"She was the nurse who took my bloods today."

"The nurse hit on you?" Halle's pitch was climbing higher and higher.

"No, I bumped into her at a coffee shop later on. We got talking, and she asked me out."

"And you said yes?"

"Yes, I did. What's with the third degree?"

"No third degree." Halle held up her hands in surrender. "You should go. I've got Fe."

"Lydia should go where?" Fe asked, swiping up one of the full wine glasses.

"She has a date."

Okay, Lydia couldn't miss the look that passed between Halle and Fe.

"It's not a big deal." If only her words rung true. For whatever reason, this now felt like a huge deal, and Lydia wasn't entirely sure why.

<u>8</u>

“I’m so sorry I’m late.” Lydia tried in vain to smooth down her hair. *God damn wind*. She’d left Fe’s looking pretty good, even if she did say so herself. But after the sodding bus broke down, she’d had to leg it to the restaurant, making her late and windswept.

If that wasn’t bad enough, Lydia’s mood was already in the toilet from her earlier conversation with Halle. What was Halle’s issue? So what if Lydia had gone back on her promise and agreed to a date? That wasn’t Halle’s concern, or Fe’s.

“No worries. I ordered you a red wine. I hope that was okay?” Zoe looked stunning in tight red jeans, a black silk top, and heels. Her hair was loose around her shoulders.

"It's perfect, thank you. I'm not normally late, I swear." Lydia regaled Zoe with her tale of woe and the danger she'd encountered to get to the restaurant. Thankfully, Zoe found her dramatics funny, which was what Lydia was going for. Being a little silly helped break the tension. And, boy, was Lydia tense.

"So, apart from your daring journey here, how have you been since this morning?" Zoe grinned wolfishly, and Lydia felt it all the way down to her toes.

"Well, it's been so long. I'm not sure I have the time to catch you up on everything that's happened since we spoke."

"We have all evening." Zoe's tone was low and sultry.

Lydia slyly pinched her arm to make sure she wasn't hallucinating. After all the crappy partners, she'd given up on finding someone. Not that Zoe was suddenly her partner, but she definitely had potential. A nurse would be understanding of Lydia's medical issues. Maybe that would make all the difference. Not that she expected Zoe to look after her or anything. Oh Jesus, she was spiralling.

"My brother-in-law is shagging his secretary." Well, that certainly did the trick. Lydia was no longer spiralling because she was dying of embarrassment instead.

Zoe's going to think I'm not fit to be around other adults at this rate. Chill the fuck out Lyds.

"Oh shit. That's awful."

"Yeah, it's pretty crappy. Although my sister, Fe, said she'd suspected for a while. It all came to blows last night, and he left this morning."

"Jesus. You could have cancelled. I would have understood. I imagine your sister is in a bit of a state."

"She's in the anger stage at the moment. Plus, she has her best friend staying over tonight."

Zoe seemed to pause momentarily. "Does that mean you don't have to rush off this evening, then?"

"No, I'm all yours." Lydia smiled internally. That was a decent bit of flirting.

"Hmm, really. All mine?" Okay, maybe she was in over her head. Zoe had mad flirting skills.

"All yours." Lydia replied smoothly.

Good answer Lyds.

"Then let's enjoy dinner. Maybe we could go to mine after?"

Swallowing thickly, Lydia nodded. She'd prepared for this. Everything was neatly groomed and waxed. A quick look at the calendar earlier told Lydia it had almost been three months since she'd had sex. Tim didn't take kindly to only being able to fuck her twice in their entire relationship.

Lydia sighed. Out loud, apparently, because Zoe was giving her concerned eyebrows. "Everything okay?"

"Yes, absolutely. I just zoned out for a millisecond."

"Nowhere nice by the looks of it."

Should Lydia tell Zoe now about her issues? It was only fair to give the woman a heads up.

"Um...okay, so this is a little awkward. It's just that, well...um."

"Are you married? Engaged? On the run?"

Smiling, Lydia answered. "No, no, and no. I have some issues with..." Lydia made a circular motion around her nether regions.

"You've got an STI?"

"Jesus, no!" Bloody hell, this was going horribly. "The reason I came in for blood tests today was to have my hormone levels checked. I'm getting tested for endometriosis soon."

"Ah, okay. I'm sorry you're going through that. My mum had a hell of a time when she was younger. I remember it vividly and prayed I'd never get my period."

"Is she alright now?"

"She ended up having a hysterectomy. But she'd already had me and my brother, so she was okay with it."

Dread settled in Lydia's stomach. Could that happen to her?

"I'm glad she's okay now. I have exploratory surgery soon. Hopefully, that will give me some answers."

"I take it the previous partners haven't understood?"

"They said they did until reality set in. That's why I wanted to be upfront with you. Um...I'd be happy to go home with you tonight, if that's where we're heading. I just can't promise I'll be able to do that often."

Leaning over, Zoe rested her hand on Lydia's. "I understand. Really. There's no pressure here. I'd like to get to know you, both in and out of the bedroom." With a sexy wink, Zoe made Lydia blush and ruin her knickers at the same time.

"I'd like that too."

With that conversation out of the way, Lydia relaxed. Zoe was so easy to talk to; attentive, social, and hella gorgeous. There were people eyeing her up left, right, and centre, which irked Lydia a little, until she remembered Zoe was here with her, and so far, hadn't taken those amber eyes off of Lydia.

Choosing wisely, Lydia ate a Caesar salad. Nothing was less flattering or sexy than a food baby. Together, they polished off a bottle of wine and were suitably lubricated for the next part of their evening. Lydia giggled at the word 'lubricated'.

"Ready to get out of here?" Zoe cooed, her lips close to Lydia's ear, making her shudder.

"Very!"

The walk to Zoe's flat was ten minutes of hushed giggling and soft touches. Lydia couldn't have told anyone what the flat looked like if they paid her. The moment the door opened, Zoe pulled her in, kissing her fiercely.

With her back now against the closed door, Lydia let herself go. Zoe was on a mission to get her clothes off as fast as possible, and Lydia was all for it.

"God, your tits are amazing," Zoe commented, as she stared hungrily at Lydia's breasts. Where her bra had gone was a mystery. Zoe practically ripped every article of clothing off her and chucked them haphazardly. "I want your nipples in my mouth."

Lydia groaned with anticipation. Not one for dirty talk, she was more than happy to let Zoe chatter away. The sensation of soft, hot lips sucking her left nipple made

Lydia's legs buckle. The slight pinch of her right nipple pulled out a few expletives.

"Zoe, if you don't slow down, I'm going to come."

"Good." Zoe growled, and sucked harder. Slamming her head against the door, Lydia was lost to the tidal wave of pleasure that started from her chest and zinged down to her crotch. Never had she orgasmed from just nipple play! But goddamn if it wasn't about to happen.

"Shit, oh God, Zoe... I—" Lydia's deep moan echoed through the hallway. She could feel wetness running down her thighs.

Zoe was panting, her eyes deep pools of hunger. "That was fantastic." Dropping to her knees, she wasted no time lapping up the droplets of pleasure making their way down Lydia's inner thigh.

"Whoa, okay." Gripping the doorframe, Lydia held on for dear life. Zoe was insatiable and had a very gifted tongue. Every swirl, suck, and nibble continued to send shocks of pleasure through Lydia's pussy. After one particularly feisty suck on her clit, Lydia grabbed Zoe's head tight. "Oh, shit!"

There was no stopping her legs from giving way after that. Slumping to the floor, Lydia lazily opened her eyes. Zoe sat on her haunches, licking her lips. A few seconds passed, and it was clear Zoe was getting ready to go again. The woman hadn't shed one item of clothing yet.

"You need to be naked," Lydia panted.

With swift ease, Zoe rose and stripped. "My pleasure. Let's go to my room. I have plans for you."

With no desire to stay on the hard floor, Lydia scrambled to her feet. Zoe pulled her down the short hall and practically pushed her onto the bed.

"Can I touch you?" Lydia was desperate to get her hands on Zoe's body.

"Yes. But not yet. Do you like straps?"

Well, that was a surprise. Lydia rarely enjoyed playing with toys until she started dating someone seriously. It was a comfort thing, but Zoe's energy gave Lydia the courage to give it a whirl.

"Yes, I do." Some of the best sex she's ever had was with a strap. Mary, her ex, had been extremely gifted when it came to wielding her silicone appendage. Unfortunately, since having problems down there, Lydia sometimes found penetration painful. Not every time. But she wouldn't know until she gave it a shot.

"Excellent. On all fours. Hold on to the headboard."

"You won't need lube," Lydia muttered, already feeling herself dripping with excitement. She'd meant to say it quietly, as an offhand comment, but the wide smile on Zoe's face said she'd heard.

Crawling onto her hands and knees, Lydia glanced over her shoulder. Zoe was already in the harness, attaching the toy. It was big and oddly shaped. A sliver of panic fluttered in Lydia's tummy. It had been a while since she'd had anything that size in her.

Please don't hurt.

"I'll go slow. Don't worry." The fact that Zoe could read Lydia so well already was a tremendous comfort, and a bigger turn on. Communication was key, whether that was in a relationship or just in the bedroom.

"It's been a while for me."

"Would you prefer to wait? I really don't mind." Zoe paused.

Weighing up her options, Lydia steeled herself. Yes, the toy was big, but it really turned her on. Looking at Zoe standing with it between her legs was something else. The woman was sex on a stick and Lydia needed her.

"I want you inside me."

Stroking the toy, Zoe approached slowly, her eyes lasered on Lydia's waiting sex. Another two strides and she was behind her, gripping Lydia's hips. "Christ, you are stunning. I want to fuck you into next week."

"Do it, then." Lydia's tone was impatient. Her head dropped to the mattress, exposing her pussy more. "I need it."

The first thrust was gentle. Still, it took Lydia a few seconds to adjust. Zoe's constant stream of dirty talk helped her relax. It wasn't physically possible for Lydia to get any more excited.

"Faster."

Zoe picked up her pace, driving the toy deeper. This was the most erotic and fun sex, Lydia had ever experienced. Zoe was so sure of herself; so sure of knowing how to please her.

"Oh shit, I'm going to come," Zoe announced. Lydia was so lost in euphoria, she couldn't answer. The sound of Zoe's hips chaotically slapping into Lydia's backside demonstrated how close Zoe was.

"Oh. My. God!" Lydia cried into the pillow as Zoe screamed her own orgasm into the room.

Dropping to her stomach, Lydia felt her whole body turn to jelly. She wasn't going to be walking anytime soon.

The smell of bacon hit Lydia's olfactory senses with a vengeance. If her body didn't ache so much, she would have sprung out of Zoe's bed to chase said bacon. Alas, her legs were still jellified, and her abs were on fire.

"Good morning, sexy."

Lydia's eyes flew open, immediately settling on Zoe, who leaned against the doorframe. With coffee in one hand and what looked like a bacon sandwich on a plate in the other.

"Morning," Lydia mumbled. "Something smells good."

"That would be your breakfast. Ready for some fuel?"

Dragging her body into an upright position, Lydia felt herself come alive. Maybe it was the smell of caffeine, or maybe it was Zoe Bell in lingerie, ready to serve her food. Whichever was the cause, Lydia was happy to be wide awake.

"I could get used to this."

"And I like the sound of that." Zoe perched on the bed next to a sleep-ruffled Lydia. "Would you want to do this again? Go on a date, I mean?"

Chewing as fast as she could, Lydia nodded through her mouth full of bacon. Finally, at an acceptable size to swallow, Lydia was free to answer with words. "That would be great. I think last night went well."

Instantly, her face heated. She hadn't meant the sex part, although that *had* gone exceptionally, in her opinion. Zoe was nice to be around. It was as simple as that. And Lydia was ready for someone nice. Hopefully, someone who would stick around.

"How about this weekend?"

"I have work on Saturday, but I'll be finished by six."

"Perfect. Now that's sorted, how about you finish that sandwich and then join me in the shower? I have to be at the surgery in a couple of hours, but until then, I'm free as a bird."

The bacon sandwich disappeared in record time. Lydia's jelly legs held up long enough to get to the shower, where Zoe did unspeakable things to her body. Again.

It took a good twenty minutes for them to say goodbye. Zoe was going to be late for work, and Lydia was positive Fe would start to worry soon. Sure, a quick text to her sister relaying her safety would've helped, but that meant tearing her lips away from Zoe for more than a second.

"Look who the cat dragged in. Glad you're not dead," Fe hollered from the kitchen.

Conscious that she was walking funny, Lydia did her best to look casual. "Sorry, I should've texted."

"I'm gathering the night went well then."

Lydia could have done without her sister's waggling eyebrows.

"It was a lovely evening."

Fe burst out laughing. "*It was a lovely evening.* Come off it, you've got two hickeys on your neck."

Lydia's hands flew to the offending area. Zoe had marked her? Oh great, now she'd have to wear a turtleneck under her work polo.

"Are they really bad?"

"Well, they're visible. Don't stress, we can cover them. So, come on. Out with it."

"Fe, I am not discussing my sex life with you." Lydia's cheeks were burning again. Fe strained to look over her shoulder, clearly checking the coast was clear. Obviously, she didn't want the kids to overhear.

"Spill!"

Huffing out an irritated breath, Lydia skimmed over her evening. Fe looked giddy, but continued to check that there was no one close by.

"Where are the triplets?"

"Mum stopped by first thing and picked them up. She's taking them clothes shopping."

So, if the kids weren't here, who was Fe looking out for?

"Why do you keep looking over your shoulder? It's weird."

"Do I?"

"Yeah, you do. Is someone here? Please don't tell me Clark came slithering back."

"Of course not. Halle is upstairs taking a shower."

"And you don't want her listening to our conversation?"

It wasn't Lydia's imagination. Fe and Halle had definitely been acting weird lately. The shared looks, the bickering, and now Fe on the lookout for Halle.

In all the years the Archers had known Halle, Lydia couldn't think of one instance where Fe wanted to keep a conversation secret from her best friend.

"Well... I...I wasn't sure if you wanted her to hear your business, is all."

Yep, definitely weird.

"Ookayy. I'm not fussed. Halle has heard worse." Chuckling to herself, Lydia set her purse down and began fixing herself a cup of strong coffee.

"Are you seeing Zoe again?"

"Yep, Saturday evening. I'll text you this time if I stay out."

"Lyds, you really don't need to stay here. I'm fine, honestly."

"Fe, I'm staying. Have you thought more about the situation with Clark?"

"You mean, if I still want to divorce his cheating arse?"

"Yeah."

"Yes, I still want to. Mum gave me the name of a lawyer she knows. I think she had a fling with him once. I didn't ask."

"Eww. I can't think of Mum with a man." Lydia shuddered.

"Halle is going to stay for a couple of days, too."

"Oh, okay. Is that your way of telling me to bugger off? Don't want to share time with your bestie?"

Lydia had been joking, but the look that washed over Fe's face wasn't one that found her quip funny.

"You can be friends with Halle."

"Um, thanks. I was only kidding."

"Lyds, I think there's something I should tell yo—"

"Ah, the wanderer returns." Halle strolled into the kitchen, her freshly showered scent filling up the room.

God, she smells great.

"Did you have a good evening?"

"Lovely, thanks." Lydia found that, in fact, she *didn't* want to talk to Halle about Zoe. Weird. "How were the three amigos?"

"Filled with Chinese and ice cream. They asked where Clark was." Fe answered.

"And you handled it perfectly, sweetie." Halle added. She always knew what to say. Lydia was happy Fe still had that kind of support. Not that she didn't get it from her sister, but sometimes a person needed an outsider to put things into perspective. Not that Halle was an outsider—oh, for the love of beans—Lydia was in her head again.

"Right, I'm going to change clothes and then we can get organised. I'll draw up a rota for the kids. On the days I'm not at the museum, I can take them to and from school. That gives you time to deal with lawyers and whatnot."

Fe hiccupped and drew Lydia in, pulling Halle along for the ride. Together, the three women stood in the kitchen, simply holding each other. Lydia's text alert finally broke the spell.

Reaching over, Lydia's heart rate increased with excitement and then, strangely, with panic. The text was from Zoe, recounting some of her favourite parts of their night together. That was exciting to read. The panic came from the looks Fe and Halle were exchanging. Halle looked crestfallen and Fe looked guilty.

Slipping the phone into her purse, Lydia made a quick getaway to the bedroom. She needed to change, so she wasn't *really* running away from whatever the hell was going on. And she was certainly not running away from some peculiar feelings that were making their presence known; feelings that had a lot to do with Halle Cartwright.

9

What was Lydia witnessing? A limp piece of lettuce hung from her fork, close to her mouth, forgotten as she looked between Cathy and Harrison. They weren't acting strangely, but there was something.

Cathy wiped her mouth and shot a quick look at Harrison. If Lydia hadn't been studying the duo, she would have missed it. Hm, something strange was afoot, indeed.

"Fancy a drink tonight, Cath?"

"Sure. You know I'm always up for a tipple or two, even on a school night."

"Harrison?"

"Sure."

The great conversationalist strikes again.

"Great, see you after work then." Reluctantly, Lydia left the table. If Norris weren't prowling the halls, she'd have happily been a little late going back to work. However, Norris was on shift and in an extraordinarily grumpy mood. Why the man didn't retire was anyone's guess. He clearly didn't like his job anymore.

"Lydia!"

Speak of the Devil.

"Norris, what can I do for you?"

"Get to the gift shop. I need you there. Benjamin called in sick."

"Righto." With a little salute, Lydia turned on her heel, happy to be assigned to the gift shop and out of Norris's way.

Breaking up two young lads getting their arses handed to them by their younger sister, via a wooden sword, was the highlight of Lydia's day. The incident reminded her so much of Jack, Jenny, and Joey. After notifying Fe she would be a little late getting home, Lydia headed for the pub. Cathy and Harrison were already seated, drinks on the table, waiting.

"Another day done," Lydia sighed. Hooking her coat on the rack close to their table, she sipped greedily on the pint in front of her.

"Is it me or is Norris getting even less patient, even with the visitors?" Cathy commented between sips of white wine.

"It's not you, Cat. That man needs to retire and find some peace." Harrison hadn't even looked up from the book he was reading.

Lydia looked from Harrison to Cathy. Cat? He called her Cat! And why was Harrison reading Shakespeare in the pub?

"Harrison, could you fetch me some Scampi Fries from the bar?" Cathy asked. Without a word, Harrison laid his copy of *Othello* down and skittered off to the bar.

"Okay, what is happening?" Cutting straight to the point, Lydia waited as Cathy sucked in a breath.

"Harrison asked me out a few days ago and I said 'yes'. We've spent nearly every day together so far. And, Lydia, it's been wonderful!"

"You said he was as dumb as a bag of rocks!"

"I was wrong. So wrong. You were right, he was just shy."

"Hang on, you need to explain this more."

"It's simple really," Harrison interjected. "I've had a thing for Cathy since I started at the museum. I finally found the courage to ask her out, and here we are. Well, she said 'no' the first time."

"You know why I said no, Harrison."

Lydia sat back and watched the two converse.

"Yeah, yeah. Age gap and all that. Nothing that matters."

"It mattered at the time," Cathy gently scolded.

"But it doesn't now?" Lydia asked.

"No, it doesn't," Cathy answered, garnering a smile from a very smitten Harrison.

"We need a girls' night, because I need all the details," Lydia laughed.

"Indeed. Because you owe me details about a certain nurse!"

"In that case, ladies. I'm going to excuse myself. I'll see you later." Harrison bent slightly to kiss Cathy on the cheek.

"Okay, I'll call you."

The moment Harrison was out of sight, Lydia rounded on Cathy. "You sly vixen. You've been getting it on with *Harrison*!"

Chuckling, Cathy took her time before answering. "I'm as shocked as you, Lyds. When he first asked me, I almost laughed at him. I mean, he's Harrison. Not exactly a wordsmith most days. But he was totally sincere. I turned him down anyway, because he's nearly twenty years younger than me. I mean, how desperate must I look?"

This was a new side to Cathy. Lydia knew her as a confident, outgoing, outspoken woman. But now, Cathy's vulnerability was shining through.

"If you were a man and Harrison a woman, this wouldn't even be an issue. Don't let anyone's opinion stop you from doing what you want."

Cathy smiled. "That's what Harrison said."

"Smart man."

"He is. Oh Lydia, he really is. I got him so wrong. Did you know he has a master's degree and is working on his PhD?"

"Jesus, really?"

"Yes. When Harrison talks, it's because he has something worth saying. I couldn't believe it when we were on our first date. Took me completely by surprise."

"Wow, I mean, I can imagine."

"And he was such a gentleman. We chatted for hours, and when the date ended, he gave me a kiss on the cheek, just like he did before leaving tonight."

"Have you...you know!"

"Lydia Archer, since when do I kiss and tell?"

"Every time. Now, out with it."

"Fine, yes, we've had sex. Let's just say the shy demeanour doesn't extend to the bedroom."

Lydia could have done without the wink, but she did ask for details.

"Harrison, the sex fiend. Nice. I'm happy for you, Cathy."

"I'm happy for me, too. We're taking it slow. Now, enough about me. Tell me about the lovely Nurse Bell."

Swallowing the last of her pint, Lydia pointed to the bar. "I'm going to need another, first."

"Did she wine and dine you?"

"She did. We went to a restaurant. It was lovely."

"Sounds like it. Bloody hell, Lyds, a bit more enthusiasm would be nice."

Cathy had a point. Lydia had been on top of the world yesterday morning. Having her libido back was something to celebrate, and she had, with Zoe, multiple times. But now, as she opened up to Cathy, Lydia realised the exchange between Fe and Halle yesterday was playing on her mind. Taking away the joy she'd felt hours before.

"There's something going on with Fe and Halle."

"Um, okay. That's an interesting change of subject."

"That's the thing. It's not—not really. I can't make head nor tail of it. When I got back from Zoe's yesterday morning—yes, I stayed the night—Fe was acting weird, like she didn't want Halle to overhear our conversation about my date, even though I've spoken to them both about this kind of thing before. And then Halle came in and there was this odd look passed between them. With their fight, and now this, I'm worried. Oh, and before Halle came into the room, I'm sure Fe was about to tell me something."

"Well, did you ask Fe about it?"

"No, I left to change. Fe was busy calling her lawyer by the time I came back down, and Halle was back to her usual self. Maybe I'm reading too much into it. I don't know what's going on in Halle's life. Fe's stressed, too."

"It could be nothing. If it's bothering you, find some time to talk to them. Halle wants a friendship with you, outside of the one she has with Fe. Well, friends talk."

"Hmm." Lydia's gut feeling was shooting out warning flares. There was something going on with Halle and her sister, and Lydia felt sure it was big. Did she want to involve herself? Was that a super selfish thing to think? After all, Fe, and Halle, were stepping up to support Lydia through her health issues. If they had stuff going on, surely Lydia should return the favour?

"Okay, okay, enough of the drama. Tell me about the sex with Nurse Hottie."

Saturday had taken far too long to arrive. Sexy text messages just weren't cutting it anymore. Lydia's sex drive was through the roof. A rarity in itself, and she didn't want to miss out on a second.

Zoe was the master of sexting. Lydia, not so much, but she gave it a valiant effort. Although she doubted Zoe blushed as hard as she did, when reading said messages. Lydia had stopped opening them when around others. Because controlling her reaction had proved impossible.

Zoe had chosen another fancy restaurant for their second date. Dressed to the nines, Lydia felt confident she looked good.

Hopefully, good enough to eat.

Of course, Zoe looked phenomenal. Lydia began to think it was the nurse's standard look, regardless of vicinity or occasion.

"You look great," Lydia commented as she reached their table. Only five minutes late this time.

"As do you! Drink?"

"Yes, please."

Zoe signalled the server and Lydia took a few seconds to calm her nerves. Silly, really, considering the positions Zoe had her in the other night. It's not like Lydia had anything Zoe hadn't already seen. But then again, sex was the simple part.

Falling into bed with someone didn't make a relationship. Neither did the quality of the sex. Yeah, it was important, but Lydia had learned the hard way, there were a million other things far more critical to a healthy relationship than shagging.

Unfortunately, most of her ex-partners didn't share her opinion. As usual, she reflected on those failed relationships. Was she asking too much of a person? Why should they wait around for Lydia, when there were millions of people out there ready to have sex 24/7?

"Earth to Lydia."

"Hmm, what?"

"You zone out a lot, don't you?" At least Zoe was smiling.

"Sorry. Yeah, I get in my head sometimes."

"Something you want to talk about?"

"Nope. Let's have some fun."

No sooner had the words left her mouth than Lydia caught sight of Halle at the bar. And she wasn't alone. The striking blonde, who looked like a Victoria's Secret model, looked comfortable on her arm.

Something akin to heartburn rose in Lydia's chest. Her hope that Halle wouldn't spot her fell to the wayside before she'd even finished the thought. There was a second of surprise on Halle's face, then something else as her gaze tracked across the table to Zoe.

They continued to look at each other awkwardly for a few seconds before Lydia waved Halle over. Why were they being weird? It's not like they hadn't seen each other on dates before.

"Halle, hi."

"Lydia." Halle greeted, kissing her cheek. "And you must be Zoe?"

"I am. It's nice to meet you."

"Are you on a date?" Lydia shouldn't have asked because it was obvious.

"Oh, yeah. First date. One I should probably get back to. You look lovely, Lydia. Have a good night."

Lydia watched Halle return to the stunning blonde before snapping her attention back to her own date, who was now watching her with interest.

"Is Halle an ex?"

"What?" Lydia scoffed. "No, not at all. I told you she's my sister's best friend."

"Sure."

Sure. What did she mean by that? Had *everyone* started acting strangely, or was Lydia missing something obvious?

"Anyway, shall we order?"

Thirty minutes later, Lydia took the last bite of her cheese ravioli when she saw the blonde leave the restaurant, and Halle at their table by herself. Zoe must have caught Lydia's wandering eye.

"Do you want to invite her over?"

"No, we're on a date."

"Lydia, it's fine. Your friend looks a little put out."

Halle looked perturbed. Had the date gone that badly? As she was about to wave Halle over, Halle stood, threw some bills on the table and stalked out, frustration painted across her face.

Lydia cast a glance at Zoe before slipping out her chair. "Um... I'll be right back, okay?"

What was she doing following Halle out of the restaurant, leaving her own date alone? Not giving herself any time to second-guess the decision, Lydia raced out to catch up to Halle.

Wrapping her arms around herself, Lydia scanned the street. Halle was a hundred metres away at the bus stop. Jogging to catch up and keep warm, Lydia ducked under the shelter.

"Lydia, what are you doing here?"

"I wanted to make sure you were okay. I saw your date leave, and you looked pissed off."

"We had nothing in common. You should go back inside. It's bloody freezing."

It *was* bloody freezing. Lydia could kick herself for not grabbing her coat. Again. "But you're okay? We're okay?"

"What do you mean?"

"Halle, something is up. I'm not blind. You and Fe have been acting weird around me."

"It's not you, I promise." Halle lay a hand on Lydia's shivering shoulder. "Please go back inside before you catch your death."

"Can we have a movie night tomorrow? Just the two of us?" Suddenly, the need to solidify their friendship was the most important thing Lydia could think of.

"If you want. Come to mine, I'll order in. Yeah?"

"Perfect. Okay then. Night."

Hesitantly, Lydia gave Halle a quick hug before sprinting back to the restaurant. Zoe sat patiently, waiting, sipping on her wine. "Everything good?"

"Yeah, terrible date. But I think she's okay. Sorry for running out on you."

"Hey, I get it. She's your *friend*."

The forced pronunciation of "friend" wasn't necessary. Was Zoe being passive-aggressive?

"She is, and now she's gone. So, shall we wrap this up and grab a drink at your place?"

Zoe raised her hand to the server. "Bill please."

Back at Zoe's apartment, things took a bizarre turn. As with the previous time they'd been together, Zoe seemed to take charge. She was aggressive, but in a way Lydia felt comfortable with. That was until Zoe had her head between Lydia's legs.

"Do you find Halle attractive?"

"What?" Lydia panted.

"She's hot. I'd understand. Maybe we could ask her to join us one night."

"What?"

"Yeah, I think you'd enjoy it. Just the mention of her name and your pussy is clenching."

Scrabbling to her elbows, Lydia looked down at Zoe incredulously. "She's my friend, and that's it. I'm in this state because you're between my legs."

"No, I think you want her. She definitely wants you. We could have fun. I'm up for it. I think I'd like to watch her fuck you."

Lydia opened her mouth to protest, but Zoe sucked her clit before a single syllable could pass her lips. The only noise she made was a gasping moan. "Oh, fuck."

"Say her name." Was Zoe out of her mind? "Scream it for me, Lydia."

"Jesus. Don't stop." Lydia pulsed with every undulation. "I—"

"Say it," Zoe growled. There was no stopping the tidal wave of pleasure that burst from Lydia's centre.

"Halle! Oh God, yes!"

This time, when Lydia woke, the smell of sizzling bacon didn't ignite her senses. The sight of Zoe standing in the door with a sandwich and coffee didn't get her excited. In fact, it did the opposite.

"Morning, ready for your breakfast?" Zoe was acting her usual self, which Lydia couldn't fathom. Last night had ended uncomfortably for her. Calling out Halle's name as she orgasmed felt right at the time, but the moment she came down from the euphoria she felt ill at ease.

"I'm sorry, I have to go. Um, I've got an early shift."

"Lydia," Zoe replied, clearly seeing through the lie, "why are you freaking out?"

"I'm not freaking out." The shriek-like answer didn't help her cause.

"So, you find your friend hot. I told you I'm cool with it. Keeps things interesting in bed, don't you think?"

"I—" Momentarily stunned, Lydia had a fleeting image of Zoe and Halle in her bed.

"Look, have some food and then go. No need to start your day off on an empty stomach."

By the time Lydia left Zoe's apartment, her head was wrecked. There had been times over the years Lydia had thought of Halle in a less than friendly manner, but they were fleeting. Halle would never be interested in her, and God forbid Fe found out Lydia had the hots for her best friend. It had never been worth the trouble, so Lydia put any feelings she had for Halle to the back of her mind and got on with her life.

Now, though, those feelings would not be stuffed away so easily. It wasn't just calling Halle's name that left Lydia feeling mixed up; it was everything that went along with it. In that moment, it hadn't been Zoe's tongue on her clit; it had been Halle's. Lydia's body had reacted so strongly, adding to what was already an intense climax.

Fe was finishing up a call when Lydia walked in. The last thing she wanted was to recap her night with Zoe. Lydia was already struggling to look in Fe's direction, terrified that her sister would know something untoward happened.

Dashing up the stairs, Lydia showered and hid with the triplets for an hour. Entertaining three hyped children was a much better idea than facing Fe's interrogation.

"There you are." Fe stood with hands on hip, one eyebrow raised.

Damn it, her cover was blown.

"I wanted some time with my niblings."

Not strictly true, although Lydia loved every second she got with the tearaways.

"Uh huh. Are you at work today?"

"Yeah, late shift, why?"

"Just wondering. Can you come downstairs now? We need to talk."

Lydia's heart seized in her chest. Fe had always been observant, but now Lydia worried her eagle-eyed sister had developed telepathic abilities and knew exactly what Lydia had done last night.

Her bum had only just touched the seat when Fe rounded on her. "I called the lawyer. Clark will be served the papers soon."

"Oh, thank Christ!"

"Wow, I didn't think you'd be so relieved. I thought you liked Clark?"

"What? No. I'm not relieved, and I did like Clark."

That was a lie. Lydia was most definitely relieved. It just wasn't related to Fe's news.

Lydia smiled and continued, hoping Fe was buying her bullshit. "I'm happy you're moving on, is all. Taking charge. The kids need stability and safety. Are you okay?"

"I'm not sure. It doesn't matter. Clark left his family, and I need to look out for the kids. I've petitioned for sole custody."

"Really?"

"Yes, really. Clark hasn't been a father for a long time. I forgave him at the time, thinking it was because he was working hard for us. But that's horseshit. He was getting his rocks off with what's-her-name while I was at home, looking after everything. If Clark wants a new life, he can have it."

10

Spending the day deliberating whether she should go to Halle's as planned, drained Lydia entirely.

If she didn't show up, that would raise questions, but if she did, Lydia would have to look Halle in the eye, which she wasn't sure was possible—not with the events of last night so fresh in her memory.

Zoe called several times, but they'd gone unanswered. Sure, a bit of kink in the bedroom was fine, and if Zoe got off on her partner thinking of someone else in the throes of passion, who was Lydia to judge? But, for Lydia, it was too much.

Halle was out of bounds for a reason. Having the woman in her life was already becoming a little difficult. The dynamics among Halle, Fe, and herself were complicated. Just forming a friendship with Halle, away from Fe, seemed to stir the pot.

There was no way Lydia wanted a reminder of her attraction to Halle, when in bed with Zoe. Therefore, she'd decided to let Nurse Hottie go. Maybe she was premature in her decision? It didn't matter, Lydia had called it off. Zoe had been extremely understanding and harboured no ill will, assuring her nothing would be awkward if Lydia had to return to the surgery.

With that done and dusted, Lydia now had to decide if she was going to knock on Halle's door. The door she'd been standing in front of for ten minutes now. This was the first time since Halle moved, that Lydia would see inside her place. She'd dropped Fe off a couple of times, but never ventured past the front step.

There was still time to turn around. Go back to Fe's place and snuggle with Monty and the kids. Or she could grab a movie in town. Then Fe wouldn't ask questions about her premature return.

"Are you going to stand out there much longer? It's just that dinner is almost ready."

Halle's voice through the door made Lydia jump enough she had to grip the handrail to stop herself from falling over.

"Jesus," she hissed, gripping the front of her coat, as if that would stop her heart from jackhammering.

The door swung open to reveal Halle, dressed in joggers and a fitted sweater. Barefoot! A flood of heat rose from Lydia's feet up to her face, which flushed. Because, why wouldn't it? This was exactly the time to look flustered. For once, she'd love her body not to react. Traitorous arsehole.

"Lyds, are you alright?"

"Yes, yup, all good." Lydia's answer was directed at the floor. How the hell was she going to get through the evening?

"Come on, then. In you come. I'm letting all the heat out."

Following Halle inside, Lydia did her level best to seem normal. "It's lovely in here."

Halle's apartment was warm and inviting. Laced with bold colours, Lydia could feel Halle in every ornament and art piece.

"Thanks. I'm happy with it. The area is so much better than my last place. Do you remember that?" Halle shuddered at the memory.

Lydia did indeed remember Halle's last residence. In a rough part of town, everyone had been glad when Halle finally moved away.

"I'm a lot closer to work now and less likely to have the tyres on my car nicked," Halle chuckled.

"Yeah, you did good at finding this place. What smells so good?"

"Dinner. I know I said we'd order in, but then I thought about all the crap that goes into takeout. It's full of sugar and won't help with bloating, so I thought it would be best if I cooked us something homemade. Is vegetable curry, okay? I got some low-alcohol beer too, because you know we can't have curry without beer. The only thing I didn't have time to make were naan breads, so I bought some. You don't need to eat one, though, if it will make you feel yucky."

"Halle..." Clearing the massive ball of emotion from her throat, Lydia placed a hand on Halle's arm. "That is incredibly thoughtful. Thank you."

You will not cry, Lydia Archer!

"No biggie. Want a beer now or later?"

No biggie? Halle had no idea how much of a biggie it was.

"Now, please."

"Take a seat and I'll be right back. I put some DVDs on the coffee table for you to choose from."

Halle was possibly the last person on earth who still used DVDs and Lydia loved it. Combing through the pile, Lydia picked her two favourite films. *The Goonies,* which was a classic, and *Cutthroat Island,* because, well, Geena Davis.

"Oh, good choices!" Halle passed Lydia a beer and sat beside her on the small sofa. "Cheers."

"Cheers."

After several seconds of silence, Lydia was ready for the floor to swallow her up. She couldn't form a sentence with Halle this close to her; not after envisioning what she did last night. Plus, Halle's scent wasn't helping. Who smelled this good, all the time?

"Dinner will be five minutes."

"Okay."

Jesus. This was painful.

"Are you sure everything's alright?"

"Are you?" Lydia's quick retort pulled Halle up short.

"What's that supposed to mean?"

"Come on, Halle, I know *something* is up. Have you fallen out with Fe again? What's with all the secret looks? Has she said something? Is it Clark? Is Fe ill?"

"Whoa, slow down. Blimey, Fe's fine. The kids are fine. We haven't fallen out again."

"Then what?"

"I was just feeling down lately, is all."

"Why didn't you say something?"

"You've got enough going on."

"Friendship doesn't work like that!" Lydia turned to face Halle head on. "If you want us to be friends, you have to treat me like one. I want to support you too. That's how it is, right?"

"Yeah, okay. Sorry."

Lydia wasn't convinced Halle was being completely truthful, but it's not like she could pin her down and force a confession. An image of Halle pinned to the bed was unhelpful, but there it was, filling Lydia's mind. A small shiver ran across her skin.

"Are you cold?" Halle's voice seemed closer than before. Refocusing her gaze, Lydia saw Halle had indeed closed the gap between them ever so slightly.

Now, if a court of law asked her what the bloody hell happened next, Lydia would claim temporary insanity. It was the only way to explain why Lydia leaned in and took Halle's lips with her own. The kiss was brief and delicious. That's until Lydia came to her senses and pulled back so fast, she almost gave herself whiplash.

"Oh, shit. Halle, I'm so sorry. I can't believe I just did that." Halle remained silent, her eyes wide, staring at Lydia. "Please, forget I did that."

"Lydia—"

"I should go. Clearly having some hormonal issues or some sort of breakdown over here. I really am sorry. I'm a mess." Lydia was off the sofa and out the door in seconds. Humiliated and mortified, she walked at a breakneck pace until she reached Cathy's door, twenty-five minutes later.

Pressing the buzzer to Cathy's flat repeatedly, Lydia cursed her own stupidity.

"Hello?"

"Cathy, it's Lydia."

The door clicked open seconds later. Cathy stood in the hall, waiting. Lydia noted the silk nightie and smacked herself in the head. She'd interrupted Cath and Harrison.

"Crap, I'm sorry, Cath, I'll call tomorrow." She was just about to walk back in the direction she came when Cathy's hand yanked her inside.

"Don't be dense. Are you okay?"

Laughing hysterically and clearly causing alarm, Lydia dropped to Cathy's sofa. "No, I'm not okay. It seems I've lost my fucking mind."

"Cat, are you coming back to bed?" Harrison's appearance wasn't a shock. The whipped cream on his nipples was. "Oh, hey Lydia."

"Harrison."

"Babe, I'm going to be a little while. Why don't you grab a shower and head to the pub?"

"No!" Lydia protested. "I didn't mean to—"

"Harrison."

"Sure, no probs."

"Cathy—"

"Stop. Lydia, this is the first time since we met you've turned up at my door. I'm here for you, and Harrison knows that. Now, want to fill me in on the crisis?"

"I kissed Halle!"

Cathy made her way to the kitchen. "I sense this conversation might need wine."

Dropping her head to her hands, Lydia groaned while she waited for Cathy to return with an enormous glass of red wine.

"Here, get this down your neck."

"I can't believe I did it, Cath."

"Why did you?"

"Everything's a bit buggered up at the minute, in here." Pointing to her brain, Lydia took a few healthy swigs of her drink. "I was on a date with Nurse Hottie yesterday and Halle showed up. She was on a first date. Anyway, we said hello and all that gumpf. We said we'd have a film night tonight. Later, as Nurse Hottie was visiting down south, she suddenly starts talking about Halle. Telling me she'd like us to have a threesome. I was already close to...you know, and then she demands I call Halle's name out as I..."

"Orgasmed... You can say the word, sweetie."

"Yes, that. Anyway, I was so far gone I did, and it was great—"

"But super fucked up at the same time?"

"Yes! I didn't just call her name, Cath, I pictured her there. Doing the things Zoe was doing."

"And now you're feeling all kinds of things you don't think you should be?"

"I know I shouldn't be! Halle doesn't see me that way and Fe would have a bloody conniption. I went round this evening, hoping everything would be normal. Oh Cath, she'd cooked me a healthy dinner and bought low-alcohol beer because she knows I struggle with bloating. We were talking on the sofa, and I think my brain short-circuited, because the next thing I know, my face is on hers!"

"Wow. Okay, and how did Halle react?"

"She sort of just sat there like a deer in headlights. I panicked and left."

"Is it really such a big deal? I mean, she looks at you like she wants to ravage you, most of the time."

"Are you insane? No, she doesn't. I've known Halle forever; I think I'd know if she was interested."

"Are you interested in her?"

"Of course. Have you seen her? But she's the *one* woman out of bounds. I've known *that* forever, too."

"Why? Because of your sister?"

"Yes, because of Fe. She's territorial, especially over Halle. It's always been the same."

"You're grown women!"

"It doesn't matter. I'm not messing with their friendship. I made a stupid mistake this evening. I don't know what's going on with me lately. I can't blame everything on my whacky hormones, even though I'd like to."

"Stress can do odd things to a person's judgement. It's possible that all this bullshit with the doctors, etcetera, has finally got to you. Don't beat yourself up. We all do dumb shit. Halle will be fine. You will be fine. Life will be fine."

"You should become a motivational speaker."

"I put it down to having great sex."

"I hope you mean with me," Harrison commented as he walked out of the bedroom, freshly showered, winking at Cathy.

"Don't go getting a big ego now."

Lydia watched fondly as Harrison kissed Cathy on the lips. They were a really cute couple and Cathy looked happy.

"I'm off. I'll be 'round for breakfast. Bye, Lyds."

"Bye, Harrison. I'm really sorry for crashing your evening."

"No worries. Take it easy."

As the door fell into the latch, Cathy sighed contentedly. "He's good for me."

"I can see that. You guys seem solid."

"You know, it's only been a couple of weeks, but he's the first man I feel... I don't know...safe with? I don't mean physically."

"I understand. You can be yourself with him."

"Yes. When we went to the pub the other night, a couple of guys flirted with me. I innocently flirted back because I just can't stop myself. And do you know how Harrison reacted?"

"How?"

"He didn't. He read his book while these guys talked to me. One of them asked for my number. I said no. They left, and Harrison simply kissed my cheek. It totally threw me. I'm used to guys getting all heated up about it. Later that night, I asked him why he didn't care that I flirted with other guys, and he said there was no need to get upset. He knew I was going home with him, and he couldn't blame men for wanting to try their luck. He's so comfortable with his feelings, and so sure of them toward me."

"Wow."

"I know! Anyway, we've got off the reason you're here."

"No, I like this, talking about each other's lives. I sometimes worry all I ever do is whine about my health issues. You know you can come to me, right?"

"Of course I do. But friendship is a balance. Sometimes one needs more than the other. You've really gone through it with that arsehole doctor buggering you about. I can't even imagine how hard it's been, so I'm more than happy to focus on you for a while. You've got your surgery soon?"

"Yes, next week. Halle and Fe both said they'd come with me. I'm not feeling that anymore."

"Say no more. I'll be there."

"What do I say to Fe? She's got enough worries, herself, with the divorce. If I tell her not to come to the hospital, she's going to ask why. I swear she's a human lie detector. I'll crumble, tell her I snogged her bestie, and then she'll hit the roof."

"Well, if she's got that much on, she might be thankful. Just don't mention anything. As for Halle, I think she's smart enough to know you'll need some space."

"Ugh, I've made such a mess."

"Oh, stop. No you haven't. It's about time you did something spontaneous."

"Hey!"

"It's true. You have been consumed with doctor visits and feeling awful most of the time, and we both know it.

Why not get a little silly and make some mistakes? At least you're living."

"I suppose."

"How did you leave it with Nurse Hottie?"

"I left it. After last night, I couldn't see her again. Not romantically, anyway."

"Shame. Ah, well, you'll just need to charge your vibrator."

"Cathy!"

Cackling, Cathy playfully punched Lydia on the arm. "Oh sweetie, you've got to lighten up. Hopefully, soon, Dr What's-her-face will give you some magic pills or something and you'll be feeling tons better. Then you can get yourself out there again."

"Or I can concentrate on myself. Maybe it's time I looked at moving."

"You love your flat."

"I do. Maybe I'm just looking for a change."

"Fair enough. Just think of all the money you'll save not having to go to the doctor's every fart's end."

"Charming," Lydia giggled.

They spent a couple of hours gossiping, which included Cathy sharing far too much information about Harrison. Overall, the evening turned out to be pretty great, even if Lydia would have to face the consequences of her earlier faux pas at some point.

Fe was already settled in her room by the time Lydia finally made it back. Sneaking into the triplets' room, she gave them a quick kiss and headed for bed. Monty sat, dutifully waiting on the bed, next to her pillow.

"Hey, buddy. Sorry I've not been around much recently. I promise that's going to change." Monty licked her ear before scooching his body under the covers.

Choosing to leave the blinds open, Lydia stared out of the window. The moon was large and bright, casting an eerie glow over the world. No matter what Cathy said, Lydia felt awful for kissing Halle. She'd hate it if someone forced themselves on her, and now she'd have to apologise again and things would be awkward.

No doubt Fe would find out, too. Maybe she should move back to her flat before that happened.

Sleep wasn't going to come, but she didn't want to risk waking her sister by going downstairs. The light on her phone, filling the room, pulled her gaze from outside. Halle's name filled her screen.

Halle 10.16 p.m.

Can we talk?

Puffing out a breath, Lydia hit the call button. They might as well get it out of the way.

"Hi."

"Hey, sorry it's late." Halle's voice was soft.

"I couldn't sleep, anyway. Look, I just want to apologise again—"

"You don't have to. I'm sorry I sort of froze."

"As if you're apologising," Lydia chuckled. "You had every right to be shocked. It was totally out of line. All I can say is I'd had a strange twenty-four hours and it messed with my judgement."

"So, you didn't want to kiss me?"

"No! I mean yes, at the time, but I know it was out of line."

"Why was it?"

Okay, the conversation was steering off track and Lydia didn't know where it was going. Did Halle like the kiss?

"Um...because."

"Can we meet up? Tomorrow evening? I still have the curry I made. We could talk."

"I have work until six." Lydia neglected to mention the appointment with the anaesthetist first thing in the morning in case Halle offered to come along.

"That's fine. Please, Lydia?"

"Alright. I-I'll see you tomorrow."

"Great. Night."

"Yeah, night."

Not how she thought the day would end! However, that ball of anxiety had unfurled and sleep was calling. Monty kicked his legs out a few times, to get in an optimal snoozing position. Curling her arm around his little body, Lydia pulled Monty closer, fully aware she had his danger zone close to her face.

"Don't fart, buddy," she mumbled.

Closing her eyes, she let the conversation percolate. Halle's tone was hard to decipher over the phone. She hadn't sounded upset or mad. But she didn't convey happiness or joy, either? Did she like the kiss? Did she hate it and swallow a tube of toothpaste after Lydia'd run away? What was there to talk about?

"This is why I should be a hermit in the woods, with animals as my only companions." Monty snored loudly, making his furry butt vibrate. "At least one of us is content," she sighed.

<u>11</u>

"There's nothing in your blood work that is cause for concern regarding the surgery. Although, your blood alcohol level was—"

"Sorry about that," Lydia blushed. "I'd had a drink the night before. But that's not usual for me."

Sure, I bet he hears that all the time.

"Okay, well then, I just need to take your height and weight and I think that will be all."

Great, standing on a scale in front of Mr Fitness was going to be fun. Why couldn't the anaesthetist be a little chubby or something? That wasn't a nice thing to think. Lydia chastised herself. She needed to stop feeling so shitty about her weight. The thought crossed her mind now and then to seek professional help. Looking in the mirror, and hating what it reflected, wasn't a healthy way to live.

Stepping onto the scales, Lydia forced herself to look at the number. Not too bad, but could be better. Next, she stood while the doctor measured her.

Yep, still short!

"Okay, Ms Archer, I think we're done here. Remember to fast after seven o'clock the night before. Only consume water."

"Great. Thanks, I guess I'll see you in a few days."

A few days, that's all it was until the surgery. Was it weird to feel so excited about the prospect of a doctor cutting into you? Maybe, but Lydia didn't care at this point.

Stepping out of the doctor's clinic, Lydia cursed her timing. Clark was across the street, and the last thing she wanted was a showdown with Fe's ex. Dipping her head, Lydia hoped he hadn't spotted her, but she wasn't so lucky.

"Lydia!"

"Oh, bugger." Slowing to a stop, Lydia turned to face the weasel. "Clark."

"She's filed for sole custody. What the bloody fuck?"

Okay, this was going to be fun.

"That's something you need to take up with Fe."

"Oh, come on. You can't think this is right."

"It's not for me to judge, Clark. This is entirely between you and Fe."

"But they're my kids."

"Yup. As I said, talk to your *wife*."

"I didn't want this, you know?"

That was a puzzling thing to hear. "You didn't want to shag Janey, and then leave your wife and children to make a life with her? Weird."

"Everything got out of control." Clark raked his hands through his short hair. "I was drowning, Lydia. I just needed an outlet."

"And Janey was that outlet?" Ew, that sounded gross.

"I didn't set out to cheat on Fe. Janey provided support for me when I was stressed. It sort of developed from that."

"Uh-huh."

"I know I hurt Fe—"

"And the kids."

"Has she told them?" Clark's voice rose in volume. People passing by cast Lydia a questioning glance. Laying her hand on Clark's forearm, she hoped to calm the situation down.

"No, she hasn't said a bad word against you. But they're intuitive and know something's up. Even before you left, they were picking up on the tension."

"I wanted to take them with me."

"But you didn't. You told Fe to keep the kids. I think you've answered your own question regarding the sole custody thing."

"I love my kids, Lydia."

"Of course you do. Fe isn't unreasonable, but she's not going to let you waltz in and out of their lives, Clark. Plus, she's fucking hurt."

"I didn't mean for this." His tone was almost pleading.

"Then what did you mean? Because you left, Clark. I can honestly say I never thought this would happen. You guys were solid. What the hell happened?"

"I don't know! It was all the little things. The kids, the house...bills. I just felt suffocated."

"Then you should have talked to Fe! But you banged your secretary instead. I'm not sure what you want to hear from me, Clark. Fe's hurting and so are the kids. You *chose* to start a life with Janey."

"I want my life back!"

"What does that mean?" Lydia was growing more frustrated by the second.

"I miss my children and my wife." Tears streamed down Clark's face.

"And Janey?"

"She was a mistake."

"Then why the hell did you leave?"

"She told me she was pregnant. But she's not. It was a lie."

"Jesus Christ." What a bloody, awful mess.

"I was scared, okay? If I didn't try with Janey, I was worried she'd threaten my job."

"So instead of stepping up and taking responsibility for the shit you started, you abandoned your family?" Shaking her head, Lydia took a step back. "I'm sorry, Clark, I shouldn't judge. I told you I didn't want to discuss this. You have to work it out with Fe."

"Will she take me back?"

"Honestly?" He nodded. "No. Not right now."

"What do I do?" Clark's brokenness was evident. Lydia felt for him, but getting in the middle of this wasn't right. Her job was to be there for her niblings and sister.

"I don't know. Give it time, I guess."

"Do you think Halle would talk to her?"

"Oh no, don't even think about it. Halle's more likely to rip you a new arsehole than hear you out, let alone advocate for you."

"I'm sorry. I'm so sorry." Wiping his eyes, Clark turned and left Lydia standing in the street, a little shell-shocked. Of all the things she'd worried about today, this wasn't one of them. Should she tell Fe what Clark said? Would Fe be pissed if she didn't tell her, or more upset if she did?

Mumbling, "Buggering hell," Lydia set off for the museum. There wasn't any time to ponder. Lydia's shift started in half an hour, and she was already on thin ice with Norris. Apparently, hospital visits weren't a valid enough reason to need time off.

The bus arrived with five minutes to spare, although Lydia ought not to have worried as every employee and visitor were outside behind police tape.

Pushing through the crowd, she spotted Cathy and Harrison. "Hey, what's this about?"

"Bomb scare," Harrison answered matter-of-factly.

"Just a prank," Cathy added. "We get them once a bloody year, at least."

"Outstanding, just what we all need. Hypothermia." Lydia moaned.

"How did it go this morning?" Cathy offered to come along, but there was no way she'd have got the okay from Norris.

"Fine, no problems. Everything is still going forward." Casting her gaze across the sea of pissed-off people, Lydia wondered if she should tell Cathy about her quick conversation with Halle last night.

"You look like you're thinking really hard there, sweetie."

"I spoke to Halle last night. She wants to meet up this evening after work."

"That's good, right?"

"I haven't the foggiest. It was strange. It almost sounded like she was okay with me kissing her." Lydia lowered her voice just in case Fe was hiding somewhere, ready to pop out and kick her arse.

"Interesting. I won't say 'I told you so'." Cathy's grin said it all too loudly, anyway.

"Stop. Anyway, I agreed to meet up. But that's not everything. On the way here I ran into Clark, Fe's husband. He had a full bloody meltdown on me."

"Jesus, is your life always this entertaining?"

"No, it's not!" Laughing with a friend felt better than worrying. "I'd quite like my drama-free life back, to be honest."

"Are you going to tell Fe?"

"That's the million-pound question, isn't it? I don't want her to think I'm on his side or anything. She's still super angry."

"Does he want her back?"

"Yep. Knows he's cocked up royally. I told him to talk to her, but she needs time. If he tries to get her back now, he'll get told where to sling his hook."

"What's your opinion on it all?"

Blowing out her cheeks, Lydia tried to figure out what she felt. Clark had always been the one for Fe. As far as she was concerned, they loved each other fiercely. She could understand that life sometimes changed a person. Fear and anxiety changed a person, but she'd never envisioned Clark with another woman. It felt so out of character for him.

Clark's broken, tear-stained face came to mind. He looked genuinely hurt, and sorry. But was that enough? He'd taken their trust and ripped it apart. Lydia wasn't sure Fe could ever get past that. She wasn't sure her sister should.

But what would Lydia do for love? If it were her in Fe's position, and the love of her life did what Clark did, would she be able to take them back?

"It's just a mess. I want my family to be happy, but I don't know what that looks like for them now. Do you think I should tell Fe what he said?"

"Tell her you ran into him and go from there. She'll let you know if she wants details."

Their conversation was interrupted by a police officer announcing it was safe for everyone to re-enter the museum.

"Thank God, I can't feel my toes."

There was nervous excitement the entire rest of the day at work. Frankly, it was a welcome distraction. As the clock ticked down the hours, Lydia became more nervous. She felt completely out of her depth where Halle was concerned.

Everything to do with the woman was a puzzle. In all the years they'd known each other, they'd never strayed into this kind of territory.

Why now? That was the question that Lydia wanted answering. There had been plenty of opportunity over the years for something to develop between them. *Or not*, Lydia thought, after a moment's contemplation. She'd kept a respectful distance from Halle so there was never a real possibility of them growing close.

So why now? Why had Halle sought a friendship with her? And why did that make Lydia feel all kinds of things? Lydia wasn't in the best place to start something, even though she'd had a few dates with Zoe. Halle was different. If they were to date, it wouldn't be a fling, or casual. It couldn't be. There was too much on the line; too many other people to consider.

Scoffing, Lydia grabbed her bag from the locker and put on her coat. Everything she came up with was guesswork. She had no idea what Halle wanted. Maybe she was going to turn up at Halle's and be told, politely, that it was never going to happen, and Lydia should refrain from planting her lips on other people without prior consent. Yup, that scenario was the most likely.

The bus was crammed. Someone forgot to put on deodorant, adding to Lydia's sullen mood. Choosing to exit the bus ten minutes early, Lydia picked up the pace. She'd end up being late, but rather that, than getting coated in stranger sweat. Gross.

Flustered and in need of a drink or two, Lydia knocked on Halle's door. Standing outside, deliberating, wasn't worth the frostbite. Might as well bite the bullet.

"Hey, come in." Halle stood to one side, looking gorgeous, of course. For once, couldn't she look less like a leisurewear model?

"Hey, sorry I'm late. I walked a fair way. The bus was stinky."

"Gross, I totally understand. Maybe it's time you got a car?"

"In London? No thanks. Plus, I can borrow Fe's anytime."

"I have a car in London."

"No, you have a *toy* car in London. You can park it on your front lawn."

"Her, I can park *her*."

Rolling her eyes playfully, Lydia handed Halle her coat. The same delicious smell of curry wafted from the kitchen, reminding her of why she was here: to talk about the kiss. Gulp.

"Beer?"

"Yes please. Um...the potent stuff this time."

Halle chuckled, but fetched a bottle of Belgian beer from the fridge. "Try this. It's one of my favourites."

Not needing to be asked twice, Lydia took several healthy swallows. Yeah, that hit the spot alright.

"Jesus, what percentage is it?" Only after she'd downed half her glass did the strength smack her in the chops.

"Six percent. Slow down," Halle laughed. "Let's eat first and then we'll talk. Is that okay?"

"Okay, yeah…great." And the nerves were back. Another two glugs of beer helped.

Sitting at the table, Lydia watched Halle dish up the food. She was so relaxed, and it was a little annoying. Lydia was harbouring psychopathic bees in her stomach, while Halle happily played hostess.

After a few minutes of awkward silence, Lydia couldn't take it anymore. "This is weird, right?"

"Why is it weird?" Halle placed the plates on the table and took a seat.

"Because everything feels awkward."

"Eat."

Having nothing else to add, Lydia shovelled a fork full of curry into her mouth. The taste was an explosion of culinary excellence.

"Holy shit, that's delicious."

A small blush crept up Halle's face. "Thanks. I'm glad you like it. There's plenty for you to take home."

Silence again. Laying her fork down, Lydia straightened her shoulders. This needed to happen now.

"I need us to talk about whatever it is that needs talking about, Halle."

Placing her own fork down, Halle took her time by wiping non-existent food from the corners of her mouth. "Why did you kiss me?"

"It just sort of happened."

"But you wanted to."

"Yes."

Halle seemed to mull over her next words. "You said you'd had a crazy twenty-four hours. What did you mean?"

Oh boy. Lydia was all up for a frank discussion, but could she be honest enough about where her head was at last night?

"I had a date with Zoe, as you know." Halle nodded. "Um...okay, this is awkward."

"Just say it. I promise I'll listen."

"Zoe said she wouldn't mind a threesome with you, and she made me call your name out when I had an orgasm!"

Lydia delivered that as carefully as a bulldozer, but it was done. She'd said it. Halle had the same wide-eyed look on her face as Lydia.

"So, when I came over to yours the next night, my head was messed up. And there you were, being all perfect, cooking healthy food for me, and your face was so close."

Halle cleared her throat. "I can't say I expected that."

"Me either! I broke it off with Zoe because the whole thing just freaked me out."

"I—I honestly don't know what to say."

"You don't have to say anything. The last thing I want is to make you uncomfortable, which I've obviously done. I'm sorry."

"When you kissed me, were you thinking of Zoe?"

"No! Jesus, no. I was thin…" Snapping her mouth shut, Lydia stared at the table.

"Hey, what were you going to say?"

Lydia shook her head. No, nope, she couldn't say what she wanted to say, out loud.

"Lydia, look at me." The warmth of Halle's soft hand lifting her chin sent tingles to Lydia's spine. "Say it."

"I wanted to kiss you because I couldn't stop thinking about what you'd done to me in Zoe's bedroom. I pictured you, not her, that's why I said your name. You were there with me. When I came over last night, I lost myself again in the thought of you, with me. I couldn't stop myself from kissing you."

In a flash, Halle was on her feet, scooping Lydia up with her. The kiss she delivered was fierce. It took a second for Lydia to catch up, but when she did, something primal surfaced.

Reaching up, Lydia grabbed fistfuls of Halle's hair, her tongue diving into Halle's mouth with force and passion. A moan escaped Halle, which spurred Lydia on further. The sounds of metal hitting the floor echoed through the kitchen, but it didn't deter them. Together they were fire, burning hotter with every passing second.

Cold air caressed Lydia's abdomen as Halle made quick work of her top. Letting go of Halle's hair, Lydia went straight for the woman's trousers. Their movements were frenzied, and it was perfect.

Lydia could feel the desire dripping off Halle. With every touch, every small whimper, Lydia grew in confidence. There was no time to worry, not when Halle Cartwright was taking her clothes off, clearly feeling Lydia wasn't doing it fast enough.

Two pairs of jeans hit the floor, knickers right after them. If Lydia had the patience to slow down and gaze at Halle's tight physique, she would, but that wasn't an option. Both women needed this to happen, now. Lydia gave a little laugh as Halle dragged her to the kitchen floor.

"Don't worry, it's clean," Halle mumbled through nips and bites on Lydia's neck. Lydia couldn't have given a rat's arse if it was clean. Halle could do what she wanted, where she wanted.

And then it was over.

"What the bloody hell are you doing?" Fe's screech filled the flat. Halle's weight lifted off Lydia as they both scrambled to find their discarded clothes.

"Fe, what're you doing here?" Halle pulled on her jeans and top. Lydia flailed about, desperately trying to clothe herself, but she was flustered, and the harder she tried, the less successful her attempts were.

"What the fuck!" Fe cried again. "I can't believe you'd do this."

Lydia looked up from her position on the floor. Fe was staring daggers at her.

"Fe, calm down." Lydia's plea fell on deaf ears.

"Calm down?"

Okay, she shouldn't have said that. No woman in the history of humanity ever calmed down when told to.

"Fe, go into the living room. We'll be right in." Halle's calm voice did little to douse Fe's rage.

"I'll never forgive you for this," she hissed at Lydia, who sat slack-jawed. What the fuck? Was it really that big of a deal?

Feeling the sting of tears, Lydia rushed to dress. With Fe out of the way, she was able to do it rather quickly. Halle stood looking unsure of what to do next. Lydia wasn't in the mood to have a full-blown argument with her sister. And she understood Halle felt torn.

"Go, it's fine."

"Lydia—"

"Please. Go and calm her down. I need to go."

Dashing past the living room, Lydia did her best to ignore Fe's continuing shouts. Her hands shook as she dialled for a cab.

Tears fell as she waited on the pavement. Alone.

12

There were a couple of ways Lydia dealt with stress. Batch cooking was one of them, and she'd really leaned into it over the past week. Her water bill was going to be through the roof. Pots and pans didn't clean themselves, as was clear by the pile stacked in the sink. But that was a consequence she'd have to suffer. It was either batch cooking, or binge drinking.

An entire week passed since the kitchen floor incident and not a peep from either Fe or Halle. Not one text, hence the three pots full of Spaghetti Bolognese. Her freezer was already full of chilli and beef stew. It looked like Cathy was in for a treat. And rightly so! Cathy had been *the* best friend Lydia could have ever asked for this week.

After breaking down in the back of the cab that night, Lydia arrived at Fe's home only to leave again ten minutes later with a sleepy Monty tucked against her chest. It had hurt not to be able to explain to the niblings why she wouldn't be around for a while, but that wasn't her place. Fe could sort that out. She'd kissed them as they slept, before leaving.

The driver was kind enough not to comment on Lydia's tear and snot-stained face, which she thought was nice of him.

As soon as she was alone in her flat, she called Cathy. Within minutes she was there, comforting, and cursing out Fe. Lydia knew her sister would be upset, but she'd never, in a million years, expected her to react like that.

Hours turned to days and Lydia fell deeper into a black hole. She'd hoped Halle would have messaged or something, but there was nothing. Fe needed time to cool down. That was fine, but after a full seven days, Lydia was getting angry. Who the bloody hell did Fe think she was? Where the hell was Halle? It hadn't been Lydia alone on that floor, naked!

So what if she and Halle had sex? What was the big fucking deal? Surely Fe should be happy her best friend and sister liked each other. There could be worse things happening!

Channelling her frustration in a positive way led to the culinary deep dive. If Lydia couldn't yell, she'd cook. And then cook some more until she felt better. So far, no amount of tomato-based cuisine had helped. Maybe lasagna would do the trick?

To add to her stress, tomorrow was the surgery. Thank God Cathy and Harrison would be there to hold her hand. Lydia was still nervous, despite the excitement of finally moving forward.

Cursing her lack of Tupperware, Lydia cling wrapped the pots. They'd be fine on the kitchen worktop for a little while. It was almost five in the afternoon, which only left a couple of hours to have some food before she went nil by mouth. The timing sucked, because Lydia was definitely a person who liked to eat her feelings, especially late at night.

Yes, she could have eaten some of the food she'd spent all week cooking, but she didn't. Instead, Lydia drowned her nerves and sorrow in pizza. Monty seemed to agree with her food choice as he sat there nibbling on a morsel of crust.

By the time 9:30 p.m. rolled around, Lydia was done for the day. No amount of pizza or TV helped distract her mind. If she couldn't think of anything nice, she wouldn't think at all. Monty wasn't as enthusiastic about going to bed so early, but he followed loyally, anyway. The quicker tomorrow arrived, the better.

Cathy arrived at 7:30 a.m. sharp. Lydia felt sick but put on a brave face, although the sympathetic look she received from Cathy said she'd done a poor job of masking her feelings.

The original plan was for Fe to pick Lydia up and drive her to the hospital. Obviously, that wasn't happening, so instead of arriving in a comfortable car, Lydia and Cathy arrived by bus.

Putting the stress of public transport behind her, Lydia readied herself. She would only be in the hospital for a few hours. Cathy already arranged for a taxi to pick them up, not knowing what state Lydia would be in. Harrison sent his apologies for not being with them. He had something crop up at university that he couldn't miss. It still blew Lydia's mind that he was a PhD student.

"Lydia, how are you?" Elise Maynard asked as soon as they saw her at the reception desk. Should she still call her Elise, now that things were rocky with Halle?

"Good. A little nervous." That was an understatement.

"No need to be. It will be over before you know it. Just fill this out and then the nurse will take you to your room. When I'm ready for you, you'll be brought to the theatre and prepped."

"Okay." That sounded simple enough.

"You haven't eaten anything since last night?"

Unfortunately, no.

"Nope, and I'm bloody starving."

The three women shared a laugh before saying their goodbyes. Cathy was allowed to wait in the recovery room while Lydia had the procedure done.

"Jesus, I look awful." The hospital gown was hideous. Why the hell did they put mirrors in the room? That was just cruel.

"They're not made to look good. Are you sure it's on the right way? I thought you were supposed to have your arse exposed in them?" Lydia slapped Cathy's hand away as she fiddled with the flap on the gown.

"Well, I presumed they'd rather have access to my front than my bum, Cathy."

"You're right, we would," a kindly nurse said with a twinkle in her eye. Had she heard the entire conversation? "Are you ready to go?"

"Ready as I'll ever be."

Ain't that the truth!

"Don't worry, sweetie, you'll be fine. And I'll be right here when you come around."

Crossing the space quickly, Lydia threw her arms around Cathy. "Thank you."

"No thanks necessary. Now, off you go." Cathy gave her a squeeze and a peck on the forehead.

Lydia drummed her fingers on the wheelchair arm the entire ride to the theatre. She also wrinkled her nose at the antiseptic smell all hospitals had.

At least it's clean.

This was it! The operating room was smaller than Lydia expected, although her experience was limited to re-runs of *ER*, so not the most realistic expectations. Following the nurse's orders, Lydia transferred over to a waiting gurney, giving the surgical team a nervous smile as she tried to stop the gown from showing her nether regions prematurely. The canular insert was awful. Why the bloody hell did a needle in the hand hurt so much?

Lying flat, she stared at the large surgical light above her. *I hope they wait until I'm out of it before turning that bugger on. It'll burn my retinas.*

"Lydia, are we ready?" Elise's masked face peered over Lydia's, causing her to jump.

"Yup, let's do it."

Doing her best to calm down, Lydia focused on the beeps of the heart monitor. It was strangely relaxing.

"Great. Now, I only intend to have a look today, however if there is anything I feel needs dealing with immediately, I'd like to sort it out whilst I'm there. Is that okay?"

"Of course. Do whatever you need to do."

"Wonderful. Now comes the fun bit. Take a few deep breaths and count back from ten."

Taking several deep breaths from the mask now on her face, Lydia counted from ten. Eight was as far as she got.

Had someone taken a wodge of sandpaper and cleaned Lydia's throat with it? It sure bloody felt like it. Opening her eyes gingerly, she tried to focus on the room. A fuzzy outline sat near the end of the bed.

"Ugh, the toaster needs cleaning."

Cathy's laugh was distinctive enough for Lydia to identify the fuzzy outline. "I think that's the anaesthesia wearing off, love. Your toaster's fine."

"Water, please."

"Here, only sip it."

The ice-cold liquid was only a temporary balm. As soon as Lydia swallowed, the pain was back with a vengeance. "My throat hurts."

"That would be from the tube we placed in your throat."

Turning her head, Lydia squinted to pull Dr Maynard into focus. "Did you find something?" Thank God, she was regaining her faculties.

"We did. I'm going to do my rounds now, which will give you time to wake up fully. When I come back, we'll go through the operation and what we found, okay? Take your time, you're in no rush. When you feel up to it, I need you to pee, and then eat. The nurse will be in shortly to check your incisions."

"Alright. Thank you, Elise."

"See you soon."

The second the door shut; Cathy whistled. "Wowzer, she is stunning. Jesus, are all medical professionals that hot?" Cathy fanned herself with a *Vogue* magazine.

"She dated Halle briefly." Mentioning her name was a mistake. Now Lydia felt a rush of emotion she'd tried to keep at bay since last week.

"Oh, darling, don't get upset. It's the meds. They're messing with your emotions."

"I can't believe Fe isn't here. After all the times I've supported her."

Ugly crying wasn't on the top of Lydia's to-do list today, but she couldn't stop the downpour. There had been such a build-up to this moment. Three years of frustration and now that she was about to get help, her sister was nowhere to be seen. And for what reason? Because Lydia had almost slept with her best friend.

"I know, sweetheart. Let it out."

So, she did. For quite some time. Enough time, in fact, for the nurse to stop by, and then Dr Maynard.

"Emotions can be a little heightened after being anaesthetised. It's normal." Elise said gently, as Lydia hiccupped and snotted into a tissue. "Would you like me to come back later?"

"No, please stay. I want to know what you found. Cathy can stay too, if that's alright?"

"That's fine." Elise pulled up a chair. "Okay, I can tell you without a doubt you have endometriosis."

A rush of air left Lydia's body. "Oh, my God." The tears were back again. Elise and Cathy sat patiently while Lydia gathered herself again. "Sorry, go on."

"I felt it was necessary to remove the tissue as soon as possible. I'm thrilled with how it went. We'll need to discuss what comes next. I want you to start a new pill. It's a much more effective medication for your condition than anything you've been prescribed. The good thing about this medication is we can start you on it immediately. No need to wait for your period. It will also regulate your hormones, which from your bloodwork, I can see are all over the place. It's a progesterone-only pill. You may find it takes several months to work, but I need you to trust me and stick with it. You're going to feel tired for a few days, but you'll be back to full capacity around two weeks' time. If you have to work, light duties only."

"I'll talk to Norris," Cathy commented.

"Make sure you keep hydrated and continue eating healthily. If you feel any pain, or you see inflammation around your incisions, come straight back, okay?"

"Of course."

"I'll look after her, Doctor."

"Good. Now, there is one other thing I think we should talk about. The endometriosis was heavily situated around your ovaries, which could have caused an issue with egg development. There's a chance that getting pregnant may be difficult."

The walls felt as if they were closing in. Could she not have babies? All Lydia ever wanted was a family of her own. Children she'd carry and cherish.

"Am I infertile?"

"No. However, if you get to a point where you want to stop the pill and get pregnant, we will have to do some further tests. It's not impossible, Lydia, I just wanted you to have the full picture."

"Thank you. I appreciate it."

"Let's get you feeling better, and then we can look at options. Lydia, please don't feel disheartened. You're on the right path and I'll help you every step of the way."

Babies. That's all Lydia could think about. A panic resided in her chest at the thought of not being able to have children. A family of her own, why was that so much to ask for? Why did it have to be her?

Tired of feeling sorry for herself, Lydia happily took the painkillers Cathy offered. They'd arrived at Lydia's flat an hour ago and Cathy hadn't stopped fussing.

"Once they kick in, you'll sleep better."

That's what Lydia was counting on. Rarely relying on medication to solve her problems, Lydia conceded defeat this time. Her brain wouldn't stop, so pharmaceutical intervention was required.

Monty lay at Lydia's feet, keeping a concerned eye on her. In all honesty, she didn't feel bad, just sleepy. Although her throat still felt raw, which was an unexpected and unwelcome side effect of the surgery.

When she wasn't feeling so fatigued, Lydia would address everything Elise had said post-op. But for now, sleep called.

Muffled voices stirred Lydia. The sun had dipped considerably, so she figured a few hours had passed since she fell asleep. Was someone at the front door? Cathy's voice rang through, clearer than whoever turned up. Lydia wasn't expecting anyone.

Pulling herself up with a wince, Lydia laid against the headboard. Those painkillers were pretty great. She'd only felt a small pull on her wounds. Rubbing sleep from her eyes, Lydia took some time to decide if she could be arsed to leave the bed and find out what was happening, or to let Cathy handle it.

Cathy interrupted her decision-making seconds later, looking harassed. "Sorry to disturb you, sweetie. You have a visitor who is refusing to leave."

"Who?" Lydia was still half asleep, and in no fit state to entertain anyone.

"Halle?"

Well, that woke her the hell up!

"What does she want?"

"To talk." Cathy did not look at all happy. "I told her you needed rest, but she is adamant she needs to see you."

"Um...okay, let her in."

"Are you sure? Don't feel obligated, Lydia."

"Honestly, it's fine."

Was it fine? Not really.

"Alright. I'll nip to the shop and pick up a few bits and bobs. I've got my phone."

"Thanks, Cath."

Lydia shuffled her bum nervously in place. Smoothing the bed covers down and then her hair, she waited. Cathy's irritation was still clear in her tone as she told Halle to go through.

Two soft knocks sounded through the bedroom door. "Come in."

"Hey."

Hey, that's it, after seven days of nada? Okay, so Lydia was finding it a little harder than expected to keep her cool. The only thing that was stopping her from erupting was the look on Halle's face as she regarded Lydia in bed, probably looking pretty rough.

"Hello. What can I help you with?"

"I deserve that. Can I come in?"

"Sure."

Halle moved closer; her steps hesitant. "I'm so sorry, Lydia. I can't believe I missed your surgery."

"It's fine. Cathy was with me."

"No, it's not fine. None of this is fine."

"What do you want, Halle? If it was to say sorry, you've done that. I forgive you. Now I need to rest."

"Please don't shut me out—"

"Don't shut you out," Lydia scoffed. "That's bloody rich. It's been over a week and nothing. You almost fuck me on your kitchen floor, and then ghost me? Why, because poor Fe is upset?"

"It's not like that," Halle protested, but Lydia was done.

"It's exactly like that. I can't do whatever the hell this is, Halle. I like you and yes, I'm attracted to you, but I don't want your drama. And with Fe, it's always drama. She's your best friend and I'm just the little sister. I hope you patch things up with her. You can let her know she won't have to worry about mean old Lydia swooping in to steal her woman!"

"I'm not her woman."

"That's what you took from all this?" Shaking her head, Lydia laughed as she finally found the clarity she'd been missing over the past seven days. "Yes, you are. Getting upset over me and you being friends, or more, is *not* normal. I'm done pussyfooting around it. It's fucking weird. I'm in my thirties for Christ's sake; I don't need this playground bollocks. No matter what, you will always be hers first, and that's fine. I need to look after myself now. I suggest we go back to the way it was before we were friends. It's easier for everyone."

"Lydia—"

"I'll deal with Fe at some point, but I'm not dancing to her tune anymore. You tell her that. Oh, and she better not think of getting mum involved. Fe said she'd never forgive me. Well, that's a two-way street. I never thought my own sister would speak to me like that."

"Lyds—"

"If you don't mind, I'd like to be left alone now. I'm tired."

"Lydia, please."

"You heard her, Halle. It's time to go." Lydia hadn't heard Cathy return, but she was so happy to see her.

Halle clenched her fists several times before slowly standing. It was taking every ounce of strength Lydia had left not to reach out and smooth the harrowed look off Halle's face.

"I'm sorry, Lydia." Halle muttered in a voice no higher than a whisper.

When Lydia was sure Halle'd left, she allowed the tears to flow. It was the right call, of that, she was sure. But that didn't stop it from hurting. It wasn't just Halle and Fe; it was the last three years of menstrual torture, all her lovers leaving, Norris giving her shit, and Lydia's life being on hold.

All of it came flowing out, but this time when the tears dried, Lydia didn't feel the oppressive weight anymore. It was time for a change; time to leave all those things where they belonged: In the past.

There were still hard times ahead. Health issues wouldn't just vanish, but at least Lydia had a competent doctor behind her. She had Cathy and Harrison, and Monty, of course.

13

Changes were afoot. Well, the planning of changes was afoot. Lydia was determined to move forward with her plans to shake things up a little.

Nearly two weeks had passed since the operation and so far, so good. Elise stopped by after work a week after the op to check on Lydia's stitches. The good doctor stayed for a coffee and a biscuit, which was unexpected but nice. They discussed Lydia's progress on her new pill, which she'd only been taking for a few days.

Apart from a little nausea in the beginning, Lydia felt fine. She wasn't bleeding yet, however, Elise warned her, that during her next period, it was likely she would bleed for longer. Hopefully, though, the pain would be a lot less and the bleeding lighter. Elise's primary concern was for Lydia's hormone balance. It could take a few months for the pill to stabilise her moods, and Elise asked her to document her feelings throughout her cycle; nothing Lydia hadn't done before.

Once the medical bit was out of the way, they chatted about daily life, agreeing to meet for a coffee one day in the week. Elise was a brilliant conversationalist, and Lydia didn't get the feeling she wanted anything more than friendship.

True to her word, Lydia was focusing solely on her own wellbeing. It was nearly three weeks since Fe went off the deep end. No calls or messages. Even their mother had kept out of it, which was surprising. But that was fine. If Fe wanted to sulk, so be it. Only the thought of Halle's dejected face sullied her mood. But she'd done the right thing, she was sure of it. Wasn't she?

Putting the "Halle situation" to one side, Lydia felt good; the best she'd felt in a long time. Which is why she knew it was time to draw up some plans. Well, a list, to be precise. First item: Look for a new flat or house. As much as she loved her home, it was time to move on. There was a constant stream of repairs, and continually having to call her landlord was a pain in the arse.

After spending over a decade in the area, she wasn't in a rush to leave. So the search for a new abode would be local. In fact, a couple of streets away was a lovely Victorian house for sale. It would definitely eat up most of Lydia's inheritance, but investing in property was smart. Or so she'd been told.

Taking the bull by the horns, Lydia did a quick Google search and found the real estate company that dealt with the listing. A few short minutes later, she was grinning from ear to ear after securing a viewing for the following day.

Second item on the list: Appearance. There wasn't a lot she could do to change her body. Eating well and doing some exercise was enough. Hopefully, her skin would clear up as the medication worked its magic. Her hair, though? That was a different matter. The last time Lydia visited a hairdresser was over a year ago, and that was to have a trim. Now she wanted a change; something sassy, maybe.

Because of her work schedule, it would be easier to find a salon close to the museum. Another few minutes of surfing Google and she was in business. Online reservation made, Lydia took a sip of her oat milk latte, sighing happily. Today was a good day.

"Lydia!"

Spoke too soon, Lyds.

"You're not paid to sit on your phone all day."

Since coming back to work, Norris had upped his snark by a thousand percent and Lydia was tired of it. He resented Lydia for taking time off to recover, even though she'd gone through the proper channels and got it approved.

"Norris, I still have 15 minutes left of my lunch break."

"You've been gone for ages. We need you back on the till in the giftshop."

"I have been gone for 45 minutes. My lunch is an hour."

"Now listen here, Missy—"

Oh, I don't think so!

"No, Norris, you listen. I am entitled to take a lunch break. What is your problem?"

"I beg your pardon?" Norris's face was slowly turning a deep shade of red.

"You heard me." Lydia was now on her feet, hands on hips. "We all work hard here, but you're never satisfied. Morale is in the toilet, and yet we still put smiles on and do a damn good job welcoming people to the museum. All you do is find fault."

"I expect—"

"The impossible. We can never live up to your standard. You've made two new employees cry this month. If you hate working here so much, why do you?"

"I've been here for years, young lady."

"I know! We all know, but that doesn't mean you can bully us all. I'm tired of coming into work, wondering what crap you're going to throw at us next."

"This is unbelievable. You'll be hearing from Sue by the end of the day!"

Sue Randal was the director of HR. A lovely woman with beautiful red hair.

"Good! Call her now. It's about time something was done. This is a hostile work environment."

Calling Norris' bluff worked a treat. The man visibly paled. "Fine, I will." His voice didn't sound as confident as he'd hoped. That was obvious.

"Go on then." Lydia glared at him, daring the man to pick up the phone.

"I'll call later! Some of us have work to do." Norris stomped off, almost taking the door with him as he stormed out.

Blowing out a cleansing breath, Lydia sat back down and finished her lunch. Returning to her list helped stave off the bad mood trying to creep in. Norris just liked to spread his misery.

Bloody Norris.

The next item on the list was more like a list-within-a-list. Lydia realised, for the most part, she'd trundled through life, not really doing anything. Her twenties were all about finding a stable job after leaving university. Paying bills took precedence over a career she loved, or travelling.

When her grandad left her money, it went straight into the bank. Then her reproductive system kicked up a stink, and that was that. Lydia just tried to get through the days without too much trouble. How sad had her life turned out?

All the things she'd dreamt of doing as a kid fell to the wayside. Well, no longer. Her list was going to rectify that. Skydiving, bungee jumping, scuba diving—she would do them all. Plus, she'd do some travelling before settling down. Her biggest dream still, was to have the house, kids, and a loving partner. She could have two out of three by herself. That had to count for something.

Jesus, her feet were on fire. After spending a few hours behind the till in the gift shop, Lydia had all but begged Cathy to swap with her for a little while. The doctor told her to take it easy, not to sit on her ass all day. Thankfully, Cathy obliged, and Lydia took her three booked-out tours.

Now her feet were protesting vehemently in her heels. Pushing open the door to the staff lounge, Lydia almost shrieked when a group of co-workers began clapping. Cathy and Harrison were standing front and centre. Cathy added a loud whistle, as if the clapping weren't enough.

"What on earth are you doing?" Lydia clutched her chest tightly.

"Everyone heard what you did," Cathy began. "Sunjit was on her way to have lunch when she overheard you calling Norris out. This is our way of saying thank you!"

"Stop it." Lydia waved her hand, blushing. "I shouldn't have spoken to him like that. He's still my boss."

"Bollocks," Sunjit injected. "The man has a chip on his shoulder the size of London Tower. That Kerry girl almost quit after he made her cry."

"Is she okay?"

"Yeah, we took her out for a pint. Managed to calm her down."

Lydia shook her head. When Norris threatened to call Sue, Lydia was happy for him to do it. Now it was obvious he was bluffing, but maybe Lydia should call her anyway. Colleagues being made to cry, to the point they wanted to quit, was outrageous.

"Well, thank you for the applause, now can you stop?" Laughing, everyone went about their business. "You guys up for a pint?" she asked Cathy and Harrison.

"As if you need to ask," Cathy playfully scoffed.

"Wonderful, I'll get my coat."

The Royal Oak was less packed than usual. Once again, they snagged the table by the fire. Harrison went to the bar, leaving Lydia the opportunity to show her list to Cathy.

"You're really going to move?"

"Yes, I think it's time. I've got a house viewing tomorrow. It's on your street!"

"Not the gorgeous Victorian?"

"Yup." A little squeal of delight left her body.

"Oh sweetie, yes! I can totally see you living there. Monty would love it. All that garden space. Can I come with you to look?"

"Of course."

"What's this next one? Appearance? You're not thinking of getting nipped and tucked, are you? Lydia, you're perfect, just the way you are."

"Alright Bruno Mars, calm down. I'm just getting a new hairstyle. I want to go shorter and...something. I'll talk to the stylist."

"Bruno sang, 'Girl you're amazing, just the way you are,' not 'perfect' the way you are."

"Whatever. It still stands."

"Why are we talking about Bruno Mars?" Harrison asked, setting the tray of drinks down.

"We're not. We were discussing hair."

"Bruno *has* got nice hair."

"Harrison, honey, we're not talking about Bruno or his hair."

"I'm confused." Taking a sip of beer, Harrison proceeded to read his book. Tittering between them, Lydia and Cathy clinked their glasses.

"So, after the haircut, your list says you've decided to kill yourself."

Lydia choked on her beer. "No, it doesn't."

"Yes. It says you're going to throw yourself out of a plane, then off a bridge, and then drown yourself."

"Bloody hell, Lydia!" Harrison exclaimed, looking alarmed.

"It does not say that, Harrison. It says skydiving, bungee jumping, and scuba diving."

"Cat, Jesus! You scared the piss out of me."

Crossing her arms over her chest, Cathy sat up straighter. "Call them what you like. It's stupid and suicidal!"

"Alright, so I won't ask you to come with me, then."

"No, and if you value life, you wouldn't do those things, either."

"Moving on," Lydia chuckled. "Do you think I'd be nuts to try to have a baby?"

"Wow, okay, back up. You've gone from a new haircut to getting pregnant?"

"No. But you heard what Elise said. It could be difficult for me and I'm already in my thirties. What if I wait too long and it doesn't happen?"

"I'll donate," Harrison chipped in, leaving both Lydia and Cathy slack-jawed.

"Harrison, that's..." Lydia didn't know how to finish her sentence. Casting a glance at Cathy, she was happy to see her friend smiling at her man. Phew, that could have gone differently.

"The offer's there, for when you're ready. Cath and I don't plan to have kids. It would make me happy to know I could help you live your dream."

A small sob popped out from Lydia's throat. "Thank you." Looking away briefly to collect herself, Lydia swigged her beer. "So, you two have talked about kids?"

"It's one of the first things we spoke of, actually." Harrison laid his book down. "It was quite refreshing being upfront from the start."

"He's right. No guesswork. We'd think of marriage, but neither of us wants children. I'd be happy to be the best aunt in the world."

"Yeah, I could be a good friend or uncle," Harrison added.

"Should I be looking for a bridesmaid's dress?"

Cathy and Harrison laughed. "Not quite. We're good right now." They shared a sweet smile and a kiss. Lydia's heart melted. They were perfect together.

"So, back to your question," Cathy piped up. "If you want a child, Lydia, that's wonderful. Just make sure you're doing it because that's your dream, not because you're scared it might not happen. You said yourself you wanted to have a little time to get yourself together. You've started with the house viewing tomorrow, and the haircut."

"I know." Sighing, Lydia picked at the beer mat in front of her. "There's still a bunch of stuff to think about. It crossed my mind, is all."

"I think it's great you're planning for the future," Harrison commented. "We've got your back, whatever you decide to do."

Who was this confident, outspoken man?

"Thank you. Both of you."

"Don't mention it. Now, next item on the pub talk agenda. Are you going to call Sue and report Norris?" Cathy asked.

"Do you think I should?"

Harrison nodded enthusiastically. "Yes. The man is a menace."

Cathy agreed with a "Uh- huh."

"I'll think about it. Although, I'm not the only one that could call HR, you know."

"Yeah, but you've rallied the troops. You're the unofficial spokesperson now."

Great.

"All original hardwood floors. New bathroom, kitchen and ensuite. They updated the electrics and plumbing last year." Meredith, the realtor, was giving it her all. To be honest, the second Lydia stepped through the door, she felt at home.

"And they want a quick sale, right?" Cathy asked as she walked around the room.

"Yes. The family has moved to Australia. They need the funds from the house."

"And is there any wiggle room on the price?" Lydia could pay the full asking price, but who did that? Haggling was part of the process.

"I can certainly negotiate a lower price, although this is a beautiful house. I wouldn't try to go too low."

"Fifteen off the asking price and I'll sign here and now."

"Let me call my clients."

Lydia waited until Meredith was out of earshot before grabbing Cathy excitedly. "I love it."

"Sweetie, it's beautiful."

"You don't think I'm being rash?"

"Lyds, if this is what you want, go for it. Investing in property is smart. And this house is a home. You could live here for the rest of your life if you wanted."

"Monty's going to freak when he sees it."

"Hell yes, he will. Have you told your mum?"

The topic was getting dangerously close to one that Lydia had no time for. Reading between the lines, Cathy was really asking if there had been any mention of Fe. There hadn't.

"I'll tell her when I visit."

"Okay, Lydia, we have a deal. Darren is keen to get the ball rolling, and considering you're paying outright, I don't think it's going to take long to complete."

"Oh, my God!" Lydia and Cathy jumped around in excitement, causing Meredith to laugh.

"Do you want to come to the office now and get the paperwork started?"

"Yes, absolutely."

This was probably the only time Lydia enjoyed sifting through a ton of paper. Her hand cramped from all the signatures she'd had to scribble. Once that was done, though, Lydia only had to go to the bank and set up payment for the deposit. After a surveyor had visited, she'd be able to close and move in.

Clinking glasses, Lydia, and Cathy drank liberally. "How're you feeling, Ms Homeowner?"

"It's not a done deal yet." Lydia didn't want to jinx anything.

"Pish. Darren, Dillan, whoever the bloke was, wants a sale. You're a cash buyer. He's not going to bugger that up. Neither is Meredith."

"Let's hope so. It would be great to move in before spring."

"We can have a moving-in party."

"We can have plenty of parties."

The server deposited their focaccia pizza before bustling off. The smell of garlic and sun-dried tomatoes was heavenly.

"How's everything going on down below?"

Lydia caught herself before she choked on her lunch. "Cathy, there's a time and a place, you know."

"Yeah, it's here and now. Who do you think is listening? Look, everyone's glued to their phones."

Casting a quick look around, Lydia couldn't argue. "Everything's fine. I'm due to start my period next week, so I'm not looking forward to that."

"But you should feel better? Less pain?"

"That's the aim. Elise says I should notice a change in my emotions, too. Hopefully, I won't be going off the deep end again."

"You'll call me if you feel down? We can have a girls' night."

"Deal." Lydia noticed Cathy playing with her food. "Everything okay with you?"

"Perfect. I wanted to ask...are you planning on talking to Fe?"

"Where's that coming from?"

"She may have stopped by the museum yesterday."

Setting her cutlery on the table, Lydia wiped her mouth. "What did she want?"

"I'm not sure, to be honest. She had the kids with her."

"And?"

"Well, she didn't ask for you, but it was pretty obvious she was looking. The kids definitely wanted to see you. Jenny kept tugging Fe's coat, demanding to see you."

"She has my number."

"And you have hers."

"Not this time, Cathy. If she wants to talk, I'll listen, but she needs to come to me. I'm tired of the game playing.

I could have handled a bit of sulking, but the way she flew off the handle was insane. I didn't deserve what she said."

"I know, sweetie, I'm not picking sides. I just know how close you were. And I know you're missing the kids."

"I am missing them. The last thing I want is for them to feel abandoned by me, but I also can't let Fe think she can use them as emotional blackmail."

If she were being honest with herself, Lydia nearly caved in every hour. Knowing her niblings were already going through a shitty time having their parents split up, gnawed away at her. They were only five, and no way near mature enough to understand the nuances of grown-up thoughts, feelings, and actions. She wanted to send them a gift, to let them know she was still around, but Cath had reminded her in no uncertain terms, a gift was no substitute for Lydia's presence in their lives.

"Agreed. Maybe you could talk to your mum. See where things stand."

"If it goes as usual, Mum will tell me to be the one to call. She'll say Fe's having a tough time of it at the minute. It's always the same."

"Alright. I just wanted to check in."

"And I appreciate it. Now, can we get back to these delicious pizzas and divine cocktails? We're supposed to be celebrating."

"Damn right. Congratulations, Lydia. Here's to a new start."

They raised their glasses. "To a new start and shaking things up."

14

Checking her watch for the umpteenth time, Lydia once again cursed British public transport. Everything was late, meaning Lydia was late. Her mum wouldn't mind so much, but that wasn't the point.

If truth be told, Lydia was feeling a teensy bit nervous. It was nearly a month since their last gathering as a trio for Sunday lunch. Lydia could no longer use her recovery as an excuse to get out of it.

No matter what they had going on in their lives, the three Archer women always sat down at 12:30 p.m. sharp every Sunday and enjoyed a good catch-up. Lydia's mum hadn't said anything regarding the break in tradition, so far, which to Lydia, spelled trouble. Something was bound to be said today. Surely?

When the bus finally arrived at her designated stop, Lydia flung her arm over her boobs and jogged the rest of the way. Turning up for lunch all sweaty and flushed, wasn't the best look, but at least she'd managed to arrive only ten minutes late instead of the fifteen it would have been, had she not risked a black eye. Maybe it was time to invest in some quality bras.

As usual, Lydia let herself in without knocking. Her mum's house was small, but growing up here had been great. It was a home; one that Lydia sometimes wished she could come back to. Being an adult, for the most part, was garbage. What she wouldn't give to be a kid again, with not a care in the world, having her mum take care of all the scary things life liked to throw at people.

I wish!

But Lydia wasn't a kid, and she had to sort her own shit out. So far, she wasn't doing such a terrible job. Having some control over her health had gone a long way in boosting Lydia's confidence. It was amazing how badly those issues had shaken her sense of being. The constant self-deprecation and low moods had taken a toll that not even Lydia had been aware of. It was only now, when she could see light at the end of the tunnel, Lydia understood how low she'd become; how out of touch with herself she had felt.

Saving the self-therapy for later, Lydia dropped her bag on the hallway floor before removing her boots and slipping on the house shoes her mum kept by the front door for them.

The coat rack was overflowing as usual, making Lydia roll her eyes. Her mum didn't know what rotating clothes meant, even though Lydia had explained it to her a bazillion times. How hard was it to put summer and spring coats away once it was winter?

Making her way to the kitchen, still tutting at the coat rack of chaos, Lydia realised there was a notable absence of smell. It was almost 12:25 p.m. The chicken should be almost done and filling the house with a delicious, mouth-watering scent. But the only thing getting up Lydia's nose was a Glade plug-in diffuser set way too high.

Those nerves she'd been feeling on the way over came rushing back. Something wasn't right about this set-up. It only took another two steps into the kitchen to see her gut feeling was spot on.

Instead of her mum, Lydia found Fe at the kitchen table, nursing what looked like an Irish coffee, if the bottle of Bailey's was anything to go by. Stopping in her tracks, Lydia weighed up her options. Was she in the mood for this?

If Fe went off on her again, Lydia wasn't sure she could hold back this time. Weeks of being ignored had manifested into an ugly feeling that was desperate to show its face. Lydia had done a grand job of keeping it under wraps.

Living with such negativity was the opposite of what she was striving for, but in the presence of the person who created it, Lydia wasn't sure she could keep her shit together.

Taking a second to breathe deeply, Lydia noted Fe didn't look so great. Her eyes had dark circles under them, and she looked as if she'd dropped a few pounds. Her hair wasn't in its usual immaculate state, but shoved up in a messy ponytail.

Obviously, Clark's absence was the reason. Lydia couldn't think of anything else that would affect her sister so much. They looked at each other for a few seconds until Fe dropped her eyes to the table.

Interesting.

"I take it Sunday lunch isn't happening?" Lydia's tone was cool. She didn't want to be a bitch, but she couldn't find it in herself, just yet, to play nice. Fe's reaction and subsequent absence had hit Lydia hard.

"Um, no, Mum's at Libby's house."

"Great." Lydia scoffed. "She could have told me before I dragged my arse across London for nothing."

"I asked her to go out." Fe's voice was a little shaky, causing Lydia's resolve to crack ever so slightly. No matter how mad she was at someone, Lydia hated seeing another human upset.

"Why?"

"Because we need to talk."

Chuckling, Lydia shook her head. "Now you want to talk, huh? Maybe I'm not ready. Did you ever think about that, Fe?"

"Please, Lydia?"

"'Please, Lydia' what? Once again, because you want something, you think everyone has to go along with your timetable. Well, fuck that, and frankly, fuck you!"

"Lydia!"

"Fe! I'm tired of your drama. I never thought you'd speak to me the way you did that night in Halle's kitchen. I never thought my sister would cut me out of her life. Never. But you did. You screamed at me and then vanished. I've always known how closely you valued Halle's friendship, but I was so utterly devastated you would choose that over me. We're not best friends, Fe, we're blood. Did my almost sleeping with Halle really warrant your reaction?" Waving her hand to ward off Fe's answer, Lydia continued. "No, don't answer that. The proof's in the pudding, I suppose."

"Lydia, I'm sorry. Please hear me out."

Were pigs flying? Maybe hell *had* frozen over, because if Lydia's ears were to be believed, Fe Archer had just apologised.

"I fucked up! All I seem to do lately is bugger up my life. I acted like a crazy person. I know that now. I'm so, so sorry. The kids miss you."

Lydia scoffed. "Ah, so you need me back on babysitting duty, is that it?"

"No! God no, Lydia. They do miss you; *I* miss you."

"I'll need more than that, sis. What the bloody fuck happened? I know you've always been weird about me being friends with Halle, but I kind of thought that would be left in the past, where it belongs. We're adults, for Christ's sake. I can be friends with whoever the hell I like, as can Halle."

"I know! I know, and believe me, she's let me know how she feels." A sob tore from Fe's throat. "Halle hasn't spoken to me since the day of your operation."

"Right. Now we're getting to the bottom of it." Lydia just couldn't let go of her anger. "This isn't about us at all, is it? Halle has dropped you and you need to make nice with me to get her back on board."

"No!" Fe scrambled to her feet, taking Lydia by the shoulders. "I swear it's not like that. I've lost the two most precious people in my life, and I can't cope."

Watching her sister crumble broke Lydia's heart and her will to stay mad. Taking Fe into her arms, she let her sister cry. Tears welled in her eyes, too, as she continued to comfort Fe.

"I'm so sorry, Lyds, so sorry."

"Let's sit down. I think I could do with an Irish coffee, too."

Lydia busied herself with making her coffee. Fe sat back down, wiping her face and nose with the sleeve of her top. "I'm a mess, Lyds."

"Okay. I'm listening, and I promise not to go off on one. Let's hash this out, once and for all, because I don't want to deal with this again after today. We put it behind us, okay?"

Nodding, Fe straightened her body. "I think I have some abandonment issues," Fe began. "I didn't realise, until Halle was shouting at me, laying it all out. She didn't hold back." Lydia sat silently, listening. "You were too young to remember the mess Mum was in when Dad left. I don't remember him, but I remember Mum crying all the time. She was heartbroken."

"I didn't know."

"You weren't supposed to. Mum did her best to be strong around us. I caught her, several times crying in the shower. At the time, I didn't see how much that had affected me. All I remember thinking is I needed to keep the ones I love close to me. I never wanted to feel what Mum did. Unfortunately, that seems to have manifested into controlling people."

"There's nothing wrong with needing control."

"Yeah, but I have this pathological need to keep people in their places, in my head, I mean. If everyone is where they should be, no one will leave."

"Oh, Fe."

"I know it sounds bonkers, and life doesn't work that way. All I can say is I've been going off the fears of a young me. I never dealt with anything. I wonder now if that's why Clark left. I was too much."

"No, that's not the reason. I promise."

"How do you know?"

"That's a different conversation. Let's sort this out first."

"Okay. Well, those thoughts and feelings are why I couldn't process you and Halle."

"Meaning?"

Fe fiddled with the hem of her sleeve. "All I could see was disaster. What if you guys got together and then split up? I'd lose my best friend. Apart from you, Lyds, Halle is the only other person who knows me so well. She's like another sister to me, and I mean nothing by that. You're a great little sister. I adore you."

"I get it."

"But then I worried that if you got together and it worked out, I'd lose you both."

"How'd you figure that?"

"You'd move in together, start a life apart from me. It would only be a matter of time before we all drifted apart."

"No offence, sis, but that's stupid."

"Is it? Think of all the friends we had growing up. How many of them are we in touch with? Hardly any, because life moves on. They got married, had kids, and that was that."

"We're sisters, Fe."

"And Dad was our father, but that didn't stop him from leaving."

Clutching Fe's hand, Lydia shifted closer, dropping her voice. "Fe, whatever happened between Mum and Dad is between them. He had his reasons, and it hurts to think we weren't a good enough reason to stick around, but that's on him. Mum stayed. She gave us enough love and encouragement for two parents. We always had each other, too. Even when I annoyed you, or you pissed me off." They chuckled. "One person leaving doesn't mean everyone will. I hate my life without you, sis. It's miserable. You're always the first person I want to tell about things happening in my life. These past few weeks have sucked."

"I'm sorry. I was so ashamed of my behaviour, I couldn't bring myself to face you."

"So what changed?"

"I lost you. And yes, I lost Halle. I feel like everything is spiralling and I don't know how to get through it."

"You've not lost me, Fe. But things need to change."

"Oh, I know. I've booked myself in for counselling."

"Really?"

"Yeah, Mum kind of made me."

"Wow, I didn't see that coming."

"I know you think she's always on my side, but it's not how it looks."

"Really?" Lydia laughed, raising her eyebrow in disbelief.

"Really! Mum knows you're stronger than me—more resilient. Look at everything you've gone through over the past three years, most of it by yourself. You are strong, Lyds. I'm not like that. Mum knows it."

"Fe—"

"No, it's true. But this time, instead of coddling me, she talked to me. We had quite the discussion last night."

"Blimey."

"Yeah. I sort of broke down on her and told her everything; about finding her crying, that sort of thing."

"That must've been hard for you both."

"More for me, I think. Did you know Mum went to a therapist?"

"Really?"

"Yup. For about five years after Dad left. That's why she told me to make an appointment."

"And you did."

"I did. I don't want my kids growing up with issues. I also don't want to drive people away because of them."

"Do it for you, Fe. That's the best reason."

"I missed your surgery."

There wasn't much of a segue, but Lydia didn't mind. Fe needed to get some things off her chest.

"You did."

"I'll never forgive myself for that, Lydia."

"Please don't say that. I had Cathy. Yes, I wanted you and Halle there, but it's done."

"I should've been there." More tears fell.

"Please stop crying. You've had just as much going on as me. We both could've done better."

"How did it go? Are you okay?"

Blowing out a breath, Lydia thought about Elise's words post operation. "They removed a lot of tissue. That should help with the pain. The doctor said I could find it hard to get pregnant." Those last words came out as a whisper. Emotion choking Lydia up.

"Oh, Lyds. I'm sorry."

"It's okay. I'm not infertile. I could still carry a baby. It just might take a while."

"I know you're gonna have babies, plural. I can feel it in my waters."

Lydia burst out laughing. "Are you eighty?"

"Grandma always said it, and she was always right," Fe grinned.

"Well, if Granny said it!"

"Have you seen Halle?"

Bloody hell, Fe was giving Lydia whiplash with the change of subjects.

"Not since she came to my flat."

"She told me what happened." Fe looked down at her hands again. Lydia waited. "Remember that day you got back from your date with the nurse?"

"Yeah."

"I was going to tell you something."

"I remember."

"God, this is hard. Okay, here goes. Halle Cartwright has been in love with you since we were teenagers. She never did or said anything because I asked her not to. Do you hate me again?"

Lydia sat stunned. "Sorry, Halle what now?"

"Halle is in love with you. Has been for nearly twenty years."

"And you told her not to tell me."

"Yes. I'm so sorry."

"Yeah, you've said that a lot."

What in the world was she supposed to do with all that information?

"It was never my position to tell you how she felt. But it was my fault she never did it herself."

"Why were you going to tell me that night?"

"Because Halle was so upset. That's why we fell out at the pub. Halle wanted to ask you out, but you said you weren't going to date anyone. Then you went out with that hot nurse and it devastated Halle. She blamed me, and rightly so."

"I...I don't know what to say."

"Do you want to slap me? That might help."

"No, I do not want to slap you. But I am pissed, Fe. What the hell? You can't mess with people's lives like that!"

"I know," Fe cried. "I fucked up. After I caught you on the kitchen floor—killer tits, by the way—Halle lost it. Once you'd gone, she got *so* mad. But the next day she came to mine, and we talked. I apologised, but I said I was still uncomfortable with you being with each other. And then we missed your surgery, and that was it."

"What do you mean? And please don't talk about my tits again." Lydia was trying hard to keep everything straight in her head.

"After you told her you wanted to go back to when you were barely friends, Halle came storming in. The kids were with Mum, thank God, because I've never seen her so angry and upset. She said I'd ruined her life. Her chance at love."

"Jesus."

"She's right. Lydia, is there any chance you feel the same for her?"

"Fe, I really don't want to talk about this."

"Okay, I get it. But if there is, could you find it in yourself to talk to her? I can't be responsible for making her miserable."

"And I can't talk to her just to assuage your guilt, Fe. I need time. I made a promise to myself to cut the crap and start looking out for myself better."

"Absolutely, I think that's great. Just don't rule it out. You might not be where she is, but I know you like her. You wouldn't have risked catching some sort of disease off the floor if you didn't like her."

Lydia flushed. "The floor was clean. And that's not the point."

"You also look at her funny."

"I do not."

"Yes, you do. I've seen you ogle her plenty of times."

"Well, she's hot. Jesus, Fe, I'm only human."

The conversation was way out of hand. Lydia had come here for a roast dinner, not a deep dive analysis of her love life.

"Do you forgive me?" Fe was clutching her mug so hard Lydia was afraid she'd break it.

"Yes, I forgive you, but it's going to take a little longer to forget. I understand there are some issues lingering from when we were kids that you need to work through, but you messed up, Fe."

"I know."

"I'll think about everything. I don't want to see Halle hurting. But I need to be a little selfish too. For now, I think it's best if we keep yours and my relationship separate from mine and Halle's."

Fe crossed her heart. "I'll keep out of it, I promise."

"Okay. Right. Is everything out in the open? Are we ready to move on?"

"I've told you everything."

"I need to tell you about running into Clark then!"

Thankful for the change of subject, Lydia relayed her conversation with Fe's ex-husband. Or soon to be.

15

"This...was...a...terrible...idea!"

"I couldn't agree more, sweetie. Are you alright? You're looking a little red over there."

"No...I...think...I'm...dying."

"Then stop, you tit. No one is making you run, Lyds. Why the hell are you running, anyway? I thought your boobs were a health hazard?"

"They are... Hang on a sec." Lydia stopped her jog/shuffle so she could bend over and rest her hands on her thighs. Head down, she did her best to draw in some much-needed oxygen. "I bought a new sports bra." Panting, Lydia could feel the stitch forming as she spoke. "Thought it would be a good plan to get fit."

"And how's that working for you?" Cathy was all smug, standing on her new electric scooter, latte in hand.

"Spiffingly, as you can tell." Wiping her hand across a very sweaty forehead, Lydia finally found the strength to stand up straight again. "I don't think running is my thing."

"Do you want a lift back on the hog?"

Chuckling, Lydia eyed Cathy's new ride. "I'd love one. She's a beauty. What's she carrying under the hood?"

"She puts out four hundred fifty watts. Twenty kilometres an hour."

Lydia gave an appreciative whistle. They were being absurd, but it was fun. "And what prompted the new ride?"

"Harrison bought it for me, from some French guy who knows one of his friends at university. They're all the rage over the pond, you know."

"Aren't they the rage everywhere?"

"Maybe, but she's an import. Special. I've called her Scarlet." Lydia burst out laughing. Cathy gave her a mischievous grin. "She's sexy. Sexy Scarlet."

"And when are you riding Sexy Scarlet?"

That sounded wrong.

"When are *we* riding Sexy Scarlet! I'm picking you up in the morning to go to work. I'll zip us to the underground."

"Well, aren't I the lucky one?"

"Hell yes, you are. Now, are we ready to hit the road?"

"Lead on." Stepping close behind Cathy, Lydia held on for dear life. After a couple of wobbles, they were on their way. Maybe she should look at getting one too? Then she wouldn't have to put up with taking the bus everywhere.

"You should buy one." Cathy locked up the scooter outside their favourite café. "We could form a club!"

"What, like the Hell's Angels, but on scooters?"

"Yes!" Cathy all but shouted, pointing excitedly at Lydia. "We'd be bad bitches."

Snorting out a laugh, Lydia pushed to go inside, where it was warm. She was bloody freezing, now that her body had cooled down from the run.

"Hot chocolate?" There was no need to ask really. Cathy loved hot chocolate on a chilly day. So did Lydia. Her mind strayed to the first day she met Nurse Hottie. That was a delicious hot chocolate, and even though, at the time, she thought it was the best hot chocolate in the UK, nothing beat the one Halle made her that night she came over and watched movies. It was a no frills, sugar-free packet mix, but the care Halle had showed Lydia made *that* hot chocolate, the best in the UK. A spear of loss pierced

Lydia's stubborn mind. She missed Halle's warmth. She missed Halle.

Nodding her agreement, Cathy nipped off to snag a table.

"Who's the new barista?" Lydia asked, setting the drinks down.

"Oh her, she's nice, right?"

"Don't be giving me eyebrows. I'm not interested."

"Fine, but you can look right? I mean, she's hot."

Peeking over her shoulder, Lydia spied the new barista. She *was* lovely. "Yes, she's hot. Now, do you want to hear about my run in with Fe?"

"Way to bury the lede. We've been together almost an hour, and this is the first time you're bringing it up? Shame, Lydia, shame."

"I was trying to run earlier. I couldn't talk *and* run. You saw what happened!"

"Well, next time, cut out the bloody exercise and get straight to the good stuff. Okay, tell me what happened."

"It was a set-up. Mum wasn't even there. Just Fe, looking...well, not great, to be honest."

"Wow, okay. Was she all pissy, still?"

"Nope, not at all. She explained her reaction to finding me and Halle...you know."

"I do know, and I am so sad you got clam jammed!"

"Thanks, anyway, she reckons she's going to therapy. Apparently, there is a load of stuff I don't remember from when our dad left, that Fe does. Seems to have done a number on her."

"Do you believe her?"

"Yeah, it makes sense. Anyway, according to her, Halle has stopped talking to her completely."

"Jesus. Why?"

This was the part Lydia was still struggling to process. Clearing her throat, she massaged her temples. "Fe says Halle has had a thing for me since we were teenagers, and it was Fe who told Halle not to do anything about it. Then, I showed interest the other week—"

"By snogging her face off."

"—and Halle lost her shit at Fe, telling her she'd ruined her chance at love."

Cathy sat back, wide-eyed. "Bloody hell, Lyds, you're living in an Eastenders episode, but the gay version."

"Fe asked me to talk to Halle."

"What, on her behalf? She's got some cheek!"

"No, not for her."

"Are you going to?"

"I don't know. I'm really serious about looking after myself, for once. I want to get to a point where I'm okay alone. Do you know what I mean?"

"Yeah, I get it. So, what's your plan?"

"Halle and Fe are like friend soulmates. I don't want them falling out. They're each other's support systems, and by the sounds of it, they both need some support. I might talk to Halle and ask her to call Fe."

"And what about the whole 'she wants you' thing? Are you going to say anything?"

"Nope. Fe shouldn't have told me. Halle would be mortified if I said something."

"So, you're just going to ignore it?"

"What choice do I have? I'm not in the right place for a relationship."

"Could you be friends again?"

"It would be tough, but yeah. Maybe that's the best place for us to be. We get on, and I do miss her."

"Can I just say one thing?" *As if Lydia could stop her.* "Don't close yourself off to the idea. I know you've got a ton of things you want to do on your own, which I completely support by the way, sweetie. Just don't hold out because you *think* that's what you should be doing. See what happens when you become friends again, yeah?"

"I will."

"So, is everything with Fe resolved?"

"I'm still mad at her, and she knows it. I've put strict boundaries in place. Our relationship is separate from any kind of relationship I may have with Halle."

"Good thinking!"

Lydia watched Cathy chew her lip. "Are *you* okay? Something on your mind?"

"Harrison wants me to meet his family."

It was Lydia's turn to get a little wide-eyed. "That's...big. It's big, right?"

"Yeah, it's huge. I'm not sure I can."

"Why?"

"What are they going to think when he brings me home? I'm a lot older. I know Harrison doesn't care, but I'm not so sure dear old mum will be so pleased."

"Maybe don't call her 'dear old mum' for a start. And anyway, would he ask you to meet them if he thought they'd have an issue?"

"It's been a long time since I've had to meet the parents, Lyds. We're getting on so well. I don't want this to torpedo our relationship. Families can spell disaster."

"Oh, I know that," Lydia laughed. "But trust him, Cath. Harrison is completely taken with you. He wouldn't put you in harm's way."

"It's a lot of pressure." Cathy looked on the verge of tears.

"Hey, look at me." Cathy reluctantly held eye contact. "You two are wonderful together. Don't let anyone or anything make you feel otherwise. If you're really uncomfortable, tell Harrison. But trust in him, and your relationship."

"I really like him."

"I know, honey. And he really likes you."

"Okay. I'll meet them. Jesus, I hope his parents drink!"

"Want another hot chocolate?" Lydia was more than happy to spend a little more time in the cosy café. Monty was with her mum, and Lydia didn't feel like going back to her empty flat. Although, she really should think about packing. The house sale was moving fast and Lydia had nothing organised.

"Sure. Can I have chocolate syrup on the cream?"

Making her way to the counter, Lydia thought about the situation with Halle. How the hell was she going to navigate it? Halle's hurt face sprung to mind, causing a cramp in Lydia's tummy. She'd sent Halle away, not knowing the full depth of the woman's feelings towards her. Now Lydia felt like a cold bitch. Should she have heard Halle out? Probably, but all Lydia could think and feel at the time was hurt, and if she were honest, betrayal; from both Halle and her sister.

Deep in her thoughts, Lydia missed the barista talking to her. "Hmm, what? Shit, sorry. Um, two hot chocolates please, one with chocolate syrup on the cream."

"Sure. Small, medium, or large?"

"Medium, please."

"I'm Shaz, by the way. I just started working here. I've not seen you before."

"I'm a regular. It's just been a few days. How are you liking it?"

"Love it. The place is cosy and the locals are great."

"Great."

Shaz made their drinks, all the time chatting to Lydia. If she weren't mistaken, Shaz was flirting.

"Here you go. Enjoy."

Lydia gave her a smile and headed back to Cathy as fast as she could. "I think Shaz was flirting with me!"

"Who the bloody hell is Shaz?"

"The new barista."

"I'd say she was. Look, she gave you her number on a napkin. Wow, do people actually do that? I've seen it in movies and in books, but wow. Yeah, she wants your body, Lyds."

"Well, this body is out of bounds."

"Shame. She could be a bit of fun."

"Nope. Now, moving on, did you get the email from Sue?"

"About the meeting? Yeah. Do you think someone actually reported Norris?"

"If they did, I've not heard. I was still mulling it over."

Cathy licked off a large dollop of cream, getting it all over her face. Leaning over, Lydia wiped it off with the napkin with Shaz's number on it.

"Well, you won't have to worry about Shaz asking you out again. I'm pretty sure she thinks we're together now," Cathy smirked.

"I could do worse." Lydia ducked in time to miss being pelted in the face with the aforementioned napkin.

"We should take bets on what the meeting is about. I bet we could get a pool going."

"You do that. I'll just hope I'm not going to get reamed out for talking back at Norris the other day."

Lydia needn't have worried. Sue from HR was not there to tear her a new arsehole for being disrespectful to Norris. She was there, however, to announce Norris had retired, effective immediately. The entire team was understandably shocked. A buzz of surprise and uncertainty flowed through the group.

"Lydia, can I have a word?" Sue was already walking to Norris' office, not even waiting for a reply. Casting a wary look in Cathy's direction, Lydia followed Sue.

"I heard about what happened." Sue was a straight-to-the-point kinda woman. "Between you and me, Norris was already on a warning for his behaviour. Once the incident between the two of you was reported, I had to take action."

"Who reported it?"

"I can't say. Anyway, how would you feel about stepping into the role of supervisor?"

"As much as I appreciate the offer, you should be asking Cathy." There was no doubt in Lydia's mind who should be the next supervisor. Lydia might have "rallied the troops"—*once*—over the whole Norris business, but it was Cathy who was the anchor.

"Okay, thank you. I'll have a word with her next." Sue ushered them both outside, cornering Cathy. Lydia smiled at her friend, hoping she'd take the job.

As soon as her shift was over, Cathy danced over to Lydia in the staff room. "I know what you did!"

"Isn't that the title of a slasher movie?"

"Stop. Thank you, Lyds." Cathy bear-hugged Lydia until she was going blue. "I took the job."

"I should hope so. Congratulations, you're going to be a great boss!"

"I know. Now, drink?"

"Can I take a rain check? I'm going to head over to Halle's."

Leaning against the lockers, Cathy observed Lydia. "So, you're going for it. Taking the plunge?"

"I'm going to have a conversation. About Fe! That's it."

"Uh-huh."

"Don't uh-huh me."

"I'll uh-huh you all I like. For just a conversation, not even about you, I might add, you're getting awfully dressed up."

Busted! Lydia couldn't help herself. If she was going to see Halle for the first time in weeks, she wanted to look good doing it. As much as Lydia tried to put Fe's confession out of her mind, it was impossible. Halle had liked her for years. Years! What was she supposed to do with that?

"Nothing wrong with looking good."

"I didn't say there was. Just remember what I said. Keep an open mind."

Rolling her eyes dramatically, Lydia closed her locker. "Good night, boss."

"Night underling. Mwahahahaha!"

Lydia was still tittering to herself about Cathy's fake malevolent goodbye when she arrived outside Halle's flat. The lights were on, so Lydia was confident she was in.

God, why did she always turn into a bag of nerves whenever she stood on Halle's doorstep? Standing tall, shoulders back, Lydia gave off the air of someone totally calm and in control. It was bullshit, but she looked the part.

Giving three rapid knocks, Lydia took a step back and waited. And waited. What was taking Halle so long? Lydia could hear her in there. Finally, after a ridiculous amount of time, the door creaked open. Halle stood there looking...sad. It seemed to take her a second to register it was Lydia standing at her door. When the realisation hit, Halle's cheeks flushed, and her eyes grew wide.

"L-Lydia, hi."

"Hey, Halle. Um, could I come in for a second?"

"What, yeah, of course. Sure, come in."

Brushing past Halle, Lydia was hit with the same smell that made her a little weak at the knees. Halle's smell.

"It's nice and warm in here." Well, that was stating the obvious and a terrible attempt at starting a conversation.

"Yeah. Um, tea?"

"Sure." Following Halle into the kitchen, Lydia couldn't help but notice the state of Halle's usually immaculate flat. Dishes piled up in the sink. Clothes lay strewn on different bits of furniture. As for Halle, she looked tired. The sad look Lydia noticed at the door was now replaced with...cautious optimism? Could you even see that kind of emotion in a person?

"Do you want to take a seat?" Halle began removing paper and plates from the table.

"Thanks." They fell silent as Halle boiled the kettle. "How have you been?"

Turning, Halle gave Lydia a small smile. "Fine, thanks. You, um, everything okay, you know, after the op?"

"I'm great. Elise gave me a new pill. It might take a while to settle things down, but I already feel better."

"That's wonderful. I'm really pleased for you, Lydia."

Silence again.

Breathing out slowly through her nose, Lydia jumped straight to it. "I saw Fe." Halle visibly stiffened. "She told me you guys have fallen out."

"Did she now?"

"Halle?"

"Lydia, it's between me and Fe. I'm surprised you're here advocating for her, after the way she treated you. After the way, we both treated you." Halle's voice dipped as she spoke the last few words. Lydia couldn't take it anymore. Halle looking so...broken, was soul destroying. Standing, Lydia closed the gap between them and wrapped her arms around the much taller woman. Halle only took a second to relax into it. "I'm so sorry, Lyds."

"It's okay." Lydia felt Halle breathing her in. Small shivers ran down her neck as Halle exhaled on her skin. Needing to keep control of the situation, Lydia slowly released her grip and took a step back. "Can we talk?"

"If it's about you and me, yes."

"Fair enough." Sitting back down, Lydia sipped her tea. "I'm sorry I didn't give you a chance to talk when we last saw each other. I was feeling hurt."

"I know."

"I want us to be friends, Halle. Real friends."

"Just friends?"

Squeezing her fingers together, Lydia powered through. God, she wanted to throw her own rules out the window and ride Halle like a bloody cowgirl in heat, all night, but she couldn't. Lydia needed to sort herself out first. Learn to be happy with herself. "Yes. Just friends. I bought a house."

"Wow, okay."

"And I made a list of all the things I want to do."

"A list?"

"Yes. I know it probably sounds a bit wonky—"

"No, it doesn't. What's on this list?"

"Um, stuff like skydiving, bungee jumping. Cathy thinks I'm nuts. I'm not. I just realised I've let myself get into a rut. I've been unhappy for so long. Unhappy with myself, if I'm truthful. For a little while at least, I need to do things for myself, and by myself."

"For a little while? Not forever?"

Dammit, Halle was making this hard. "Not forever, but I don't know how long I need."

"I can wait, Lydia."

Good grief, this woman. "Halle—"

"I'll wait, and in the meantime, we can build a friendship. No pressure. No expectations."

"You really want to be friends? That's enough?" Lydia needed them to be on the same page.

"Yes. Being your friend is more than enough."

"For how long?"

"For as long as you need. I'm not going anywhere, Lyds."

Was this a good idea? Could they really stick within the bounds of friendship? That night on the kitchen floor sprung to mind. Knowing what Halle's lips tasted like, Lydia wasn't so sure they could stay platonic.

"Okay. Friends." Sticking out her hand, Lydia smiled when Halle shook it. "You need to sort things with Fe. There, that's my first bit of friendly advice. She misses you."

Halle puffed out her cheeks. "She crossed the line, Lyds. I don't want to go into it, but she really fucked up."

Lydia knew how badly Fe had buggered up, but she couldn't tell Halle that.

"She's going to therapy."

"Really?"

"Yeah. Even Mum had a word!" Lydia grinned, hoping Halle would see the light side of her comment.

"Yeesh. Mrs Archer getting involved! That's—"

"Unheard of," Lydia chuckled. "But clearly needed. Please, just think about talking to her."

"All right. I'll think about it. Can we stop talking about Fe now, though? I need to process before I'm ready to do anything."

"Sure. Want to know about my new house?"

16

"How is everything so far, Lydia?" Elise Maynard asked, looking as wonderful as ever, sitting behind her large desk. Did she just wake up looking that good?

"Good, great actually. I started my period two days ago."

"And how have you found it so far?"

"Great!" Lydia never thought she'd use that adjective to describe how she felt towards her period. How times had changed. "I had some discomfort, but nothing close to what I felt before." Being able to function like a regular human was wonderful.

"Any vomiting? Cramps?"

"No vomiting. I actually slept through the start of it, which is a first. A few cramps, but nothing too bad."

When Lydia had woken to find she was bleeding, the first thing she felt was panic, wondering when the pain would start. After an hour of mild discomfort, she dared to believe this was her new normal. Nothing could have censored her joy that day.

"And your mood?"

"I haven't experienced the black cloud at all. I still felt hungry, but I ate sensibly until that feeling passed. I'm bleeding, but it's a lot lighter."

That was an understatement. Instead of using the extra heavy pads she was accustomed to, Lydia could pop in a panty liner and be safe from leaks.

"That's a great start, Lydia. Remember, you might bleed for longer than usual. Don't panic, it's quite normal."

"I'm prepared." Lydia took a second to quell her rising emotions. "Elise, I just have to say thank you, once again. It's no exaggeration when I say you've changed my life. I know there will be difficulties, but I already feel so much better. Like I have my life back again. I don't know how to repay what you've given me."

Elise gave Lydia a soft smile. "I don't need you to repay me. Seeing you like this is all the reward I need."

"Well, that may be so, but would you allow me to buy you a drink? I'm meeting up with a bunch of friends later. Halle included. I'm sure she'd be happy to catch up. Plus, we never got 'round to grabbing that coffee."

"Sure, why not? I'm comfortable to discharge you to a GP now. You'll need to visit them every six months to get a new prescription. Dr Pritchard will take care of you. That's if you're still okay to attend his surgery."

"I'm fine with that." It would be a tad awkward with Zoe to begin with, but Lydia was confident they'd move past it.

"Wonderful! In that case, you're no longer my patient. Although if you have any concerns, you can always come to me."

"So, you'll have a pint with me?"

"Sure. I'll meet you there if that's okay. I have a few things to get finished first."

"Perfect. I'll see you at The Royal Oak around six?"

"Lovely."

Lydia breathed a sigh of relief. Things were moving in the right direction. Meredith called that morning to set a firm moving date. Two weeks from Saturday and Lydia would sleep in her very own home.

Fe brought the triplets to the museum several times since their heart-to-heart. Lydia appreciated her sister's effort and was more than happy to hear therapy was helping. The triplets were as insane as ever, which made Lydia happy. They seemed to be coping better with their parents' divorce. Fe didn't look so stressed out, even though Clark was trying his best to win her back. Which apparently, Fe didn't want.

The only hitch now, in her perfectly laid out plan to live her best life, was Halle. Well, remaining *only friends* with Halle, to be exact. The more time they hung out, the harder Lydia found it to keep her boundaries in place.

Foolishly, Lydia thought if they hung out in a group setting, it would make the situation easier. That was until Lydia had the opportunity to watch Halle interact with Cathy and Harrison. She was so effortlessly charming. Lydia was putty in her hands. It was only when Cathy nudged her—hard—in the ribs, Lydia realised: one, she was practically drooling over Halle, and two, how hard she was finding their predicament.

Halle wanted Lydia. And Lydia wanted Halle, but she wasn't there yet. Plus, Lydia wasn't entirely convinced Fe wouldn't do a one-eighty and lose her shit again.

Shooting off a message to Cathy and Halle telling them to meet her at the pub, Lydia made her way home with a small skip in her step. Shoving through the front door, Lydia called to Monty. The poor little guy was dwarfed by stacks of moving boxes piled around the place.

The sound of his paws skittering through the maze of cardboard brought a smile to her face. A loud yip announced Monty's displeasure of his kingdom being overrun by these brown towers.

"Sorry, buddy. Not long now, okay? You'll have loads of room at the house, and a much bigger garden. This is just temporary."

"Does he ever answer you back?"

Screaming, Lydia swivelled round, launching her purse at the intruder.

"Lyds, shit, it's me."

Breathing hard, Lydia focused on a cowering Halle. "Fuck, why'd you sneak up on me?"

"I didn't. You left the door open. I thought you heard me!"

"Well, I didn't, clearly!"

"Yeah, I got that from the face full of faux leather! Jesus, you've got quite a throw."

"I played rounders as a kid."

"Yeah, I remember now. Anyway, is it safe to enter without getting pelted with accessories?"

"Yes. I just need a second to bring my heart rate back down. It's currently somewhere in the bloody stratosphere."

"Hey, Monty-moo!"

Lydia grinned through her palpitations as Halle knelt to roughhouse with her dog. Monty gave her his best "love me" eyes and Lydia lost their attentions for a few minutes.

"Did you scare the shit out of me just to fuss with my dog?"

"No, I thought we could grab a pizza before going to the pub. I was only around the corner." Halle stood, wiping Monty's hair off her jeans.

"How come?"

"Ben got discharged. I popped in to give him one last check-up. Remind him to keep up with his physio."

"Wow, he's home. That's great."

"Yeah, I'm so proud of him. So, pizza?"

"Sure. I invited Elise to the pub too." Why had she blurted that out?

"Oh, really? You guys are friends?" Lydia didn't miss the edge in Halle's voice. Did she really think Lydia had something going on with the doctor beyond friendship?

"We're becoming friends. It was tricky when she was my doctor, but I've been discharged now and it's only right that I buy the woman a drink."

"Of course." Halle's face still looked stricken.

"Halle, we're just friends."

"Lyds, it's entirely up to you who you see. I'm not being weird, I swear."

Yeah right!

"I owe you, too. Although I don't think a drink will suffice."

Lydia still hadn't worked out how to thank Halle for sticking her beak in, as Halle so eloquently put it one time.

"You owe me nothing. And we're not gonna bleat on about it either. Why don't you get changed and I'll call for a pizza?"

Sensing Halle's metaphorical foot being put down, Lydia sighed. "I'll be ten minutes."

"Is this the list?" Halle asked, waving a piece of paper as she spoke. Pulling on a boot, Lydia hopped over to the kitchen table. Plonking down rather ungracefully, Lydia peered at the flapping page.

"Yup. What do you think?"

The doorbell rang, halting further discussion temporarily. Halle shot off to collect the food.

"It's not a very long list. And what does "appearance" mean?" Halle asked as soon as she was back in the kitchen, holding a huge pizza box.

"I just wanted to change things up a little."

"Well, the haircut was a good shout. You look great!"

Sensing her cheeks heating, Lydia busied herself with the pizza box so as not to make accidental eye contact. Any compliments from Halle were too much at the minute.

"Thanks."

Actually, Lydia was over the bloody moon with her new hairstyle. Instead of bedraggled brown locks, she now sported healthy layers that sat just above her shoulders. It was a simple style but gave her a little edge. Everyone she'd come across had complimented her hair, apart from Halle. Which at the time upset her a little, but now she wondered if Halle was trying to play it cool.

"So, you can tick the moving one off. What about the others? Have you found a place to chuck yourself out of a plane? Or off a bridge?"

"Not yet. Anyway, they were just the first things that came to mind. There are plenty of things I want to experience."

"What about that charity dog sled you always wanted to take part in?"

Lydia sat silent for a few seconds. *She remembered?*

"Y-yeah, that's still something I want to do. How the hell did you remember that?"

"Lydia, you spent six months bombarding Fe and I with pictures of cute Husky dogs."

"I was twelve."

"And? You were pretty determined that's what you wanted to do. You should put it on the list." Halle handed the paper over, tapping it with one finger, whilst handing Lydia a pen with the other.

"Okay, that's added."

"What else?"

"I'd like to visit the fjords in Norway, too."

"Well, there y'are! It's a two for one. You could make a holiday out of it. It'd be a real adventure."

"I suppose so."

"I had a patient who was from Norway. I'm still in touch with him. I'm sure I could call and ask for some travel advice."

"Why?"

"Why what?" Halle looked perplexed.

"Why would you do that? This is my list."

"Shit, I'm butting in again, aren't I?"

"No! I just wondered why you're so into helping?"

"Cause it's something important to you, Lyds. Everyone should have the chance to live their dreams. It's unfortunate that so many people never get to."

"What are your dreams?"

Smiling, Halle held Lydia's gaze. "That's a discussion for another day."

"That's not fair," Lydia pouted. Halle smiled her megawatt smile and Lydia melted a little inside.

"Eat your pizza."

Blowing a raspberry, Lydia shoved a piece of pizza in her mouth. Halle belly laughed at her antics. Exactly what Lydia hoped would happen. Halle had the best laugh.

Finishing the last crust, Halle tidied everything away. "Ready for a pint?"

It took Lydia a few seconds to remember they were supposed to be meeting people at the pub. A not-so-small part of her was disappointed. Hanging with Halle was always fun and easy.

"Yes, let's go. See you soon, Monty."

"Fancy walking by the park first? It's a pleasant night."

"Sure." *Because that's not romantic at all!*

They were the last to arrive at The Royal Oak. Lydia ignored Cathy's raised eyebrows. Instead, she hugged Elise and then Harrison. While Halle was busy saying her hellos, Lydia leaned into Cathy's embrace.

"Stop looking at me like that," she whispered.

"No idea what you're talking about, sweetie."

"Hmmm. What's everyone drinking?"

"I'll get this round, Lyds. You relax." Halle was making her way to the bar before Lydia had the chance to argue. Unable to control herself, she tracked Halle's supple arse across the pub. Only Cathy's unsubtle throat clearing snapped her back to the table.

"Everyone had a good day?" Lydia stuttered.

Cathy sniggered. "Smooth. Why were you late?"

"Oh, um, we took a detour to the park first."

"Really? That's...cosy."

"Not really. Just taking advantage of the dry weather."

Even Lydia didn't believe her own bullshit, the walk had been romantic. And even if Halle didn't mean it to feel that way, it had. Lydia couldn't help but feel they were edging towards...something.

"Here y'are," Halle announced, setting a large tray in the centre of the table. Everyone reached over, taking their respective orders. "Did Lyds tell you she's going to Norway?"

"Halle," Lydia laughed.

"When?" Cathy shrieked.

"Not anytime soon. Calm down. Halle is getting way ahead of herself."

"Am I?" Halle challenged, a twinkle of mischief in her eyes.

"Yes," Lydia laughed.

"Want to fill in the rest of the class?" Cathy demanded. She really wasn't on board with Lydia's list, convinced Lydia was going to get hurt.

"There's a charity dog sled event in Norway. I've wanted to do it for a while—"

"Try twenty-plus years," Halle interjected.

"And I've always wanted to visit the fjords. We were talking about it, that's all."

"When did this happen?" Elise asked, looking amused.

"About an hour ago," Halle smiled. "I said Lyds should go on a big adventure in Norway. Tick off two of her wish list items."

"On your own?" Cathy's voice was increasing in decibels every time she opened her mouth.

"Why not? I'm a big girl!"

"But—" Cathy was pale.

"She'd be fine, Cathy. With plenty of planning, there's no reason to worry. Plus, we'd all know her itinerary, right Lyds?"

"Of course. I'd be happy to share my imaginary itinerary with you! Cath, honey, calm down. Nothing is happening in the near future. Okay?"

"You'll tell me though, right? When do you want to do it? We need a plan!"

How had Lydia's list become a group thing?

"Did you really have to tell them about Norway? Shit!" Lydia stumbled over nothing, looking at the offending pavement before straightening herself out. Maybe that last pint wasn't such a good idea.

"What's the problem? It's exciting, right?"

"Yeah, but I've not planned anything. It's just a list right now."

"It doesn't have to be, Lyds."

"You say it like it's the simplest thing in the world," Lydia laughed. Her head felt floaty.

"It is that easy. You want something, so just go for it. You've already done it with the house."

"It's not quite the same." Lydia wobbled, catching Halle's attention. A strong arm circled her waist, keeping her upright. A low burn erupted in a very delicate area. Lydia had struggled all night, to be honest. This whole 'let's-be-buddies' trope wasn't working. Halle had been the perfect gentlewoman. No shenanigans, just friendship. It was Lydia who had her mind in the gutter. Every time she caught a whiff of Halle's delicious scent or gleaned a peek at her powerful arms, Lydia turned into a puddle of lust.

"Of course it is. The house is a new adventure. Sledding in Norway is an adventure. You just gotta plan it and do it."

They were interrupted by Halle's phone. Lydia caught the guarded mask that slid over Halle's perfect face.

Stop it!

"Hey," Halle answered. Her eyes darted to Lydia. "No, I'm not home. Yeah, I'll be there in half an hour or so." Lydia did her best to not eavesdrop. "I'm walking Lydia home." Pause. "Uh-huh. Yeah, talk later."

"Wrong number?" Lydia joked.

Halle smiled. "Fe."

"Oh, right. Um, are you guys okay now?"

"We're getting there." They walked in silence until they reached Lydia's flat. "Fe knows where I stand regarding you," Halle suddenly blurted.

Lydia turned. "And what does that mean?"

"That she has no say. None."

"And she was okay with that?" Lydia was suddenly nervous.

"It doesn't matter either way," Halle said in a whisper, moving closer.

Lydia's heart drummed dramatically. Halle, being so close, completely unravelled her and depleted her resolve. "I–"

"Good night, Lydia." Leaning forward, Halle dropped the softest kiss on Lydia's cheek.

Lydia watched Halle leave, stunned by how affected she felt. Given an extra few seconds, Lydia would have dragged Halle to her flat and picked up from where they left things in Halle's kitchen. But once again, Halle kept her promise and kept things in the friendzone.

Letting out a stuttered breath, Lydia headed inside. Monty didn't move, which was fine. Lydia had something to take care of.

Kissing the top of Monty's head, Lydia headed straight for her bedroom. With her heart still beating hard, she stripped. Crawling under the bed covers, Lydia reached over blindly to the bedside table where her toys lived.

It had been a while since she'd indulged in a night of self-care. It wasn't the ideal time. Lydia was still bleeding slightly, and under those circumstances, she wouldn't usually entertain doing anything sexual, but this was an emergency situation.

Having the foresight to grab a towel from the bathroom, Lydia raced back to bed, repositioning herself. Switching on her Cstar vibe, Lydia took a deep breath. It wouldn't take long, which was fine. It was the exact reason she'd chosen this toy. Lydia always came hard when her clit was stimulated and that's what the Cstar was for.

For once, she was happy Cathy had overshared and introduced her to this little beauty. Tonight wasn't about soft and sensual. Lydia needed it quick and powerful.

Flicking through the vibration setting, Lydia stopped on her favourite: A strong pulse. Pressing it close to her clit, she sucked in a breath. It was always a shock the first time the vibe made contact.

Screwing her eyes shut, Lydia's mind focused on the thing she wanted the most: Halle Cartwright touching her. In her mind's eye, Halle was the one deliciously sucking on her clit, with unparalleled skill.

"Oh God, yes." Moving the vibe a little higher, Lydia's back arched. "Yes, Halle, right there."

Only a couple of minutes passed between Lydia pressing the vibe to her clit and her screams of ecstasy. Breathing heavily, she tossed the vibrator to one side, bringing a hand to her face. Her face was hot, but it was more than the lasting effects of the orgasm that had ripped through her pussy with a force she wasn't expecting. It was Halle.

The effect that woman had on her... Should she feel bad for thinking of Halle that way? Maybe. After all, it was Lydia who had stopped things from progressing past friendship.

Would Halle be upset if she knew how Lydia used her to reach climax? Would she be turned on?

"Oh, Lyds, what are you doing?"

17

Considering the adventure in Norway was going to cost a bloody fortune, and she'd just spent that already on buying a house, Lydia opted to wait a year or so to commit. Instead, she'd focused on the smaller experiences. Namely, skydiving to begin with.

Winter wasn't the ideal time of year, but looking at the advanced weather forecast, the UK was supposed to get a week's worth of winter sun; clear skies and little wind. That was good for hurtling towards the earth at terminal velocity, right?

Now and then, Lydia questioned her sanity, especially after any length of time talking to Cathy, who was still vehemently against the idea. But in the end, curiosity won out. Enough that one Saturday morning, Lydia googled the closest place to skydive and booked herself a slot for the following weekend.

Nerves steadily built throughout the week, but Lydia was determined to do it. The Friday before the big jump, Lydia set herself up for a night of relaxation. Meditation had never held much appeal, mostly because Lydia ended up giggling nervously, nine times out of ten. Was she really that uncomfortable in her own head?

Friday, however, she was giving it another go. Her body was overly excited, and terrified, for the following day, and Lydia would try anything to calm down. Even Monty was picking up on her anxiety. His little yips of unease sealed the deal, so Lydia lit some candles, dimmed the lights, and opened up the meditation app she'd downloaded the previous day.

It took her several seconds to stop the automatic grin from becoming a laugh, but eventually she did it. The melodic female voice ensconced her living room. Lydia concentrated on it, letting the velvet voice fill her up. It wasn't so much a meditative state as a light slumber, but at least she was chill now.

Peeking out from heavy eyes, Lydia bit her lip to stop the bark of laughter breaking through the tranquillity.

Monty was sitting beside her, eyes closed, head up. He was doing a better job of it than she was. Shaking her head, Lydia refocused just as the bodiless voice told her to *feel her body*. How did one *feel* their body? Did she mean physically? No, surely not. Thankfully, the app clarified she was supposed to feel her body through her mind's eye, whatever the bloody hell that meant.

Just as Lydia was settling into the music, and not feeling so weird about sitting on the floor internally checking out her own body, everything went dark and silent. Wow, had she reached a total state of transcendence?

Lydia's mobile rang, scrapping any notion she'd travelled into the depths of her psyche. Opening her eyes, Lydia reached for the phone, accepting Halle's call. Forgetting it was hooked up to her Bluetooth speaker, Lydia was certain she had a minor stroke when Halle's voice boomed through her apartment.

"Lyds, you okay? The power's out."

"Hey, yeah, hang on a sec." Fumbling through to the phone's settings, Lydia finally disconnected the device. "I'm going to put you on speaker so I can use my phone lamp to find my candles."

"Oh, no, it's cool. The power is back," Halle commented, leaving Lydia frustrated. Her power was not back on. Heading to the window, Lydia curtain twitched, checking the buildings in her street. Every light was back on, apart from hers. "Shit!"

"What's up?"

"I still don't have power. Everyone else's back on, by the looks of it."

"Hold on, I'll be there in ten."

Disconnecting the call, Lydia searched high and low for the candles she knew she bought. Or did she? Thinking back, Lydia remembered putting them on her shopping list. When was that? Crap.

Halle knocked on the door several minutes later, comically calling out she was there, and that Lydia should put away any purses she'd prepared to launch.

"You're hilarious," Lydia deadpanned.

"I have my moments," Halle grinned.

"You know where the switchboard thingy is."

This wasn't the first time Lydia had needed someone taller than her to flip on her electricity. The landlord, for some unfathomable reason, installed the main electricity doo-flop at the top of Lydia's boiler cupboard.

"I got it, one sec." Pushing past, Halle headed for the cupboard, torch in hand.

She's always prepared.

"Um, Lyds, when was the last time your electrics were serviced?"

"Uh, I didn't know they were supposed to be. What's wrong?"

"What's wrong is you're one short-circuit away from having an electrical fire. You can't put it back on, Lydia, not like this."

"Are you shitting me?"

"I shit you not! It's not safe."

"Well, that's just fan-bloody-tastic." Throwing her hands in the air, Lydia stormed off to the living room. Her landlord was about to get a mouthful.

As soon as the call connected, Lydia launched her attack. "The electrics are going to kill me, Brian! Apparently, I'm one short away from dying in a house fire. What the hell?"

"Lydia, calm down. Blimey, no need for the dramatics. I'm sure it's not that bad."

"You need to get someone here ASAP, Brian. I can't live without electricity!"

"It's the weekend, Lydia. I'm not paying double the rate. I'll get my mate Bongo round Monday morning."

"Bongo! Are you serious? Is he even an electrician?"

"He knows how to wire stuff." Brian answered casually. "He'll do you a good deal."

"Me? There is no me in this. You're the landlord. It's your responsibility to keep the place safe and habitable. Which, let's be honest, hasn't been that way for a really long time, Brian."

"Nonsense."

"Nonsense?" Lydia screeched. "I've had tepid water for a year. The sink leaks in the bathroom. The taps in the kitchen are leaking. The ballcock thing is broken, which causes the toilet to fill with water continuously. Each room's windows need to be resealed. All of which I have reported to you, and you've done sweet fuck all."

Why had she allowed herself to live like this?

"I've put it in my diary," Brian argued.

"Well, that's chuffing brilliant. What good is that to me? I've needed these repairs done for years. It's not my job to pay out of pocket. That's what my rent is for. You'll be hearing from my lawyer. I'll be requesting my deposit and the first month's rent back. I will also vacate the property tonight, instead of next week. And before you try anything, Brian, I have documented evidence that I sent in the repair requests, plus photo and video evidence that, to this day, you have not completed them."

"Lydia, hang on. No need to talk about lawyers. I'll get someone out tonight, okay?"

"Nope, too late. I expect to see a return of funds in my account by the end of next week. Don't push me, Brian, I've had absolutely enough." Jabbing the End Call button far too hard, Lydia breathed in deeply, a growl emanating from deep inside. *Fucking Brian!*

"Holy shit, Lyds, that was outstanding!" Turning on her heel, still breathing rather heavily, Lydia caught Halle staring at her wide-eyed. "It's about time you stood up to that useless prick."

Nodding, Lydia let the weight of what she'd just done settle on her shoulders. Halle might be impressed, but Lydia felt herself slipping into panic mode. Yeah, she'd given Brian a telling off, but in the process, she'd made herself homeless. There was still another week to go before she collected the keys to her house.

"Shit, shit, shit." Lydia paced back and forth, Monty's head following her every step. "Well done, Lydia," she muttered angrily to herself.

"Lydia, will you stop moving?" Halle laughed, taking her by the shoulders. "What's got you worked up?"

"Um, I just told Brian I'd be leaving tonight, Halle."

"And?"

"And I don't have anywhere to go." Calling Fe crossed her mind, but Lydia wasn't sure she was at the stage with her sister where she could comfortably share a space.

"Stay with me?"

Of course, Halle would offer. Lydia should have seen that coming from a mile away.

"You live in a one bed, like me."

"The sofa turns into a bed. It's only until you get the keys to your house. Plus, I'm closer to the museum, so that will help. Come on, Lyds, it'll be fun!"

Fun? More like torture.

"Look, why don't you grab some things, and we'll go to mine? If you're really uncomfortable, you can call Fe tomorrow, or your mum."

Looking at the time, Lydia gave in. It was already getting late. Fe would be neck deep in getting the terrors to bed, and her mum would already be in her dressing gown, watching reruns of *Poirot*. Cathy wasn't an option. Lydia didn't need to see Harrison's nipples again.

"Fine. I'll grab some stuff."

Lydia was packed and ready to go in under half an hour. Halle scooped up her bags, allowing Lydia to carry Monty, who was not impressed his bedtime routine was being ruined.

"Do you want me to help you pack the rest of your things tomorrow?" Halle asked as she drove them to her place.

"Oh, um, no, that's fine, thanks." Lydia hadn't told Halle she was planning to skydive in the morning. Perhaps she should reschedule?

"I don't mind. I've got the weekend off."

"I've actually got an appointment tomorrow morning. Uh, maybe we could sort the flat out in the afternoon?"

"Sure. Going anywhere nice?"

Fiddling with Monty's ears, Lydia mumbled her answer, unsure why she didn't want to tell Halle.

"I've got good hearing, Lyds, but not that good. You don't have to tell me if you don't want to."

"I'm going skydiving."

"Why wouldn't you want to tell me that?" Halle looked genuinely confused.

Sighing, Lydia looked out Nora's little window. "I don't know. Cathy has been getting me all nervous. Fe's not much better. I was trying to calm myself tonight, you know, preparing my mind. It was going great until the power went out. Then you heard all the crap with Brian, so I'm feeling less than *at one* with myself. I didn't want you piling on. I know everyone thinks I'm nuts for wanting to do this stuff, but it's important to me."

"I know that," Halle responded in a small voice. "I never thought you were nuts."

"Ugh, that was stupid. You're the only one who actually understands. I shouldn't have thought like that."

"It's cool."

"No, it's not. I struggle to let other people in. Even if it's silly things like this." Why was she regurgitating all this? Halle wasn't here for an impromptu therapy session.

"Why do you find it so hard, if you don't mind me asking?"

Lydia spent a second mulling it over. The answer was simple. "Because people leave. I've relied on friends and family for too long, and I always end up hurt."

"Family?"

"Yeah. Look how Fe has been lately. I finally opened up to accept help from her and she threw it all back at me. I know I'm supposed to be getting over it, but sometimes, Halle, I feel like a bloody doormat. Then there's Mum, who until recently never took my side. On anything. Always wanting to be the peacekeeper, even though she always backed up Fe. So I stopped going to her. Cathy is great, and has been a rock, but she's with Harrison now, and I'm not going to keep bugging her with my stuff. Plus, I get a headache when she shouts at me for wanting to try new things she classes as 'fucking moronic.'"

"What about me?"

Lydia turned. Halle was watching the road but kept flicking her eyes across to Lydia. "What about you?"

"I know I messed up after...you know, but I'm here now. If you need help, Lydia, I'm there for you."

This was becoming a habit between them. General chit-chat ending up somewhere deep and meaningful. A place Lydia knew they shouldn't be.

"Do you want to come with me tomorrow?"

The question clearly threw Halle. She looked back and forth from the road to Lydia. "Really?"

"Yeah, if you want to. Honestly, I could do with the support," Lydia laughed. "Who knew jumping out of a plane could be stressful?"

"I'd love to come with you. Can I join in?"

"You want to skydive?"

"Only if you're cool with it. Totally understand if this is something you want to do alone. I can watch from the ground. I'll bring a flask of something strong for when you land." Halle grinned.

"No way. If you're willing to scream with me as we hurtle towards the ground, I'm happy with that."

"Ah, Lyds, you say the nicest things."

"Jesus, are we really doing this?"

"Hell yeah, we are. I'll hop on to the website as soon as we get back to book my spot."

❦

"I think I'm going to be sick."

"Lydia, you are not going to be sick. You don't have to do this," Halle reiterated for the tenth time, as they drove at breakneck speed in Nora.

"Not because of the skydive, Halle. Because of your driving. We will literally be crushed like a Coke can if we crash."

"Oh, calm down," Halle laughed. "It feels fast because Nora's small. We're closer to the ground. I promise I'm doing the speed limit."

"How long until we're there?"

"Five minutes. Are you ready?" Halle asked, wiggling her eyebrows. The woman had been a ball of energy all morning. God knows what time she got up. When Lydia shuffled into the kitchen—purposefully not looking at the spot on the floor where Halle had almost ravaged her—she was amazed to see the table adorned with every breakfast food available.

Halle sat munching on toast, with scrambled egg and bacon on a plate. Lydia couldn't even contemplate food. But, through sheer persistence, Halle got her to eat a slice of buttered toast with jam. That buttered toast was sitting heavy in her stomach, threatening to reappear as Nora zipped along.

"Here we are! And in one piece."

"Yeah, just," Lydia muttered.

"Wowzer, you are *not* a morning person."

Lydia wanted to argue, but Halle was already slipping out of Nora, smiling excitedly. Scrubbing her face with both hands, Lydia took three deep breaths. "You can do this, Lyds! You can do it!"

"Yeah, you can!" Halle called from outside. Well, that was embarrassing. Lydia was used to Monty being the only one who heard her muttering to herself.

"Shall we do this?" Lydia sounded a hell of a lot more confident than she was feeling.

"Onwards!" Halle called, marching off. Scurrying after Halle, Lydia did her level best to take everything in. The whole point of these experiences was to...well...experience things. There was no point in any of it if Lydia couldn't remember a damn thing about the day because she'd got herself into a tizzy. Using breathing techniques she'd briefly learned while listening to the meditation app, Lydia centred herself and looked around.

The sun was blazing, although giving off little heat. There was nary a cloud in the sky, which meant they would have excellent visibility. Halle headed towards a hangar with Lydia following close behind. There were four guys waiting outside. One looked as nervous as Lydia, so she presumed he was there for his first jump, too. The other three guys had the company logo on their jumpsuits.

"Hi, we're here for the jump," Halle chirped. "I'm Halle and this is Lydia."

"Hi, and welcome. Let me introduce us—I'm Jimmy, this is Angel, and that rough-looking guy is Bob," Jimmy winked.

"Rude," Bob laughed. "Is this your maiden voyage?" Lydia simply nodded. "Great, meet Roy. He'll be jumping with you today. It's his first time, too."

"Hi, Roy," Halle greeted enthusiastically. Roy nodded, looking green. "This is going to be ace!" Halle grinned. Her energy was infectious, and Lydia felt herself getting amped up.

"Alright, people! Let's get this show on the road," Jimmy shouted. They all high-fived, which made Lydia laugh.

After a very thorough lesson, Lydia felt quite relaxed. She would be jumping tandem with Bob, who turned out to be a funny guy. The camaraderie between the instructors put everyone at ease. Bob constantly checked in with her, making sure Lydia was in the right frame of mind. After all, this was supposed to be fun.

Flight suit on, Lydia made her way to the plane. Halle was right by her side, almost tucked into her body. "How're you feeling?" she shouted over the engines.

"Fantastic," Lydia shouted back, smiling widely. Holding up her palm, Halle gestured for another high five. Lydia rolled her eyes but obliged.

They strapped in and waited as the plane taxied. Everyone was in high spirits. Lydia glanced over at Halle, who had buckled in on the other side. Her face was so open and happy, Lydia felt her stomach flutter, and she knew it had nothing to do with the upcoming jump.

Jimmy stood, signalling it was time for everyone to get into position. Roy and Angel were first, followed by

Lydia and Bob, leaving Halle and Jimmy until last. Roy still looked like he wanted to hurl. His brow showed visible beads of sweat.

Looking nervously at Angel, Lydia could tell Roy was close to backing out. Waving to get his attention, Lydia gave him her best smile and two thumbs up, hoping it would give the guy a little encouragement. They held eye contact for a few seconds until Roy nodded. Straightening himself, Roy stood in front of Angel, allowing himself to be clipped in.

Jimmy slid open the door. The wind and noise physically took Lydia's breath away. Giving the signal, Jimmy tapped Angel on the shoulder. Without pause, he gripped the edges of the door and threw himself and Roy out of the plane.

"Holy shit!" Lydia cried.

Lydia then realised it was her turn. Bob clipped her harness, giving her one last questioning look. It was the "Are you ready to do this?" look. Lydia smiled at Bob and then looked at Halle, who mouthed, "I'm so proud of you."

Swallowing the sudden rush of emotion, Lydia let Bob guide her to the door.

It was now or never.

18

Gripping the dew-soaked grass between her fingers, Lydia stared up at the cloudless sky. Her heart was still in her throat and probably wouldn't calm down any time soon. She'd done it!

Closing her eyes, Lydia envisioned the moment Bob pushed them out of the plane. The intensity of the wind and noise still coursed through her ears.

Instead of feeling as though she were falling, Lydia remembered the sensation of flying; soaring above the world, seeing earth in a whole new way. Adrenaline pumped through her system as they flew faster and faster.

Bob pulled the chute earlier than Lydia wanted. It was an experience she never wanted to end and was quite possibly addicted to now.

After they'd landed safely, Bob unclipped them and patted Lydia on her back, who was still in a state of awe. Unable to hold a conversation yet, which Bob and Angel found rather amusing. They moved away from the landing area, waiting for Halle and Jimmy.

Halle was beaming as her feet touched the ground. Jimmy hardly had time to unclip them before she raced over to Lydia, scooping her up and twirling them around.

"That was incredible!" Halle squealed.

Lydia laughed uncontrollably as they spun. Eventually Halle put her down to high five and chat with the instructors. Lydia dropped to the ground and starfished, enjoying the last remnants of dopamine in her system.

A shadow blocked Lydia's view. Squinting, she focused on Halle looking down at her. "You all good down there, Lyds?"

"Completely!"

"Can I join you?"

"Sure," Lydia sighed happily.

Dropping, Halle rolled to her back, mimicking Lydia. They lay silently, staring up at the sky. It was only when Lydia felt Halle's hand gently take her own, lacing their fingers together, that she broke her gaze.

Halle was staring up, smiling. Lydia let her eyes wander across Halle's face, tracing the outline of her nose, down to her chin. Halle's bronze skin glowed in the morning sun; or Lydia was that taken with the woman, and she was seeing things!

"You did it, Lydia! How do you feel?"

"Amazing! Just… God, I'm speechless. I can't believe I finally did it. What did you think?"

Halle turned to look at Lydia. "I think it was one of the most enjoyable things I've ever done. I want to jump on the plane and do it all over again."

Lydia laughed, "Oh my God, me too!"

"You ladies okay down there?"

Lydia and Halle raised their heads to look at an amused Jimmy.

"Bloody brilliant," Lydia called.

"Fan-sodding-tastic," Halle added.

"That's what we like to hear. You wanna come into the hangar for a cuppa? You're gonna freeze your bums off if you stay down there too long!"

Halle jumped up, offering her hand to Lydia, who took it willingly. Halle hauled her up and straight into a hug.

"Thank you for letting me share this with you, Lyds."

"I wouldn't have wanted to do it with anyone else." How true those words were.

After two cups of piping hot tea and several digestive biscuits, Lydia and Halle bid the instructors farewell and left. They had a couple of hours in Nora to get through before reaching Halle's place.

"Jumping out of a plane is less scary than your Mini!"

"Hey, stop hating on Nora," Halle laughed.

"I'm not. I'm hating on your driving."

"I'm a fantastic driver," Halle argued playfully.

"Uh-huh. Oh, fancy stopping for some pub grub?"

Halle veered off unexpectedly, taking a sharp left. Lydia hung on for dear life.

"There's a nice pub not too far," Halle commented, completely unaware of Lydia clinging to Nora's door. Swinging the car into a parking space, Halle jumped out, racing round to open Lydia's door. "You okay?"

"Super," Lydia muttered. "Just need to slot my organs back into place."

Laughing, Halle led Lydia to the pub by her hand. When had they started getting so touchy?

Scanning the menu, Lydia warred with herself. Her stomach and taste buds were crying out for a steak and ale pie. Her waistline, however, required something a little less carb-orientated.

"Get the pie," Halle said, still looking at her own menu. Lydia looked up, confused. "You want a steak and ale pie with chips instead of peas. I'll make you a salad tonight if you want."

"How did you—"

"Pie is your favourite food, but you only eat it on a special occasion. Today is definitely special, so I know you want the pie."

"Wow, busted," Lydia laughed, until Halle looked up, a fierceness in her eyes.

"You look amazing, Lydia."

"Um—"

"I just wanted you to know that. You have a beautiful body. So have the pie."

"O-okay."

Holy hell, is it hot in here?

The pie was friggin' delicious. Hell, Lydia even indulged in a wedge of steamed treacle pudding with custard. Sure, she'd have to be careful over the next few days, but Halle was right. Today was special.

Halle paid for the meal, standing to hold Lydia's coat open for her. "Shall we get back to yours and start packing?"

"You can just drop me off, Hal. It won't take me long."

"I just figured we'd get it done quicker, leaving us time to plan your next adventure!"

"And which adventure would that be?" Lydia smiled.

"Jumping off a massive bridge, obviously."

"Is there any reason you have three Furbies?" Halle shouted from inside the built-in wardrobe. That was literally the only redeeming factor to Lydia's apartment.

"I bought them for the triplets, thinking they'd enjoy a retro toy, but they freaked out. Fe said they didn't sleep for a week."

"Oh, shit! I remember that."

Lydia heard Halle moving some more things into a box. Lydia had already packed the majority, so she really didn't need help, but Halle seemed quite insistent.

"They can go to charity. Most of the stuff in there can!"

"Hey, did you see these photos? Oh, shit," Halle laughed. "Lyds, you have to see these."

Placing down the box she was currently stuffing full of dog toys, Lydia joined Halle on the floor in the walk-in.

"What photos?"

Lydia didn't recall having an album or anything. Halle had a green shoe box on her lap. Lydia's eyes went wide. Oh crap, that was Lydia's memento box. It was pretty much a shrine to Halle. Wow, it'd been a few years since she'd seen the thing, but Lydia remembered it clearly.

At the tender age of twelve, Lydia started to notice girls. One girl in particular, but, as stated previously, Halle was way off-limits. Obviously, Lydia had dealt with her unrequited longing by collecting tokens that reminded her of the older girl. Ticket stubs. Polaroid pictures of days out. Christ, she even had a sweet wrapper, Halle discarded. How fucking creepy was that? Looking at the memory box now, it was clear as day, Lydia was infatuated with her sister's best friend. Would Halle come to the same conclusion?

"Sheesh, look at my hair in this one," Halle laughed. Lydia peered over and smiled.

"I liked it like that!"

"No way."

"Yes way. You were alternative."

"If you say so," Halle chuckled. "Is that the ticket to the carnival we went to?"

"Yup." Did Lydia sound calm and breezy? Hopefully. "It was a great night. I had my first kiss there."

Lie! Lydia didn't have her first kiss until a year later. The carnival ticket reminded her of Halle winning her a stuffed elephant that she still had, FYI.

"Wow, these are great memories. We obviously spent more time together than I realised."

"Fe was there," Lydia commented. Fe was always bloody there.

"True, but if I remember correctly, Fe buggered off to chase some boy at the carnival. It was me and you that spent the evening riding all the attractions. I got you that elephant. Do you remember?" Lydia nodded. "And here," Halle pointed to a picture of them at the beach, "Fe didn't want to get her feet wet, so me and you went looking for shells. We found that jellyfish and you screamed like a bloody banshee."

Lydia cracked up. "I'm such a wuss."

"No, the thing was sodding huge, Lyds. Like a proper sea monster."

"A sea monster?"

"We were kids. Of course, it looked like a sea monster!"

They spent the next half an hour sifting through the box. Lydia did her best to remain chill, even when it looked as if Halle had cottoned on to the fact the box was dedicated to her.

It took several trips to and from Lydia's apartment, but eventually they were on the last load of boxes. Monty yipped excitedly when they returned. Halle's mum stepped out of Halle's apartment, smiling just as brightly as her daughter.

"Hey, you two. How was the jump?"

"Holy cow, Mum, it was outstanding. You'd love it!"

"I might give it a whirl one of these days. What about you, Lyds? Same as Halle?"

"Yes! A million times yes. It rocked. Thank you for watching Monty for me."

"Oh, sweetie, that little one is a charmer. You're lucky I didn't have my big purse on me, otherwise he'd be coming home with me."

Lydia laughed, scooping up Monty, who bathed her in soggy kisses. "He has that effect."

Together, they hauled Lydia's boxes into Halle's living room. Lydia grimaced, noticing just how much room she was taking up with her belongings.

"Relax," Halle whispered in her ear.

A shiver ran down Lydia's neck. When did Halle get so close?

"I can see you worrying. You get the keys in a week and then we'll get you moved into the house. We can cope with the boxes for a few days."

Halle's doorbell stopped Lydia from doing something stupid, such as turning around and shoving her tongue down the aforementioned woman's throat.

"I'll get it," Halle's mum called, already on her way. There were several shrieks of excitement, and a scurry of little people. Lydia laughed the moment the triplets fell through the living room door. They squealed louder when they noticed their aunt standing by the sofa.

"Aunty Lydia, you're here!" Jenny screamed, loud enough for Monty to whine.

"Yes, I'm here," Lydia chuckled. Seconds later, Fe walked through the door. The look of surprise was clear on her face as she took in the scene.

"Do you live here now?" Jack asked, throwing himself on the sofa.

"No, silly. I have my own house now, remember? I just can't take all my things there until next weekend."

"What happened to your flat?" Fe asked.

"She told Brian to stick it," Halle laughed, completely unphased. "The electrics in her flat never came back on after the power outage. I went round and discovered she was one trip away from—"

"It wasn't good," Lydia said pointedly, nodding towards the kids. The last thing anyone needed was the triplets flipping out about house fires.

"Yeah, it wasn't good," Halle finished.

"I called Brian, and he was his usual useless self. I just had enough and told him to shove it."

"Then she realised she was homeless for a week," Halle grinned, "and I told her to come here. So, she did."

"Right. Good, that's good." Fe nodded comically, entirely uncomfortable but doing her best to keep it together. Years of controlling Halle and Lydia's relationship towards one another were hard to let go of, evidently.

"We went skydiving today!" Lydia blurted. "It was great."

"Today! You went today?"

"Yeah, it was so cool."

"You did it too?" Fe asked Halle, eyebrows raised.

"Hell yeah, I did. Couldn't let Lyds have all the fun."

The wink that followed caused Lydia a little problem in the knicker department.

"Wow. I didn't think you'd actually go through with it." Fe replied. The comment stung.

"I knew she would," Halle interjected. "And next, it's bungee jumping. Speaking of which, what's your schedule this week, Lyds?"

"Oh, um...working Monday through Wednesday. Thursday, Friday off. I was going to spend some time cleaning up the flat before officially vacating, but I'm not doing it anymore. Brian can shove it!"

"Hear, hear," Halle called. "So, how about we look at getting you a reservation to bungee on one of your days off?"

"So soon?" Fe asked.

"Why not?" Halle said, her eyes on Lydia. "You're going to be busy with the house after the weekend. It could be an excellent opportunity to check another item off the list?"

"Let's do it!" Lydia was completely onboard. "Will you do that with me, too?"

"If you want me to, then yeah."

"Since when have you wanted to chuck yourself off a bridge?" Fe scoffed at Halle.

"Since I'd do anything Lydia wanted me to!" Halle shot back hotly. Fe shrank back, realising she was walking a thin line. Halle and Fe had only just started getting to some sort of normal.

"Sorry, sorry," Fe mumbled. "Okay, kids, let's leave Aunty Lydia and Aunty Halle to it."

The triplets moaned loudly. "But we wanna stay," Joey whined.

"I want ice cream," Jenny announced.

"You can stay, Fe." Halle's tone had softened. "We can order in, and the kids can watch TV. It's been a while since we all hung out."

Halle was offering an olive branch, knowing Fe's fear stemmed from thinking she would be left behind. Lydia started tickling her niblings, making them laugh.

"Yeah, plus I need some time to torture these three!" she laughed maniacally causing the triplets to squeal in delight.

Laughing, Fe agreed. It was the first time in weeks Lydia felt good about the situation. Halle's comment to Fe was firmly lodged in her head. Did Halle really mean what she said? She'd do anything Lydia asked?

After two large pizzas were consumed—the vast majority eaten by the triplets—Lydia, Halle, and Fe shared a bottle of wine in the kitchen. Halle searched for a location to bungee jump, and to everyone's surprise, including her own, Fe agreed to do it with them the following Thursday.

"We're fucking insane!" Fe declared as the trio stood looking out over a terrifying canyon. "I mean, literally insane!"

"You don't have to do it, Fe," Lydia said reassuringly. Fe regretted her drunken promise immediately but had kept her word to do it, anyway.

"Seriously Fe, there's no pressure here," Halle added.

"Are you two doing it?"

"Yes," they said in unison.

"Well, I'm not backing out then." Crossing her hand over her chest defiantly, Fe took several deep breaths. "Can I go first?"

Lydia and Halle exchanged a look. "Of course, knock your socks off, sis," Lydia smiled.

The bungee guy did his best to be open and friendly with Fe as he strapped her up. Fe was having none of it. She glared at him until he shut up and secured her harness.

"Jesus, she's got a face like stone," Halle muttered.

"I've only ever seen her with that look once before, and that was when she was giving birth. Jenny was stubborn and wouldn't come out. The next thing you know, Fe slips into that stone face and Jenny zips out. It's her sheer determination face, and I'm pretty sure she can do anything when she's in that mood."

They watched as Fe listened to the guy explaining what she needed to do. The moment he gave the okay, Fe flung herself off the edge. Lydia gasped; Halle cursed. They both leaned over and watched Fe scream in delight as the cord snapped her back inches from the water below.

"Jesus," Lydia laughed.

Fe continued to whoop and scream all the way until she was back on terra firma. "Whoa!" she screamed. "Ladies, that is insane!"

"Me next," Halle shouted, already approaching the instructor.

"Fe, oh my God. That was nuts!"

"I can't believe I just did that." Fe was coming down from her high and possibly going into shock.

"Of course you did it. You're a badass."

"Lydia, I'm sorry. I'm sorry for all of it and I know I've said it before." Fe looked over her shoulder at Halle getting kitted up. "I was stupid to think you guys would ever abandon me. You would make a great couple. She adores you, sis, and you adore her. I've known that for a long time too. Please don't let my silly issues stop you from going for it with her."

Lydia stood silent, shocked at her sister's sudden outburst.

Fe barrelled on. "And for what it's worth. You're ready to be with her. I know you want to be in a better place. But sometimes we need our person with us to get to that better place. Know what I'm saying?"

Lydia nodded. If she were honest with herself, Fe wasn't telling her anything new. Waiting until the right moment hardly ever worked out for anyone. The past few days, it had become abundantly clear Halle made Lydia feel better about herself, to the point where Lydia had the confidence to look at herself in the mirror and be less disgusted with what she saw.

Obviously, that wasn't the end goal. Lydia wanted to love her body completely, but sometimes that just wasn't possible. She would always see her broken parts, but having Halle like her for exactly who she was, helped more than any diet ever could.

"I know, Fe," Lydia finally answered. "I've got it under control."

Fe smiled and winked. "Course you have, Lyds." Their attention snapped to the edge of the bridge as Halle screamed all the way down.

"You're up, sis!" Fe called from the barrier. It was Lydia's turn. Not just to launch herself off into oblivion and hope the cord stopped her from being squished, but to take another chance; To be the one that had the courage to finally ask Halle out.

That was the biggest adventure after all, right? The thing Lydia wanted most: to be loved by someone. Maybe it was time to stop hoping, and make it happen.

"I'm ready," Lydia called to her sister. She was so ready!

<u>19</u>

"F e?"

"In here Lydia."

"Why is there smoke?"

"We were cooking."

Lydia entered Fe's kitchen. The triplets had identical aprons on, with flour covering ninety percent of their bodies. Fe had a smattering of flour on her cheek. The air was thick with smoke. Lydia located the source when she spotted the smouldering trays on the kitchen counter.

"Um, this isn't cooking, sis. This is arson!"

"Funny," Fe deadpanned. "We were trying to make muffins."

"Chocolate ones," Jenny coughed. "We left them in for too long and now they're burned."

"I bet I could still eat them," Joey muttered, eyeing the black rocks.

Lydia began opening windows, hoping the smoke would clear out quickly. "Fe, you can't cook!"

"Hey!"

"What? It's a fact. You broke three microwaves at Mum's house."

"Mummy broke ours, too."

"Traitor," Fe whispered to Jenny, and Jenny snickered.

"And she set the oven on fire at Christmas," Joey chimed in, still looking at the incinerated muffins.

"All right, jeez," Fe grinned. "Here I am, just trying to do my motherly duty and teach my kids some life skills, and this is the thanks I get?"

"Fe, *you* need to be taught those life skills before trying to pass them on!" Lydia laughed. "Come on, let's get cleared up and we'll start again."

An hour later, the kitchen smelled of succulent chocolate. Joey was practically vibrating with anticipation as he stood watching them like a hawk. "Can I have one now?"

"No, they're still too hot, love. Ten minutes, okay? Go play. I'll call you when they're ready."

The terrors stomped off, but didn't make too much of a scene.

"They seem to be doing better," Lydia commented, sipping on her Irish coffee.

"Clark and I talked to them. They know we're getting a divorce."

"Wow, so you finally decided, huh?"

At one point, Lydia was sure Fe would take Clark back, but clearly some things just couldn't be moved on from.

"The trust is gone, Lyds. I don't want to live my life always wondering if that late meeting is really a lie and he's knobbing another secretary."

"Totally understandable."

"And I actually want to take a leaf out of your book for a while."

Furrowing her brows, Lydia continued to drink her coffee, wondering where her sister was going. "Explain."

"I want to get right with myself. I need to prove to myself I'm strong enough to stand on my own two feet. If you think about it, I've always had a fella to fall back on. I don't want that to be who I am. I've got three kids who look up to me. And, especially for Jenny, I want her to see what a strong, independent woman looks like. I mean, she already looks up to you. I'd like to be the other person she admires."

This was possibly the deepest conversation they'd ever had. Lydia repositioned herself on the chair.

"That's... Wow, Fe, that's great, but you know they look up to you. Those three love their mum."

"I know that! But look how we are with our mum. Let's be fair. We saw her as a superhero growing up."

"True."

"I kind of want the terrors to look at me that way."

"Maybe stop calling them terrors," Lydia grinned.

"Let's not get silly, Lyds. They *are* terrors, and they know it."

"But the tantrums have stopped?"

"Mostly. Sometimes one of them has a bit of a wobble when they're missing Clark, but we agreed the kids could call him anytime and he would pick up the phone."

"And is he sticking to it?"

"So far. He knows he's on thin ice, and not just with me. The kids really took him to task when we all spoke. Considering their age, they were quite clear about how they were feeling."

"Good for them! So, no dating?"

Shaking her head, Fe made a chopping motion with her hand. "Nope, no men."

"Can we also say no cooking, too?"

"I might take some lessons."

"That's a great idea."

"Would you come with me?"

"Yes, obviously. What about Halle?"

Fe shook her head again. "She's an amazing cook. I don't need her showing me up."

"Good point, although, does that mean you think I'm crap and you aren't threatened by my culinary skills?"

"Yes." They stared at each other for a second before laughing. "Let's be honest, we didn't get Mum's cooking skills."

"Was Dad a good cook?"

Looking sad, Fe deflated slightly. Lydia wanted to kick herself for bringing him up. It was clearly still a sore issue for her sister. "I don't remember."

"Sorry," Lydia mumbled.

"No, if you have questions, Lyds, ask them. My therapist thinks it's a good idea to talk about him. I've kept everything so locked up, it's not been good for the old grey matter."

"I don't really have questions," Lydia began. "But if you ever want to talk. I'm here."

"Speaking of. Are you going to ask Halle out or what?"

"How is that 'speaking of'?"

"I couldn't think of a segue to get us on the topic, so I just jumped straight to it."

"I don't know if we should be talking about it, sis."

"Sure, we should. I just don't want any sexy details," Fe gagged. "You're my actual sister, and Halle is as close to one as it gets. I don't need to know about body parts mushing together or anything."

"Ew, stop talking." Lydia threw her last bit of muffin at Fe.

"Come on, tell me. One second you were staunchly against the idea and now you're thinking of asking her out. What changed?"

Blowing out a breath, Lydia pondered on the question. "Well, first I stopped feeling like a crazy person. I have Halle to thank for that. She was the one who got me in front of Elise. I'm feeling so much better in myself, mentally, on these new pills."

"That's great, Lyds. And I know I didn't help with the whole Halle situation."

"No, you didn't. But we're past that. I suppose I realised I didn't want to be someone who missed out on being with a great person out of fear. And that's what it came down to. Halle has always supported me. I just wouldn't let myself see it. And I was terrified she would leave."

"Why?"

"Maybe I have some dad issues of my own," Lydia laughed humourlessly.

"Your experience with dating didn't exactly help, though, Lyds."

"True. Halle has been a constant in my life. Even if I put the possibility of us ever being more, out of my head, she's someone I rely on."

"You two have gotten close, quickly?"

"Yeah. It's crazy to think we both distanced ourselves for years, but it has taken, what? Weeks for us to become close friends."

"Ugh, I feel so shitty, Lydia. You guys could have been together ages ago."

"Maybe, or maybe not. There's no point thinking like that."

"Still, I hope you know I support you, one-hundred-percent."

"Well, can you support me by telling me how to ask her out? I'm worried she's going to think I'm having a meltdown or something. I've been so opposed to anything other than friendship. This is going to give her whiplash."

"People change their minds! It's as simple as that and that's all you have to tell her."

Lydia played with her now empty coffee cup. There was still one thing that worried her enough to think asking Halle out might be a mistake. Not for Lydia, but for Halle.

"Hey, what's up?" Fe stilled Lydia's fidgeting hand.

"I'm still bleeding. So, my womb issues aren't totally solved yet."

"Okay?"

"What's the point in asking her out when I know I'm going to disappoint her by not being able to...you know."

"Have sex?"

"Yeah."

"Oh, Lydia." Fe chuckled. Lydia furrowed her brows again. "Halle has loved you for years without the sex part. You think she's going to have a problem with waiting a little longer?"

Lydia hadn't thought of it like that. "Yeah, but what happens if things go well but I still can't have regular sex?

Sometimes it's weeks. I mean, hopefully this pill will settle down soon, but I don't want to get my hopes up."

"Then Halle will support you through it. That woman would be happy to sit and eat a family bag of Doritos with you in front of the telly. She just wants to be with you."

"You're *such* an arsehole, Fe Archer!"

"Hey, you said we were moving past it!"

"Yeah, and then you say shit like that, and I get pissed again."

Lydia still felt Fe's past behaviour keenly, but she wasn't really mad. Maybe 'sad' would be a better descriptor.

"Fair enough. I'll make it up to you somehow."

Fe, making it up to Lydia, consisted of a barrage of text messages the following day, suggesting ways she could ask Halle out. When an inflatable T.rex costume came into it, Lydia had to beg her older sister to desist. It was moving day and the last thing Lydia needed was Fe blowing up her phone with increasingly ridiculous messages.

Halle was up and at it far too early, in Lydia's opinion. She wasn't due to pick up the keys until noon, but Halle insisted she organise the boxes, readying them to load into the rental truck Lydia ordered the week before. Moving big boxes in Nora once, was enough. She really didn't want them to do it again.

"Okay, we have all the bedroom boxes here, kitchen there, and living room by the front door," Halle announced. Lydia was unsure if she was talking to her, or just muttering to herself.

"Fabulous. Now, can you take a break? It's like eight in the morning on a Saturday. We shouldn't even be conscious yet."

Halle chuckled playfully, pushing Lydia towards the kitchen. "Sit down. I'll make breakfast."

The week living with Halle had been pretty exceptional. Lydia had healthy, home-cooked meals daily. Halle was a caretaker, for sure. To make sure Lydia was pulling her weight, she did all the washing up and tidying. They quickly fell into quite the domestic routine.

Shoving her nose into her coffee mug, Lydia inhaled deeply. Even Monty looked bloody knackered. They were both used to sleeping late on a weekend if Lydia was off work.

"I love coffee so much," Lydia muttered, staring adoringly at her cup. Halle's eye roll could have been seen from space. "Don't roll your eyes at me, Halle Cartwright! You're just as bad."

"Sure," Halle grinned. "Do you want a Full English or a bacon butty?"

"It's going to be a long day. I think we'll go for the Full English."

"Sound choice. Okay, let's do this." Flipping on her Bose speaker, Halle found an upbeat playlist and set to work. Lydia was more than happy to sit back and watch, especially with Halle wearing fitted joggers and a T-shirt that left little to the imagination.

As usual, the food was delicious. Lydia noted Halle grilled the bacon instead of frying it. The eggs were poached, too. Halle never made a fuss about Lydia's need to watch what she ate. Instead, she simply went along with it.

Midday rolled around and Lydia was handed the house keys. Halle insisted she have a dozen pictures taken outside her new home. In the end they got ridiculous, with Halle photobombing and using Monty, who thoroughly enjoyed the attention.

Unlocking the front door, Lydia drew in a breath. "Here goes," she muttered, stepping over the threshold.

"Just think, Lyds, you're going to have hot showers and dripless taps," Halle commented seriously.

"You've no idea how bloody good that sounds."

"Oh, I do. You spent half an hour a day in my shower. It was like a bloody steam room by the time you finished."

Flushing slightly, Lydia knocked Halle's shoulder. "I was defrosting. It's been years since I had hot water."

"I'm only messing. Now, shall we get these boxes unloaded?"

Halfway through unloading, Fe stopped by. She hadn't had the chance to check out Lydia's new digs yet. It would have been better to choose a different day to visit, but that was Fe. The kids tore through the house, instantly picking their bedroom. Thankfully, Lydia had already earmarked the one they chose.

"Oh, Lyds, this is magnificent," Fe gasped. "Bloody gorgeous."

"I know, right?" Lydia couldn't hide her excitement. "I can't wait to decorate the place. Make it my own."

"Oh, we can have a deco party!" Fe clapped. "They're all the rage."

"Where?" Halle asked, amused.

"Everywhere," Fe scoffed.

"Do you mean you saw someone on a TV show do it?" Halle grinned.

"Shut up. Please, Lyds, please?"

"Jesus, all right. We can have a deco party."

"We can help," the triplets chorused as they bounded into the kitchen. "I'm great at painting. Mummy said," Jenny added.

"Let's get unpacked before we start trying to paint anything, guys," Lydia chuckled.

"And on that note, we have to go," Fe announced.

Lydia stared, mouth agape, as Fe rounded up her brood and promptly left.

Halle burst out laughing. "You didn't think she would actually stick around and do some work, did you?"

"Well, after the deco party idea, yeah, kind of."

"Lyds, my sweet. Fe will bring party food and then walk around telling everyone else what to do. I would bet Nora, she won't even pick up a paintbrush."

Halle was spot on. Fe would become the unelected leader and get her bossy pants on.

"Shit. Why did I agree to do it?"

"Because you're excited and rightly so. Instead of a deco party, just turn it into a housewarming. Me, you, Cathy, and Harrison, can get the place decorated."

"You think Cathy is going to paint? Ha! And Harrison is not exactly the handy type."

"Good thing I am, then. We can start whenever you want. Have you got an idea?"

"A few. But honestly, I'm in no rush."

"You're just excited to be here, right?"

"Right!" They stood smiling and staring at each other for a few seconds. Lydia's heart ramped up. "Um...I...had another idea for my bucket list."

Not what she'd actually wanted to say, but, hey ho!

"Really? I thought scuba diving was next?"

"In the Atlantic? In winter?"

"They do it in swimming pools too, Lyds," Halle smiled.

"If I'm going to do it, I want to see fish. Anyway, I was thinking, and it might sound really lame but..."

"But?"

"I'd like to get all dressed up and have afternoon tea at The Ritz."

Halle gave a low whistle. "Damn, that's a good one. Have you ever been to The Ritz?"

"Nope. I always wanted to." Pausing, Lydia knew this was a good time to see if Halle was open to a date. "I was thinking...you could be my date."

"Sure, let's get it booked." Halle whipped out her phone and began tapping away.

Lydia felt a little deflated, knowing Halle hadn't picked up on her meaning. "I mean a proper date," she blurted.

Halle's fingers stilled. Her eyes slowly rose from the phone screen. "You mean... Sorry, what do you mean? I don't want to presume."

"Halle, will you go out with me?"

These little staring sessions were becoming a thing. Halle searched Lydia's face, whilst Lydia tried to keep a confident stance. Was her eyelid twitching?

"Yes, I'd like to go out with you."

The rush of air Lydia expelled was audible. "Great, good. Great. Um...I'm going to take my bedroom boxes up. Right, yeah, okay."

Blithering idiot!

In her new bedroom, she faceplanted on her new four-poster bed. The execution was far from elegant, but she'd achieved her goal. Lydia and Halle would go on a date; a fancy one, at that.

Although, as Lydia mentally catalogued her wardrobe, she knew there wasn't one piece of clothing suitable for such a glitzy place. Picking her phone from her back pocket, Lydia sent a message to Fe.

You 2:00 p.m.

I did it! I asked.

Fe 2:02 p.m.

Yes, girl!

You 2:02 p.m.

Please never use that expression again. Anyway, we're going to The Ritz for afternoon tea.

Fe 2:03 p.m.

Wowzer, that's posh!

You 2.04 p.m.

I have nothing to wear. I don't think they appreciate lounge wear.

Fe 2:05 p.m.

Instead of replying, Fe called. Hitting the accept button, Lydia buried her head back in the bed. "Hi," she said, muffled.

"Where the hell are you?"

"On my bed. I kind of ran away from Halle when she said she'd go out with me."

"Dear me, Lydia. You should have just passed her a note, asking her to circle 'yes' or 'no'. It would have been less dramatic than running away, you tit."

"I didn't realise I was going to ask, and then I did ask, and she looked at me all intense. My heart nearly fell out of my arse."

"Such eloquence. Look, sis, the main thing is she said yes, and knowing Halle, she's downstairs chuckling at your daft reaction."

"She looked shell-shocked, Fe."

"Well, yeah! She's finally getting a shot with you. What excuse did you give before running?"

"I told her I was taking boxes to my room to unpack."

"Not a terrible excuse. Maybe unpacking is what you need. Work off your nerves. Then you need to get your bum back downstairs and act normal."

"That's easier said than done, Fe. Now I'm properly allowing myself to open up to the possibility of us, I can't stop thinking about her... In not-so-innocent ways."

"La la la la la la la la la!"

"Fe!"

"Nope, I don't want to know about you getting feelings in your knickers for Halle. That's the rule, remember. Call Cathy if you want to talk like that."

"Good call! She's much better at sex talk than you are!"

"Hey, I can talk sex, just not with my sister; it's wrong."

"Whatever. Can we talk shopping?"

"I'll pick you up Monday morning. You've got an afternoon shift, right?"

"Yup. I'll see ya then. Love you."

"Love you, too. Now stop acting weird. It's unsettling."

Laughing, they hung up. Fe was probably right. Halle would definitely be mocking her for running. That's okay, though, because Lydia had some idea of how to shut Halle up.

20

"Fuck, fuckety, fuck." Lydia was still bleeding. Three weeks she'd put up with it, and now, on the day of her date with Halle, she was really over it!

"That's a lot of profanity, sis," Fe called from Lydia's bedroom.

"Sorry. Just frustrated."

"Still got the Red Devil?"

"Gross, but yes. I think I need to call Elise."

"She did say it could take months."

"Yeah, and that was fine before."

"Ah, you're getting pissy 'coz you want a bit of 'bow chick-a-wow-wow'."

Chuckling, Lydia finished in the bathroom. Still in her dressing gown, she was almost at the point where she needed to slip into the exquisite, yet disgustingly expensive, dress she'd bought whilst out shopping with Fe.

"No, well, yes, I want that. But I don't put out on the first date."

"Lydia, you almost put out on her kitchen floor!"

"Christ, I'm never gonna live that down."

"Nope." Fe said, giving the "p" in nope an extra pop.

"It's not about getting laid. I'm tired of having to wear tampons and pads. I feel frumpy."

"Give over! You look stunning. I've seen you in that dress, Lyds."

"I can't help the way I feel, Fe. I'm just tired of bleeding."

Fe stood from the bed and took Lydia in her arms. "Sorry, I shouldn't dismiss how you're feeling. Maybe it is time to make an appointment with the hot doctor."

"You think Elise is hot?"

"I've got eyes."

Stepping out of the hug, Lydia looked at Fe with interest. "You rarely comment on hot ladies."

"Just an observation. Now: hair and make-up. Time's-a-ticking."

"Shit." Lydia's nerves were at an all-time high. What was she thinking, asking Halle to attend The Ritz with her? That, in itself, was anxiety inducing. It's not like Lydia screamed wealth or class. She was getting all dolled up to be judged by fancy people, and now she'd tacked on a first date! Talk about pressure.

With her hair and makeup done, Fe helped slip the half-sleeve vintage green cocktail dress over Lydia's head. It was fancy, but not over the top. Next came the shoes: two-inch lace-up high heels that kept in line with the era of the dress.

"Wowzer!" Fe exclaimed, wolf whistling. "Halle's going to pass out."

"Stop," Lydia laughed.

"No, seriously. Lydia, look at yourself in the mirror."

This was the bit Lydia had wanted to avoid. She was getting better at being kind to herself when faced with her body, but at a time like this, the pressure made her only see flaws.

Fe took Lydia by the shoulders and moved her to the long mirror in the bathroom—Lydia's archnemesis. Drawing in a breath, Lydia brought her eyes up from the floor and looked.

"What do you see?" Fe asked softly.

Lydia had recently opened up to Fe about her body dysmorphia. To her utter surprise, Fe had been wonderful.

"I... Wow, okay, I look good."

Fe's bright smile lit up the bathroom. "Lyds, you look gorgeous. I think you've really nailed your style. Vintage suits you."

Nodding, Lydia continued to survey herself. The dress fit snugly but didn't cling to the point it felt uncomfortable. Sure, she could see areas where a few extra pounds sat, but the overall look of the dress and shoes overpowered the self-criticising part of Lydia's mind.

"I love it," she all but whispered.

"I'm so excited for you! What time is she picking you up?" Fe squeezed Lydia's shoulders in her own excitement.

"Half two. Our sitting is at half three."

"Oh, hark at you. *'Our sitting is at half three,'*" Fe mocked in an aristocratic tone.

"You idiot," Lydia laughed. "That's what they call the time you book. It's a sitting."

"Have you prepared?"

"Of course. I read the menu online four times last night. I'm not daft enough to walk into The Ritz without doing my homework first."

"Did Cathy tell you to book a room?" Fe smiled, waggling her eyebrows. Fe and Cathy had become closer recently. In fact, Fe was hanging out a lot more; not just with Lydia, Halle, and Cathy, but with other mums she knew from the kids' school, as well. It seemed Fe was serious about getting right with herself and with standing on her own two feet.

The triplets were still running amok ninety percent of the time, but Fe was calmer and more laid-back. It was looking as if splitting from Clark was the best thing to have happened to her sister.

"Yes, she did! She told me to pack a go bag."

"What's a bloody *go bag*?" Fe made herself comfortable on the bed once more.

"A sex go bag! She told me to take accessories and naughty lingerie with me."

Fe's hand went to her mouth in surprise and then she belly laughed for a solid five minutes. "Shit, you really would kill Halle, if you did that!"

Throwing her make-up sponge at Fe, Lydia shook her head. "I'm doing nothing of the sort."

"So proper," Fe cackled.

"We haven't even had a first date. Blimey, Fe, I wouldn't use accessories with someone I've been dating for several months, let alone one."

"You don't like toys?"

Throwing up her hands, Lydia looked at the ceiling in exasperation. "Oh my God, why are we talking about this?"

"You brought it up. I was just wondering. Clark didn't like toys either."

"TMI, sis!"

"Christ, Lydia, I thought I was the uptight sister!"

"You are!"

"Clearly not, anymore."

"Fe, you specifically told me I wasn't allowed to talk about sex with you."

"True, but I think I can handle it now."

Squinting, Lydia tried to read Fe's face. It occurred to her this was more about Fe's need to talk about sex, than Lydia's. They really were entering unknown territory now. Was Fe interested in something...or someone? Why the sudden change of heart where sexy talk was concerned?

Lydia settled on the bed next to Fe. "Is there something *you* want to talk about?"

Fe was fiddling with the bedcovers. It was an Archer trait when nervous. "Not specifically. I don't know. I was just wondering if there's stuff I've missed out on."

Lydia couldn't believe she was about to ask this question. "Did you have good sex with Clark?"

"I think so."

"You think so? Not exactly a ringing endorsement."

"Well, I mean, yeah, it was good."

"But?"

Fe's fidgeting became worse. "Clark never wanted to explore. Now I'm wondering if that's why he cheated. Maybe he wasn't sexually attracted to me, or I was a duffer in bed."

Curse Clark for making Fe feel this way about herself. "That's not possible. Us Archer women are dynamite in bed."

Fe tittered. "Oh, yeah?"

"Yes. And you can put that crap out of your mind about not being sexually attractive. You know you turn heads, Fe. I've been jealous of you our entire lives."

"Lydia, what? Why?"

"Oh, come off it. You got the height, the waistline, and the gorgeous skin from Mum. I looked like a bridge troll compared to you growing up."

"Take that back right now, Lydia Archer!" Fe's tone made Lydia reel back slightly. "I will not have you say such things anymore. You are beautiful, just the way you are. Yeah, I got the height, but you got those curves. I know you see them as a curse, but I wish you wouldn't. You enchanted Halle from the get-go! And that girl had every lesbian, from here to Scotland, wanting a piece. But she only had eyes for you. Ha, actually, she mainly had eyes for your killer boobs."

"Oh my God," Lydia laughed.

"The point is, Lydia, you need to stop comparing yourself to me, or anyone else. You are a fox."

"That was one good speech, sis."

"Then listen to it." Fe ordered.

"Okay, then you listen to me when I say it's not your fault Clark strayed. That's on him. And now is definitely the time to explore, sexually, if that's what you want."

"I don't know, Lyds. My vibrator is older than the kids. I'm not exactly with the times. Missionary was as exciting as it got for us."

"Ugh, that's no good. We need to get you some supplies. You don't need a partner to explore, Fe."

"Do you have accessories?"

"Yes. And I've got recommendations. Hey, why don't we have a girls' night with Cathy? She's the one who steered me in the right direction."

"Outstanding. Okay, now back to the date. You have exactly ten minutes before Halle shows up. Do you want a shot?"

"Can I have two?"

❧

Fe was wrangled into the kitchen. Lydia did *not* want her first interaction with Halle to be overshadowed by a hyperactive sister.

"Stay in here—with the door closed."

"Oh, come on, I want to see what Halle looks like. And how she reacts to this." Fe waved her hand up and down the length of Lydia's body.

"Fe, please. Just this once, will you do as you're told?" Lydia's palms were sweating at this point.

Fe evidently saw the very real stress her sister was experiencing. "Okay, okay. Calm down. I'll stay here. Can I at least look through the blinds when you've left?"

"Yes. Do that." Their conversation was interrupted by Lydia's rather fancy sounding doorbell. "Crap."

Laughing, Fe twirled Lydia round by the shoulders and shoved her towards the door. "Go get her, tiger!"

Smoothing the dress down unnecessarily, Lydia took a steadying breath before unlatching the door. In a slow-opening sweep, the door revealed Halle, standing with a bunch of wildflowers.

Accustomed to seeing Halle in leisurewear, Lydia bit her tongue to keep in the very sexual growl building in the back of her throat. Holy hell in a handbasket, Halle looked divine.

"Lydia, wow!" Halle was scanning every inch of Lydia's outfit, her eyes wide.

Lydia swallowed loudly. "Right back at ya!"

Halle stood at least six inches taller in gorgeous black patent leather heels, fitted red trousers, and a white button-up shirt underneath a long woollen coat. Her usually shaggy hair was slicked back, with a side parting. Dark makeup gave her a dangerous vibe and Lydia liked it. A lot!

"These are for you!" Halle stepped forward as she handed over the flowers. Completely captivated, Lydia took them automatically, her eyes never leaving Halle's.

"Thank you, they're beautiful."

"Beautiful flowers for a beautiful woman."

"Wow, that was one hell of a line, Halle Cartwright," Lydia replied, grinning. Halle's eyes sparkled.

"Get used to it. Are you ready to go? Our ride is waiting." Peeking over Halle's shoulder, Lydia noticed the black cab.

"No Nora?"

"Not today. I'd like our date to start off complaint free." The wink Halle gave produced a heavy thud in Lydia's heart.

Oh boy.

The cab pulled up half an hour later, but not at The Ritz. Confused, Lydia looked to Halle, who was already paying the fare. Outside, Lydia noted they were at St. James's Park.

"I thought we could take a walk first. We're early, and it's a beautiful day."

"Wonderful. I haven't been to St. James's in a while."

They set off silently at a slow pace. They were both adjusting to the new direction their friendship was taking. With a shot of confidence, Lydia slid her hand around Halle's upper arm. Halle looked over, smiling. So far, so good.

The temperature was just above freezing, but the sun was out, and nothing could stop Lydia from enjoying herself. Halle began remarking on different things around the park. Happy just to listen to Halle's sexy voice, Lydia strolled along.

Conversing with Halle was always easy, not taking into account the times things got a bit skew-whiff between them. Over the years, they'd covered most topics, meaning they didn't have that awkward, getting-to-know-you portion of a first date. They were able to ease into their time together, and even though they were chatting like they usually did, there was a definite air of expectation.

With five minutes to spare until their scheduled sitting, Lydia and Halle arrived at The Ritz.

"I can't believe we're doing this," Lydia gasped. "I know it's only fancy tea and sandwiches—"

"It's more than that, Lyds. It's an experience, and one I'm just as excited as you, to take part in."

Inside, Lydia did her best not to look completely out of place. A handsome young man in a server's uniform took their coats. He even had on white gloves. The walls of the tearoom were white with gold leaf everywhere. Marble pillars framed the room. Circular tables, adorned with white cloths that draped to the floor, filled the ornate space.

"This way, please," Mr Posh Server said, directing them to a table in the centre of the room. Halle waited for Lydia to be seated before sitting down herself.

"That was very chivalrous," Lydia grinned, rolling her lips in, suppressing a nervous giggle. This was a side to Halle she'd never seen.

"Just being polite."

"Well, I like it."

Halle winked. "Good to know."

A silver cart was rolled over, brimming with heart attack-inducing goodies.

"Oh yeah, okay, now we're talking." Halle said with an appreciative look.

Small sandwiches in brioche buns caught Lydia's attention first. As her eyes tracked over the tray, her taste buds came alive at the mere sight of the delicate cakes and scones. Jesus, they even had fresh clotted cream.

"I'm going to have to spend a week in the gym, but it's so going to be worth it!"

"I'll be right there with you, 'coz I plan to eat a lot of this." Halle declared.

Their voices were low as they discussed the best way to attack the cart without looking like gluttons. Casting a wary gaze around the tearoom, Lydia couldn't miss how refined the other guests ate and genteelly they drank their tea.

"Are you feeling a bit like a fish out of water, too?" Halle mumbled.

"Yes, completely."

"Well, bugger them. This is our tea sitting. I say we tuck in!"

Without preamble, Halle slid three sandwiches on her plate. A fourth was added as she unceremoniously shoved a cheese and pickle bun in her mouth, moaning sensually.

"Holy crap, Lyds, this is delicious!"

It wasn't out of embarrassment that Lydia flushed. It was the noise Halle was making. Once again, she was inciting a riot in Lydia's knickers.

"Champagne?" a voice said close to Lydia.

It only then occurred to Lydia she was staring, transfixed. The server's appearance hadn't even registered.

"Please," Halle answered, smiling up at him. "Here's to new experiences," Halle toasted, holding her flute up to touch Lydia's.

"And to first dates," Lydia supplied with a wink of her own. Yeah, she could do sexy, too... sometimes.

They ate far too much and drank enough tea to warrant bathroom breaks every ten minutes, but it was worth it. Once Lydia stopped worrying about how she would be perceived by others, the afternoon tea at The Ritz became one of the most memorable days of her life. It wasn't one specific thing, just all the little details: Halle's wit and charm, the ambiance, and the grandeur of it all, including laughing at Halle smearing clotted cream across most of her face because she was in such a rush to eat the scone, piled high with the cream and some strawberry jam.

Buttoning up her coat, Halle's eyes were downcast when she spoke. "Would you like to walk for a little while?"

Was that a hint of nerves showing?

Repeating her earlier move, Lydia wrapped her hand around Halle's arm. "I'd love to."

"Did you enjoy yourself?"

"So much. Thank you, Halle. It wouldn't have been the same with anyone else."

"It was truly my pleasure, Lydia."

Before she knew what was happening, Halle stopped, whirling Lydia around so they were face to...well...boob. Halle's extra height put Lydia in an interesting position. Clearing her throat, Lydia averted her eyes. A soft finger under her chin shifted her face up. Halle's eyes were shining, staring down at Lydia's lips.

This is how it felt to be wanted. Lydia could feel it coming off Halle in waves as she continued to gaze longingly at her. This was their moment, and what a bloody wonderful moment it was when Halle finally gave in, capturing Lydia's mouth.

Obviously, this wasn't the first kiss they'd ever shared, but it was completely different to the lust-filled snog they'd had in Halle's kitchen. Halle possessed Lydia, wholly. The passion they felt before was still as strong as ever, but a layer of tenderness added to what became the best kiss of Lydia's life.

Halle pulled back minutes later, panting. Lydia was grasping at Halle's coat like her life depended on it. That, and also, she was sure if she let go, she'd probably fall arse-first to the floor because her legs had turned to jelly.

"Can that be our official first kiss?" Halle whispered, her face still dangerously close to Lydia's. All it would take would be a slight shift, and they'd be lip-locked again. This time, though, Lydia wasn't sure she'd be able to stop.

"Yes. And wow!"

"I was definitely going for 'wow'."

Jesus, how Lydia wished they were somewhere private. She'd do all sorts... No, wait, she wouldn't because she was still bleeding.

God fucking damn it!

"Hey, what's that face for?"

Jolted from her frustrated mind, Lydia sighed, looking back at Halle. "Nothing, sorry, just wandered off for a second."

"Don't do that, Lyds."

"Do what?"

"Censor yourself with me. Please tell me why you looked so pissed. Did I move too fast?"

"God, no." Shaking her head, Lydia pulled Halle back to her body. "If you must know, I was thinking that I'd like us to be somewhere private."

"We can do that," Halle murmured, nipping Lydia's bottom lip.

"But then I remembered…"

"Being somewhere private doesn't mean we have to have sex, Lydia."

"Yeah, but I want to." Lydia's tone was almost petulant, causing Halle to laugh.

"Lydia Archer, what kind of woman do you take me for?"

"Are you kidding me right now?"

Capturing Lydia's face in both hands, Halle gently brushed her nose against Lydia's. "I want you, Lydia. Make no mistake. But I gather it's not an option right now, and I don't want you feeling angry or frustrated. Let's go back to your place, play with Monty for a bit, and watch a crap movie. It would be the perfect end to a perfect first date."

21

Cathy raised her Screaming Orgasm in toast, "To a naughty girls' night in!"

"Couldn't we have had something like margaritas or something?" Fe asked, eyeing the cocktail suspiciously. Fe wasn't exactly the adventurous type. A good Pinot was her limit.

"Absolutely not. You wanted a naughty night, and that's what you're having."

"No one, apart from you, has said it's a naughty night in," Lydia commented, already halfway through her drink.

Damn, that's creamy!

"When you call me up and tell me you want a girls' night in to educate your sister about sex, it's gonna be a naughty night. And for your information, Lyds, you really sounded like you were coming on to me when you asked me to host this evening. I mean, you're not my usual type, but I was tempted."

"You said I need educating about sex?" Fe screeched.

Rolling her eyes and wincing because Fe had almost reached sonic level, Lydia finished her Orgasm.

"I didn't say that. So thanks, Cathy. And just for *your* information, you'd know if I were hitting on you." Lydia raised a playful eyebrow. Cathy winked, chuckling. "I said you wanted to explore a little. I told Cathy what you told me, about Clark, and his—"

"Lacking abilities," Cathy finished.

"I didn't say that, either. Christ, Cathy, zip it."

Cathy continued to enjoy the cocktail and the mayhem she was creating.

"I said it was a little vanilla, and how you were interested in broadening your horizons."

"See, it's a naughty night in. And I'm thrilled. Harrison is going to get a workout later, that's for sure." Both Archer sisters grimaced. "Oh, don't look at me like that! I'm over forty, not dead. Maybe if you two unwound yourselves a tad, you'd be enjoying the pleasures of a good

man, too. Or either, in your case, Lyds. How is Halle?"
Pumping her eyebrows, Cathy bopped Lydia on the
nose.

After their first date, and reality-altering kiss, Halle
dropped Lydia off at her door, giving her a simple peck
on the lips before leaving. They'd both decided a movie
would probably lead to something else, and that it was
best to say goodnight early. Lydia was so ramped up she
practically booted Fe—who hadn't bloody left—out the
house so she could get rid of the sexual tension that was
tying her up in knots. After taking care of *that*, Lydia
called Cathy to gush over her perfect date.

"You know she threw me out of the bloody house,
right?" Fe cackled.

"I had something to take care of," Lydia grinned.
Talking to Fe about sex was becoming less weird.

"How many times did you take care of that
particular thing?" Cath asked.

"Three times."

"With the Cstar?"

"What's the Cstar?" Fe asked, finally sipping her
cocktail. The moment the creamy goodness hit her lips,
Fe practically downed it.

"It's a toy—a very efficient toy," Cathy answered. "I have a friend who sells them. I recommended it to Lyds and she's never looked back, right?"

"Nope, it's great. It was the only thing I could use for a while."

Looking back and forth between Cathy and Lydia, Fe looked confused. "Why?"

"I often found penetration painful. Now I know it was to do with the endometriosis."

"So, should I try one out?"

Cathy could see she needed to tread a little lighter. "Only if that's something that interests you, sweetie."

Fe might come across as brash, and confident, but underneath the façade was an inexperienced woman.

"I don't know. Clark never wanted to use anything. Before him, I'd only slept with one other guy, and that wasn't anything to brag about. God, I feel like I'm missing out."

"Good job you're here now, then!" Cathy commented, sliding over her iPad. "Let's do some shopping."

"Now?" Fe looked panicked. "But I don't know if I'll like anything."

"We can window shop for now. Look. This is my favourite online shop. It has tons of toys, for all different tastes. Have a drink, scroll through, and see if anything stands out."

"No pressure, sis," Lydia added. In her life, Lydia never expected to be sitting and coaching her older sister through sex experimentation. "Cathy, make another drink, love."

Shooting to the kitchen, Cathy made another round of Screaming Orgasms. Placing the drinks on the table, Cathy smiled and winked as she passed one to Fe. "Hopefully, tonight will be the only time your screaming orgasms come in the form of a drink."

"Window shopping, remember?" Fe smiled, already scrolling. Lydia and Cathy suppressed their smirks when Fe's eyes widened at something on the page.

"So, while she's doing that," Cathy began, "care to tell me what your plan is with Halle?"

"Plan?"

Damn, these cocktails were good. And boozy.

"Yeah, plan. You want to fuck, right?"

"Do you have to be so—"

"Yes, we're big girls, we can say 'fuck'," Cathy glared comically.

"Whatever. Regardless of the word you want to use, yes, I want to do that with her, but my body is still being an arsehole."

"Aunt Flo still hanging around?"

"More like her annoying cousin. I'm not having a full period, but I'm still bleeding."

"Okay, so learn to edge," Cathy said, rather blasé in her tone. "If you can't go full-on, do other stuff. Get each other worked up. Then, when the time comes, so to speak, you'll both be quivering messes and it'll be explosive."

"I really think you've missed your calling," Fe muttered, eyes still on the screen.

"I agree, Cath."

"Nah, I love the museum. This is just fun. But, in all seriousness, I strongly believe people should invest in their sex lives through knowledge. Sex should be fun and satisfying. There's no time for anything less, in my book."

"Amen," Fe added.

"So, what do you think I should do? Plan a seduction?"

"Why not? Not only will it drive Halle nuts, but you'll feel confident *and* sexy. Both of which you need to work on."

"You don't think I'm sexy?"

Wow, that kinda hurt.

"Oh, *I* know you're sexy, Lyds. It's *you* that doesn't!" Cathy exclaimed. "The moment you see what you do to Halle, and I mean *really* see the effect you have on her, you'll find your power. And it's not about needing someone else to validate you; it's about you seeing yourself through their eyes, Lydia."

"She's right, you know," Fe chimed in. "I might need to learn a thing or two about sex, but you need to learn how to love your body, sis."

"How the bloody hell has this turned into a conversation about me?"

"It's a conversation about all of us, Lydia," Cathy soothed. "Fe is currently surfing for vibrators, so we've got her covered for now. It's your turn."

"I don't know what you want me to say. It's not something I can just switch off. Frankly, even when I'm in the mood for sex, and available, so to speak, I don't often feel sexy."

"Why not?"

"My mind just fixates on my wobbly bits. So if I'm thinking about that, what must the person I'm with, be thinking?"

"Oh, love, I doubt they're thinking anything. I'd imagine their minds would be well and truly occupied."

"Maybe, but that worry is where my head goes."

"Have you ever voiced those thoughts to the person you're with?"

Lydia let out a bark. "Ha, obviously not!"

"Halle will know," Fe said pointedly. "She knows you better than anyone, I'd guess. She's got a freaky way of reading you."

"Gee, thanks, that puts me at ease, Fe. Christ!"

"Why's that a bad thing?" Fe shot back.

"Can we please move on? Halle and I will sleep with each other when we're both ready. And what I think about myself is my business."

"Okay, okay, this is supposed to be a fun night," Cathy interjected. "Let's get back to what we gathered here for. Fe, how's window shopping coming along?"

Lydia leaned over Fe's shoulder, her eyebrows shooting up when she clocked Fe's online basket. "I'd say she's doing alright!"

Cathy joined Lydia, smiling devilishly. "Oh my, Fe Archer. I think we've just found your naughty side."

There was so much pain! There'd be less pounding if Lydia had her face strapped to a bass speaker. Curse Cathy and her evil cocktail ways! Mixing alcohol had been a terrible idea, but Cathy was on a roll. They'd sampled no less than six different cocktails, all with naughty names, of course. God forbid they strayed from the theme of the night.

It was between Lydia's third '69' and first 'Blow Job' where things got fuzzy. There was dancing at one point. Monty had gotten involved; he loved a good boogie. It's possible Lydia had also paraded round in lingerie. Or maybe that was just a dream.

"Oh, you look like you're in pain." Jesus, the hangover must be bad if Lydia was hearing Halle's voice. "Want some coffee and painkillers? I have both."

Cracking open an eyelid—with a substantial amount of difficulty—Lydia waited for her eye to focus. Standing by her bed, in comfy looking joggers and a crewneck sweater, was Halle. She wasn't a figment of Lydia's dehydrated mind.

"S'not you?" Lydia slurred.

Snickering, Halle sat on the edge of the bed. "Here, take these pills and drink this coffee. Fe and Cathy are already downstairs."

Christ, her tongue felt like sandpaper. Doing her best to sit up without falling or vomiting, Lydia took several deep breaths. In the pit of her stomach, she felt something bad had happened last night. Something she wasn't going to live down anytime soon, judging by the humour in Halle's eyes.

Silently taking the pills and coffee, Lydia shut her eyes, downed her drink, and prayed. Several minutes later, she painfully, shuffled downstairs. Cathy and Fe looked as horrendous as Lydia felt.

"I hate you." Lydia couldn't even shoot daggers because it hurt her eyeballs.

"No one forced you to drink," Cathy replied, her voice scratchy.

"It's still your fault," Fe grumbled, clutching her head. "How the hell did we end up at your place, Lyds?"

Sitting at the kitchen table, Lydia's head dropped to Cathy's shoulder. Halle's laughter rang through the room, causing the three suffering women to moan.

"Do any of you remember what happened last night?"

"Nope," they chorused unenthusiastically.

"Shall I tell you then?"

Lydia's head snapped up, her eyes a sea of confusion. "How would you know?"

"Oh, because I was here," Halle grinned wickedly.

"No, you weren't."

"Yes, I was. Harrison and I arrived around eleven. Just in time to see you three in full swing."

"No, you weren't," Lydia repeated stupidly. Her mind was too tired to come up with something better. There was no way Halle saw her last night! No way!

Oh, buggering crap balls.

"Harrison is here?" Cathy asked, just as perturbed as Lydia.

"He's nipped to the bakery to grab something nice and greasy for you all."

"Ugh, please stop talking," Fe interjected, her hand coming to her mouth.

"Yummy butter. That'll sort your stomachs out," Halle continued, delighted in the effect she was having on her best friend.

"You suck," Fe replied, before running to the downstairs loo.

Reaching over, Lydia took Halle's cup of coffee and drained it. "That was mean."

Grinning again, Halle poured more coffee for them all and settled next to Lydia. "That's payback, sweetheart."

"So, are you going to tell us what happened, then?" Cathy reached into her purse as she spoke, pulling out a compact mirror and face wipes. In a matter of minutes, she'd wiped her face and reapplied fresh makeup.

Lydia regarded Cathy in wonder. "How are you putting your face on right now? I can't even lift my head!"

"Out of necessity, sweetie. Harrison does not need to be seeing me in this state."

"Too late for that, Cathy," Halle laughed.

Dropping her head to the table, Lydia braced herself. "Oh God, what did we do? Just tell us."

Setting her cup down, Halle rubbed her hands together. "Let's set the scene. It was a frosty night, and I'd just settled down with a cup of Ovaltine—"

"You don't drink Ovaltine. Cut the crap and tell us," Lydia huffed.

"Snarky! Okay. I really was settling down for the night, sans old lady drink, when my phone rang. Guess who it was?"

"Me?" Lydia raised her finger, head still on the table.

"Nope, my bestie. She tells me she's just purchased a shit ton of sex toys that will be delivered to her house in two days' time."

"Oh shit," Fe moaned, dragging herself back to the chair. "I spent so much money. I remember that!"

"Indeed. But we never got to discuss that because Cathy, here, took the phone from you and ordered me to come to her house."

"Did you?" Cathy asked, looking a lot more human than the other two.

"No, I did not. You were all hammered."

"Then how did you end up here?" Lydia muttered.

"I'm getting to that! So, we disconnect, but minutes later Harrison is on the blower telling me you three wanted to start decorating Lydia's house. Apparently, you stumbled your way here. Harrison was concerned and asked me to come over. He wanted to make sure you were safe."

"He's a good one," Fe remarked. Cathy smiled in acknowledgement.

"So I did my civil duty and came over."

"Well, that doesn't sound too bad," Cathy shrugged.

"And when I arrived, you three were dancing in sexy lingerie."

"Oh God, it *was* real." Lydia's pained moan elicited chuckles from the group. The front door opening gave them a few seconds of reprieve.

"Hey honey, I'm home," Harrison called, dumping three bags of baked goods on the table. Leaning over, he kissed Cathy sweetly. "How you feeling, Cat?"

"Better now."

"Good. Did Halle tell you what happened?"

"She was just delighting us with the story."

"Excellent, carry on."

Leaving Harrison to dish out breakfast and fix more coffee, Halle continued, far too happily, in Lydia's opinion.

"As I was saying. You three were shaking your arses in underwear. Harrison arrived seconds after me. At first, neither of us knew what to do, to be honest. You ladies get feisty when you drink cocktails."

"I still have scratches," Harrison commented.

"Scratches?" Cathy's eyebrows furrowed.

"Yes, scratches. You tried to climb me like a bloody tree, woman."

"Oh shit," Fe laughed.

"As that was happening, you two," Halle pointed at the Archer sisters, "thought it was a good idea to do a show-and-tell with Lydia's Cstar."

Any ounce of colour left in Lydia's face, drained. *Please, God, no!*

"Oh, sweet Jesus," Lydia whispered.

"Fe had passed out on the living room floor by the time you got back from your bedroom, Cstar in hand," Halle smiled, raising an eyebrow.

"Please tell me I passed out next." Lydia was fucking mortified.

"Nope. You proceeded to show me how effective the thing was."

Lydia's eyes grew to the size of dinner plates. What the hell had she done?

"Don't panic. You simply held the thing to the tip of my nose, changing the pulse settings. You were quite insistent I tell you my favourite one, Lydia."

What in the motherfucking hell was Lydia supposed to say to that? "I... Oh, Jesus."

Cathy burst out laughing. "And did she find out your favourite?"

"That's for Lydia to remember," Halle laughed.

"It was certainly entertaining," Harrison added, sitting at the table with his book.

Fe and Cathy left a couple of hours later. Halle stubbornly refused to go, even though all Lydia wanted was to disappear. She was surrounded by a fog of embarrassment and shame. It was rare for her to let go like that. Clearly, Lydia had a good reason to limit her alcohol intake.

"Will you please look at me?" Halle asked for the tenth time. Lydia decided hiding in her room under her duvet was the best way to deal with the aftermath of last night.

"No."

"Lyds, come on," Halle laughed.

"I can't look at you, Halle."

"That's silly. Lydia, you were drunk. It's no big deal."

Throwing off the covers, Lydia sat bolt upright. "No big deal? Halle, I paraded around in lingerie and then attacked your face with my clit-sucking vibrator. That *is* a big deal!"

"Well, when you put it like that," Halle laughed.

"Halle!"

Pulling Lydia closer, Halle gently took her by the face. "It's no big deal. We all get daft sometimes. Plus, you looked super sexy in your underwear."

Looking away, Lydia shook her head slightly. "You don't need to say that."

"You think I say things I don't mean?" Halle's tone changed from jovial to serious in the blink of an eye. "Lydia, you are the sexiest woman I have ever met."

Opening her mouth to form a protest, Lydia let out a surprised gasp when Halle kissed her forcefully. Wrapping her arms around Halle's neck, Lydia leaned into the kiss that was quickly picking up steam.

It would have been better if Lydia were still clad in scanty underwear instead of baked bean-stained T-shirt and pyjama trousers, but this is what she was working with. Plus, Halle didn't seem to mind.

The soft brush of Halle's fingers over Lydia's nipple drew out the first moan. The pinch that followed, elicited the second.

"Halle," Lydia breathed.

"Mmmm?"

"Oh God, I want you to touch me."

"It would be my pleasure." Tearing her lips away, Halle sucked and nibbled her way down Lydia's neck.

"Wait."

Halle immediately pulled back, both hands dropping from Lydia's body. "I'm sorry."

"No, I want this, but I'm still bleeding."

Halle was breathing heavily, her expression almost pained that they'd stopped, but Lydia saw the resolve in her eyes. She wouldn't push. "Then we'll wait until you're comfortable."

Tugging on the bottom of Halle's sweater, Lydia collected all the confidence she had. "Can I touch you?"

Halle studied her for a second. "Do whatever you want, Lydia. I'm yours."

22

The tremble in Lydia's hand could easily be ascribed to dehydration, but she knew better. It was the thought of intimately touching Halle that had Lydia's hands shaking, not the aftermath of a boozy night. The bravado she'd summoned moments ago was quickly ebbing away. Intrusive thoughts began circling like a shark in chummed waters.

"Lydia, we can just relax in bed. Nothing has to happen."

Fe was right; Halle knew Lydia well. Reading her emotions and moods seemed to be a gift Halle possessed, and one Lydia found entirely destabilising. Flashes from the girls' naughty night in swarmed Lydia's mind. A vague recollection of a conversation with Cathy circled the periphery of her memory.

Concentrating, Lydia willed herself to remember. They spoke about seduction—yes—that was it. Cathy thought Lydia should try to seduce Halle. What was it she said?

"The moment you see what you do to Halle, and I mean really see the effect you have on her, you'll find your power. And it's not about needing someone else to validate you; it's about you seeing yourself through their eyes, Lydia."

Right now, Lydia needed to find her power. It was inconceivable, that the first time she got to be with Halle, her mind would try to sabotage her with toxic self-doubt. No, she wouldn't let that happen.

"Halle, can you go downstairs for twenty minutes?" Lydia had a plan! Halle looked confused and concerned. "Please, it's important. Twenty minutes."

"We don't have t—"

"Halle Cartwright!" Finding her inner Domme seemed to do the trick.

"Oh...bossy. I like it." Lydia raised her eyebrows. Halle held up her hands in surrender. "Okay, okay, I'm going. I'll keep Monty company."

"Twenty minutes."

"Aye, aye, Captain." Leaning forward, Halle pecked her on the lips. Lydia forced herself to lean back and allow Halle to leave. As soon as the bedroom door closed, Lydia shot off the bed like a rocket. Luckily, she had fully unpacked her ensuite. It was time to beautify!

"See, this is why you should shave more," Lydia muttered to herself, running both hands up her stubbly legs. "God, I look like a fucking grizzly."

Turning on the shower, Lydia jumped in, cursing herself for not waiting until the water was above freezing. Shaving legs with one hand while washing hair with the other was fun, said no one ever!

Talk about multitasking.

With ninety percent less hair on her legs, Lydia concentrated on her bush. "Christ, it's a good job she can't visit there for a while," Lydia scoffed. "I need to book in for a wax or see if the local gardener has space for a hedge trim."

Chuckling to herself, Lydia did her best to tame the bushy beast. In under fifteen minutes, Lydia was smooth and clean, a far cry from the trash panda she'd resembled first thing this morning. Drying her hair and attempting to moisturise at the same time was an experience. Regardless, with five minutes to spare, Lydia was almost ready. Now for the lingerie.

The last time Lydia bought anything remotely sexy was almost four years ago, and even then, she only wore it once, for all of five minutes. The moment she saw herself in the mirror and spotted the thong cutting into her hip fat, she'd taken it all off and stuffed the garments in the bottom of her drawer, never to be seen again.

Steeling herself against the black thoughts that were bound to surface the moment the red-and-black lace covered her body, Lydia headed for her knicker drawer. It took several precious seconds to locate the required undergarments.

Closing her eyes, she slipped on the thong, and then closed the clasp on the front-closing push-up bra. Walking to the dreaded bathroom mirror—that for some unknown and masochistic reason Lydia had reinstalled in her new ensuite—Lydia regarded herself.

Of course, her eyes snapped to her hips. The thong still cut into her skin, but Lydia was determined to keep the lingerie on. A quick check of the clock on her bedroom wall told her she needed to haul ass. Halle would come back upstairs any second.

Skipping to the bed in unbridled excitement and nerves, Lydia momentarily paused. Should she lay on the bed? Stand at the end of it? Drape herself across the armchair in the corner of the room?

"Jesus, seduction is a full-time bloody job!"

"Lyds? Are you talking to me?" Halle's muffled voice rang through the door.

With her heart trying to climb out of her throat and butterflies attempting to fly out of her arse, Lydia was feeling anything but seductive. Oh, add the tampon string, trying to cut her in half, and things weren't off to the sexiest start.

"One second!"

Okay, she could do this. Crawling onto the bed, Lydia stayed on her knees, widening her stance. Putting her hands on her hips, Lydia did her very best to convey confidence and sexual prowess. One last fluff of her hair and she was ready.

"Come in."

If a door could open any slower, it would set a world record. Steadying her breath, Lydia watched as it opened, centimetre by centimetre. The anticipation of witnessing Halle's reaction was giving her palpitations.

Cathy was right. Lydia felt power instantly surge through her as she watched Halle become breathless.

Frozen in Lydia's doorway, the moment her eyes landed on Lydia's half-naked form, the feeling was almost physical.

Halle exhaled, "My God, Lydia, you are breathtaking."

Maybe for the first time, Lydia actually believed what she was hearing. Past lovers often commented on her body, usually her breasts but when they uttered words such as "hot, stunning, fit, beautiful," the compliments always fell flat. Lydia knew they were saying what they thought she wanted to hear.

And of course, who wouldn't want to hear such compliments, but Lydia needed the words to mean something deeper; something that went beyond the immediate physicality of the situation. She needed to hear the sincerity. Halle had just given her that.

"Come here." Crooking a finger, Lydia beckoned Halle closer. A smile crept onto her lips as she watched Halle stumble to get closer. As soon as Halle reached the foot of the bed, Lydia held up her hand. "Wait there."

Crawling on all fours, Lydia sensually moved to Halle, who was almost hyperventilating. Walking her fingers up Halle's torso, Lydia returned to her knees. Their faces were close, and Halle was clearly fighting the urge to take Lydia by the face and kiss her senseless; another reason for Lydia to smile.

Empowered, Lydia brushed her nose gently against Halle's. Jesus, this woman smelt good. Was there such a thing as an odour fetish? Tentatively, Lydia swiped the tip of her tongue across Halle's bottom lip.

"I'm going to touch you now," she whispered.

"Yes, please do," Halle replied with a gasp and a rapid nod, as Lydia bit down on her lip. Pulling back a few centimetres, Lydia looked Halle square in the eyes as her hands pulled up Halle's jumper. As the expanse of copper skin was unveiled, Lydia did her best to continue her seduction, when all she now wanted to do was pull up a chair, grab some popcorn, and stare at Halle's mouth-watering abdomen for the rest of the day.

Dropping the sweater to the floor, Lydia's hands went straight back to work. Using both index fingers, she dipped just below Halle's jogging bottoms. Halle's hips swayed unconsciously toward Lydia, seeking purchase.

Grinning widely, Lydia watched Halle close her eyes, tilt her head towards the ceiling, and breathe deeply, through her nose. Halle Cartwright was losing control, and plain old Lydia Archer was the cause. Well, maybe not so plain, after all.

Taking advantage of Halle's weakening state, Lydia brought her lips close to Halle's ear. "Hold on tight," she breathed.

Fingers that once probed the jogging bottoms now removed them swiftly.

Fuck me, she's not wearing underwear.

Clearly, Halle had a few surprises of her own.

Making quick work of Halle's sports bra, Lydia leaned back to take in the full wonder that was Halle, naked. "Oh, Lord, you are perfection."

"Lydia..." Halle's tone was pleading. Lydia was better at this whole seduction malarky than she'd thought. Straightening her back, Lydia pressed her torso forward. A frisson of lust snaked between their bodies as skin touched skin.

Sucking gently on Halle's collarbone, Lydia let her hands explore. Dark nipples brushed the top of Lydia's breasts, causing goosebumps. The feeling was too much. Those nipples needed to be in her mouth, ASAP.

"Oh," Halle moaned the second her left nipple touched Lydia's warm lips. "Oh, yes!"

Did Cathy happen to say what Lydia was supposed to do when she was drunk off her new sexual power? Lydia wanted to bottle it and make sure she had an endless supply.

This shit was addictive. Every moan that fell from Halle's mouth added to Lydia's surging carnal omnipotence.

Continuing to tease Halle's nipple, Lydia's hand dropped to the fine hair between Halle's legs. As much as Lydia wanted to stretch this out, she was struggling. Her own overwhelming excitement was so intense, she was pretty sure she would internally combust if she didn't touch Halle's pussy soon. It seemed Halle had similar thoughts because the moment Lydia brushed past pubes, Halle thrust her pelvis forward.

Not one to deny pleasure, Lydia bit down gently on Halle's overworked nipple the second she felt wetness glide over her fingers. Lydia slid back and forth a few times before entering Halle with a bit of force, inspired by her excitement.

The response was immediate. Halle's hands flew to Lydia's head, pulling her face up. Lips crashed together as Lydia pumped her fingers. Halle matched the rhythm perfectly, widening her legs as her climax built.

Apparently, Lydia was into her hair being pulled. Halle was probably unaware she was doing it, considering the woman looked a little unhinged, as pleasure ripped a scream from her throat. As Halle tightened around Lydia's fingers, so did her grip on Lydia's head.

Throwing an arm around Halle's waist, Lydia held on for dear life as Halle's body vibrated.

"Lydia!" Halle screamed one last time, before her body, completely depleted, slumped forward. Lydia slowed her fingers. Her own breath was ragged in exertion.

They stayed locked in each other's embrace. Halle's head resting on Lydia's shoulder, her lips brushing sensitive skin. Lydia's desire to be touched was inescapable, but Halle already knew she was "out of order," so to speak. Well, technically, only penetration was off the table.

Lydia never found the prospect of sex on her period in the least bit exciting, so she normally shied away from any form of intimate contact during that time. However, that had been before she'd had the privilege and satisfaction of touching Halle. Now, her body screamed for release.

Sensing Lydia's energy, Halle lifted her head slightly and gently sucked on Lydia's damp skin with her full lips.

"Mmm."

"You like that?" Halle quietly enquired, continuing her ministrations. Lydia slowly nodded her head. "What about this?"

Lydia's whole body clenched as Halle brought her hand up to Lydia's breast, squeezing it firmly. "Mmm, I like that."

"Can I take this off?"

Another nod, and Halle shifted to get to work. Lydia spilled out of the bra the second Halle flicked the clasp.

"Jesus," Halle mumbled to herself, her eyes fixated on Lydia's breasts. "They're a work of art."

"They're just big," Lydia chuckled, used to this sort of reaction.

"No. They're perfect. Art!"

"If you say so." Lydia could feel her old insecurities resurfacing. This is how it went. The breasts impressed, and the rest disappointed.

Halle drew Lydia's head up. "Your body is exquisite. I have wanted you for so long, Lydia. I'm in awe I finally get to see you, touch you, if that's what you want. I can stay above your thong."

Nodding, Lydia cupped the back of Halle's neck. Slowly, she guided Halle down until she was over Lydia completely.

"I won't last long," Lydia admitted.

"The first time," Halle commented, bending forward to capture Lydia's lips. With her hips between Lydia's legs, Halle wasted no time setting a gentle roll. If Lydia didn't calm herself, and quickly, she'd be coming quicker than a virgin after a school disco.

Gripping Halle's hip, Lydia pulled her down harder. "Mmm, oh yes."

"More?" Halle asked, her breath short.

"More!" Biting her lip, Lydia buried her head in Halle's neck as she felt the rhythm increase and the pressure build. It was no use. Lydia's clit was pulsing when she'd made Halle come minutes before. Now it was throbbing almost painfully. Lydia was powerless to stop the orgasm from crashing through her body like a wrecking ball. Miley Cyrus got it right. That shit did damage, but in the best kind of way.

Wiped of all energy and cognitive thought, Lydia sunk into the mattress. Halle stayed put, her weight like a comfort blanket.

"Are you okay?" Halle's voice was soft and filled with emotion.

It struck Lydia then that as meaningful as this had been for her, for a myriad of reasons, it had also been that way for Halle too.

"I'm perfect."

Halle nipped her throat. "I think it's time to go again."

"Again?"

Halle's eyes took on a mischievous glint. "Oh, yes. That was just the beginning. I want to play."

"Play?"

"Hmm. You were drunk when you told me your favourite setting. Let's see if it matches now."

For a second Lydia thought Halle was talking nonsense until she realised what Halle was referring to. Of course, her face immediately flushed.

"Don't worry, it won't be your nose I'm playing with." Halle added with a grin.

"Arsehole," Lydia laughed. "You...you really want to use it?"

So much for waiting a few months to use toys. That's what she'd told Fe last night, wasn't it? That it took her months and months to get comfortable with a sexual partner to even consider 'playing?' Zoe had been the only exception to the rule, so far.

"If you're comfortable. I understand if you want to wait."

"No, no. I'm more than comfortable, and more than ready. It's in that drawer." Lydia pointed with her head.

Giving Lydia a nip on the nose, Halle leaned over, reaching for the drawer. A giggle broke free the moment

Lydia heard Halle switch on the vibrator, mumbling, "Nice."

"Okay, Ms Archer," Halle began, sitting back on her haunches and wiggling her eyebrows, holding the Cstar aloft. "Time to tell me which setting is your favourite, or I could try them all out!"

"You'd kill me if you tried that," Lydia laughed. "I'll tell you my two favourite rhythms."

Sitting up, Lydia took hold of Halle's hand, the one which held the toy. Applying some pressure, Lydia turned it on, using Halle's fingers.

"This first one is straight to the point. If I want to get off quickly, this is the one I use." That internal self-confidence was flowing again.

Halle's widening eyes sent a thrill straight down Lydia's spine.

"This one," she continued, using Halle's fingers to press four times and causing the vibrator to change its rhythm, "is the one that causes me to scream the loudest."

They silently listened as the toy buzzed—*buzz, buzz, Buzzzz, buzz, buzz, Buzzzz.*

"I think I want to use that one," Halle rasped.

"Mmm, me too." Slowly lying back down, Lydia widened her legs suggestively. Halle gulped, taking a few seconds to process what was happening.

"Would you like to leave your thong on?"

"Is that okay?"

"Of course. I can put my underwear back on if that's better."

"Don't you dare," Lydia glared playfully. "You're to stay naked for as long as possible."

Halle grinned. "Well, okay then."

Seconds later, Halle's lips travelled up Lydia's legs, the vibrator trailing slowly behind. Lydia was on tenterhooks, her lower half already feeling like jelly. And then those gorgeous lips stopped, but the toy kept on travelling.

Unconsciously, Lydia had closed her eyes in anticipation, but the lack of soft kisses was enough for her to open them up again. Halle was sitting back on her haunches again. One hand on Lydia's bent knee, the other slowly moving the vibrator closer to its goal.

"I want to watch you."

No one had ever purposefully watched Lydia come, and she wasn't sure how she felt about it now. Once again, the corrosive thoughts tried with all their might to invade Lydia's head.

Fat, spotty... Stop!

All Lydia had to do was look into Halle's eyes and she saw the truth. She might never be fully comfortable with her body, but Halle wanted her, desired her, and made Lydia feel beautiful, even if it was for just one moment in time. It was enough to stave off the negativity.

"Then watch."

Lydia was safe here with Halle. She had to trust that feeling and run with it. The Cstar slipped under Lydia's thong, seeking its target. There was no power on this earth that could stop Lydia from closing her eyes in pure ecstasy as Halle expertly manoeuvred the toy. Lydia's breath caught in her throat as it sucked rhythmically on her clit.

"Oh...oh, oh yes. Halle!"

Gripping the bed covers, Lydia's back arched. She felt Halle's grip tighten on her knee. True to her word, Lydia screamed loudly, and for a long time. The orgasm just kept on coming. Wave after wave. Christ, she was going to have abs like the bloody Hulk if she continued to tense for much longer.

With a raw throat, and exactly zero energy to move her muscles a single second longer, Lydia's body collapsed back to the bed.

Soft kisses on her stomach stole her attention, but she still couldn't move enough to see Halle working her way up her torso until a head popped above Lydia's.

"That was incredible." Halle said with awe.

"You should have been on this end of it," Lydia mumbled, already feeling herself drifting off.

"I think we should play with that again," Halle answered, nuzzling Lydia's neck and wrapping around her body until Lydia was completely cocooned.

"You might need to give me a week," Lydia chuckled, her eyes drooping.

Hell, she might need a month after that workout. Halle ignited something in Lydia that could possibly kill her from sexual overexertion. Lydia made a mental note to google if that was a possibility. She'd make preparations if needed.

23

"Not today, Satan," Lydia growled, turning over to beat the shit out of that infernal "vintage", otherwise known as heart attack-inducing, alarm clock her mother had bought as a moving-in gift. It was the fucking worst!

The roll, however, was cut short as Lydia hit the other body in her bed. The one she'd momentarily forgotten was there. Instead of Halle's eyes, though, Lydia was face deep in cleavage.

"I've never had my boobs referred to as 'Satan' before."

Lydia should really pull back and answer, but the smell of Halle's skin, as previously discovered, was becoming one of Lydia's favourite things to waft up her nostrils. Plus, Halle was warm, and soft, and delicious.

Chuckling at Lydia's silence, Halle rolled slightly to shut off the devil clock. Expecting her to sit up, or shift away, Lydia grinned maniacally when Halle shuffled back down, gently guiding Lydia's face back to her boobs.

Relishing in Halle's pillowy delights for a few seconds longer, Lydia finally moved back and up, resting her head on the pillow, level with Halle's face. It was a weird habit Lydia had in bed. For some unknown reason, she always ended up slipping down and off her pillow during the night.

"That clock is Satan," Lydia mumbled, her voice still marred with sleep; a dream-filled sleep that left parts of her body feeling more than alert this morning.

"Why use it then?" Halle gently shifted a piece of hair from Lydia's face, tucking it behind her ear.

"Mum bought it for me."

"But she's not here to see you use it, Lyds. Does she know how loud it is?"

"I doubt it. Maybe I should sneak it into her room and let her find out."

"Oh, you're grumpy. Poor baby."

"I'm not grumpy," Lydia pouted.

Halle smiled, leaning in, "It's okay, I know how to turn that frown upside down."

Monty's scratching broke them apart before Halle could show Lydia all the ways she wanted to make her smile.

"Shit, I need to let him out. I'll be right back."

"Take your time," Halle smiled, watching intently as Lydia slid out of bed, searching for something to put on. Lydia could feel Halle's gaze all over her, and God, if it didn't make her shiver in delight.

Monty was not happy. He had a propensity to sulk when he didn't receive his allotted amount of cuddle time. And yesterday, the poor little guy had almost none. Lydia and Halle stayed in bed for the entire afternoon and evening, only leaving the bedroom to use the bathroom, let Monty pee, and grab a few snacks.

"Sorry, buddy. Please don't be mad." Monty trotted off towards the back door without even a backward glance. Lydia was in the shit. "I'll cook you some bacon. You love bacon."

"I'll ask again. Does he ever respond?"

"Fuck, Halle. Who the hell moves without making a sound? That's twice you've frightened the life out of me. You're like a fucking ninja, for Christ's sake."

"Um, in my defence, the first time, you left the door open. And this time, it's because of your super soft carpet. I assure you; I usually clunk around, making all kinds of noise."

"I might have to fit you with a bell or something."

"Oh, collars, interesting…"

"I didn't mean like that."

Monty's irritated bark made Lydia wince. "Sorry, lad, off you go. I'll start your breakfast."

"No, I'll do breakfast. We both know which one of us is the cook."

"Halle, you don't have to make my dog breakfast."

"How about I cook it for all of us? Fry-up sounds pretty good right now. I'm famished."

"Okay, fine. Do you mind if I grab a shower? I've got a shift this afternoon, and I need to spend some time with Mardy Arse out there before he starts chewing my shoes or something else, in protest."

"Go. I'll sort his majesty out and play with him for a while." The kiss Halle gave her felt so natural, like they did it all the time. Waking up, making breakfast, looking after the fur child, etc… all very domesticated, and oh-so-comfortable.

Lydia mulled over those feelings as she showered and dressed. There was still plenty of time before she had to get to work, meaning there was still plenty of time to spend with Monty and Halle, if that's what Halle wanted.

Crap, now that they'd slept together, what *would* Halle want? Was that it? She'd fulfilled a teenage dream; got the girl, so to speak. So, would that be it for her? Would her interest wane now?

"You're looking deep in thought. Are you alright?"

Lydia hadn't realised she'd stopped outside the kitchen. Standing there, just staring, was obviously disconcerting to witness. Shaking her head to dislodge her train of thought, Lydia smiled. "All good. Is Monty still being a grump?"

"Nah, two bacon bits and he got over it pretty quickly."

"That's my boy. I also get over things pretty quickly with bacon bits, FYI."

"Noted. Now, let's eat."

As with earlier, everything was easy. They passed each other sauces and other condiments, chatting about the day ahead. Halle fed Monty her toast crusts and Lydia fed him her egg whites. All of it was just so *normal*.

Lydia expected to have some sort of conversation about them sleeping with each other. The fact they hadn't, left her confused. Was it a good thing? Or did it mean Halle was afraid to hurt Lydia by telling her the truth? The truth being: She wanted nothing more to happen. Had Lydia been a shitty lay?

Halle left an hour after breakfast. Apparently, she was supposed to visit her mum. Was that the truth? Or did she just need to get out of there without Lydia causing a scene?

Jesus, her head was a mess. All the thoughts she'd successfully tried to keep at bay, were now battering down the door to be let in, and Lydia could do nothing to stop it.

The commute to work passed by on autopilot. The ease and simplicity Lydia felt this morning was long gone. Now, all she felt was hollow. Those uglier thoughts had crept their way in and constricted all the happiness she'd felt mere hours ago.

Halle would leave. Or she'd get fed up with Lydia's insecurities and broken bits. Something! There would be something that would give Halle an out. That's how relationships went for her.

"Are you still hungover?" Cathy's voice pierced Lydia's darkening mind fog.

"What? No, why?"

"Because you look like shit, sweetie. Are you having problems again, you know, down south?"

"No, I'm fine," Lydia snapped. That was the wrong thing to do; on two levels. One: Cathy was a dear friend and never deserved to be snapped at. Two: She was Lydia's boss, and they were at work. "Sorry, sorry, Cath."

"My office." Cathy's tone was level, not outwardly hostile, which worried Lydia more, if she were honest. Dropping her head in shame, Lydia followed Cathy silently to her office.

"Ca—"

"What happened, Lydia?" Cathy sat back in her chair, arms on her desk, face soft. She wasn't mad; Cathy was concerned, which made Lydia feel like more of a bitch for snapping.

"I slept with Halle."

"And it was bad?"

"No, it was perfect. She was perfect."

"And that's causing you to look like the world is ending?"

Well, when it was said like that... "No. But we didn't even talk about it this morning. We acted like... Well, I don't know. We had breakfast together, chatted, all the usual stuff, but that's it. It was lovely, don't get me wrong, but it could have been a regular Saturday, for all we knew."

"Really? Does Halle often wake up next to you and then follow that up by making you breakfast?"

"Obviously not, but…"

"What were you expecting?"

"I thought we'd talk about it."

"So did Halle act as though it never happened?"

"No, we kissed this morning. Actually, we were heading into more sexy time, but Monty was upset with the lack of human interaction." Why was Cathy looking at her like that? "What?"

"Well, I might be wrong, but I think that *was* you guys talking about it!"

"What do you mean?"

"The fact you both felt comfortable waking up, having a few kisses, and then the possibility of more *was* the conversation. Look, Lyds, you and Halle know each other. You were never going to have the awkward conversation after a night of sex, the same as you might with a stranger. And I think you know that, so what's bugging you, really?"

"Well, what happens now?" The question all but shot out of Lydia's mouth. "Halle left after a very pleasant morning and fantastic afternoon-slash-evening of sex, without a word as to where we go now."

"Well, why didn't you ask her?"

"Because... I don't know!" Lydia was becoming vexed, and she couldn't put a finger on exactly why. "Look, I need to get to work."

Sensing Lydia was done talking, Cathy simply nodded. Unable to look her friend in the eye, Lydia made a hasty retreat, more than happy she would get to spend all day taking tour groups around the museum. That kind of task would keep the demons quiet for a little while.

Lydia worried her lip as she sat in the staff room, tea in one hand, phone in the other. Halle messaged, asking if Lydia was free tonight. That was a good thing, right? Clearly, Halle wasn't done with her just yet. But maybe Lydia should create a bit of distance; slow things down a little.

Jesus, any slower between you two and you'll start going backwards.

Responding, Lydia asked if they could take a rain check until the following evening. Nothing good would come of Lydia seeing Halle tonight, not when her head was playing silly buggers. See? This was why she'd decided not to date for a while. Why had she gone back on that? Clearly,

Lydia needed more time to sort her shit out before she was ready to... God, she'd said all this to herself before. She was going round in circles.

Okay, today needed to end. Lydia needed sleep. That would help clear the mud...she hoped.

Monty yipped excitedly as soon as Lydia stepped through the door. Why was the kitchen light on, and what was that smell? Dropping her bag, and kind of wishing she knew self-defence, Lydia creeped down the hall. Huh, Halle was right; the carpet really sucked up all the sound.

Speaking of Halle. "Um...hi?"

Wheeling round, spoon in hand, Halle smiled brightly. "I'm not here."

"Then I'm having some sort of episode." In the pit of her stomach, Lydia felt the knot she'd had all day begin to loosen. That was a recurring thing, too. Halle's presence soothed her. What a conundrum it was; how being near Halle both helped and hindered Lydia's equilibrium.

"No, I mean, obviously, I *am* here, but I'm also *not*."

"Halle, have you been drinking?"

Chuckling, Halle set the spoon down on the worktop, fiddling with the gas hob before turning to give Lydia her full attention.

"I know you wanted to rain check tonight, and I heard you, I promise, but—"

"But?" Lydia cocked a brow.

"Lydia, you have no food! I found out this morning when I was making breakfast. I looked in your freezer for some hash browns and I was stunned. You have one frozen broccoli floret. I mean, how? I tried, okay, to, you know, forget about it, but I couldn't. What the hell have you been living on?"

"Wow," Lydia laughed, taken aback by Halle's tirade.

"I thought I could cook you a few things to freeze. That's why I'm here like a crazy person, even though you told me you needed space."

"Uh-huh."

"That's not right? I messed up, didn't I? Yeah, I did. I should have waited. Shit. Um, okay, let me just clear this up. Um, you get on with your evening, and pretend I'm not visible. I'll slip out as soon as I'm done."

"Halle—"

"Sorry, Lyds. Jesus, what a prat." Halle was muttering to herself now. Unable to watch Halle berate herself, Lydia did what felt natural. Closing the gap, she slipped her hands around Halle's neck and kissed her with everything she had.

Once again, it was as if the day's worries and torments slipped away without a trace. How did Halle do it? The kiss remained heartfelt, and although it could have easily turned into something more, neither Halle nor Lydia pushed for it.

"Okay, wow. Should I stalk you more often?"

"It was more like breaking and entering," Lydia mumbled against Halle's lips. "And, yes, you can do that whenever you want. Especially if you're cooking me food."

"So I should carry on cooking this moussaka?"

"Yes, and then you should sit down and eat some with me. If you're not busy?"

"No, not busy. But are you sure? I've totally hijacked your night. Which is something I keep doing."

"You've never hijacked my night."

"No, just your doctor's appointment. And your bucket list. And the house moving."

Pulling back, Lydia studied Halle. "Are you seriously worried that's what I think?" Halle's shrug said it all. "Halle, you're never an intrusion or unwanted. I've loved doing my bucket list with you, and if you hadn't intervened with the doctor, I would still be a mess."

"I find it hard to take a back seat where you're concerned. But that's *my* deal. I want to respect your boundaries, Lydia."

A shot of laughter filled the room. Was Halle serious?

"Halle, you are the most respectful person I have ever met! Like, ever!"

"Clearly not."

Lydia was flummoxed. She'd never heard Halle be self-deprecating, and she didn't like it.

Taking Halle's face in her hands, Lydia did her best to convey just how serious she was. "Do you know what I've been thinking today?"

"No."

This was it. The turning point. Instead of letting things fester, Lydia was going to open up. Halle deserved Lydia being courageous and honest right then, because she was the most respectful, reliable, and supportive person Lydia had the privilege of knowing. And she would be damned if she'd let Halle spend a second longer thinking she was anything else.

"After you left, my mind went completely wonky. I honestly thought because we didn't talk about our night together, you'd had your fill of me and that was the end of it. Of any chance of us." Lydia held Halle's face tighter, stopping the woman from rearing back in hurt and surprise. "Let me finish." Lydia waited for Halle's compliance. "I've been so used to people getting what they want and then leaving when things get real. You know that, because you've been there for it."

"I didn't ask you out again because I didn't want to pressure you. I'd nev—"

"I know. But sometimes insecurities take over. I've come to learn, I'm not the most stable of people," Lydia laughed. "Sure, a lot of that was because I was feeling crazy with my manky hormones, but I know it's more than that. I have body dysmorphia, I have abandonment issues, and probably a host of other shit. And I learned to cope with it, alone. For right or wrong, I'm just a bit broken in places."

Dropping her hands, Lydia gripped the front of Halle's shirt. "You, Ms Cartwright, have shown up for me time and again, even when I didn't realise it. Over the years, you've been my steady person, even from afar. You were the person that saved me from months of agony by being my pillar of strength in that doctor's office. You have made me feel wanted and sexy, which is an almost impossible feat. And you did it so easily."

Lydia took a breath. Wow this was hard, yet quite...liberating.

"I pushed you away after Fe caught us because I thought you would inevitably leave anyway. But the more I see you, the more I come to understand you and the way you treat me, I know I have been so, so wrong. I want you to hijack my life, Halle. I want to conquer my demons and not let them get the better of me, but it won't be easy. I want you to know what you're signing up for."

"I know exactly what I'm getting into."

"Then I want to give this—us—a real shot."

"Do you really not find yourself sexy?"

"No."

Shaking her head in disbelief, Halle kissed Lydia's head tenderly. "Can I speak now?"

"Sure."

"None of the people you dated were worthy of you, Lydia. I know you'll scoff and try to laugh off my comment as something ridiculous, but it's true. You are beautiful, inside *and* out, and I've wanted to be by your side since we were teens."

Lydia searched her eyes, only seeing raw truth.

"I remember the first time my stomach got butterflies around you," Halle continued. "Fe was being her usual self, giving you shit for hanging around. I looked over at you and I swear to the Spirits, I was struck by lightning."

Lydia could only smile as Halle held her and threw more gorgeous words her way.

"You were wearing a summer dress and your hair was down, in long brown ringlets. My heart thudded so loud I was scared you could hear it. In that second, I knew you were the girl for me. Unfortunately, Fe disagreed, and stupidly, I went along with it."

Halle's past hurt was clear to see, and once again Lydia cursed her meddling sister.

"That's one of my biggest regrets, Lydia: not telling you sooner. We could have been together for years, and I would have been able to support you the way you deserved when your health problems began. For that, I'm sorry. I was a coward, too scared to change the status quo."

"No, Halle—"

"It's my turn." Halle playfully squeezed Lydia's waist. "I *was* a coward. Fe was like a sister to me. We'd gone through everything together and I chose to keep her happy, over myself, and you."

"I could have said something, too."

"No, you'd have never put yourself out there like that. Looking back, I could already see you had insecurities, which mystified me then *and* now. You are smart, funny, humble and loving. Those are what I find the most attractive about you, Lydia. Plus, I'm not blind. You *are* breath-taking to me. You always have been."

"Halle, Jesus," Lydia hiccupped.

"After the last jackass dumped you, something in me broke. That resolve I'd built to stay away, crumbled. I wanted to be the one comforting you, cooking for you, loving you, and nothing Fe said anymore could change how I felt."

Tears pooled in Lydia's eyes as Halle pulled her even closer.

"I want to be the one who fights your demons *with* you. I want to show you how bloody sexy you are, even in baked bean-stained pyjamas!"

They both chuckled, and Lydia felt as light as a feather.

"I need you to remember all this when those voices make you feel you're anything but perfect to me. I'm not going anywhere, Lydia. It's taken me twenty-odd years to get here!"

24

Lydia shuddered as the last vestiges of her orgasm dissipated. The moussaka would definitely be cold by now.

"That one was strong."

"That was fantastic. This little thing is efficient." Halle remarked, holding up the vibe.

"Oh, yes, it is. But I think you should find out for yourself."

Halle shuffled down the bed, starfishing. "Let me have it, baby."

"Oh my God," Lydia laughed. "You're an idiot."

"True, but I'm *your* idiot, so who really wins? Me!"

Lydia paused. "You really mean that, don't you?" She scooted down the bed, half draped over Halle's long body, their faces just inches apart.

"I told you, and I'll keep telling you until you believe me. I'm yours. Have been for a while now. Does that freak you out?"

Lydia bit her lip. "It feels foreign. But it doesn't freak me out."

"I don't want to come on too strong. Even though we've known one another for years, we need to get to know each other as lovers and partners."

"I think we're getting to know each other quite well," Lydia murmured seductively.

"Oh, we've definitely got this part covered. But what about the big things?"

"You don't think sex is a big thing?"

"It's one part of us, sure. But not the biggest. And I knew we would be good in bed together."

"You did, did you?" Lydia nuzzled Halle's nose with her own.

"Yes. There is no way we would be anything other than fantastic."

"So, what are the big things you want to learn?"

"Do you want to get married? Have kids? Join a reading group? You know, the big things."

Okay, wow, they were getting to it. The big questions already.

"Yes, I want all those things. But...the kids could be an issue."

"Not impossible, though, right? That's what you said." Halle leaned up on an elbow, kissing Lydia sweetly.

"Not impossible."

"Would you consider other methods, such as adoption? Or..."

"Or?"

"Well, not to get too ahead of myself, but I have a womb, too."

"You'd carry our baby?"

"Of course I would."

"Wow, okay. So, we're getting married and having kids. That's what I got from this," Lydia grinned.

"Hold your horses," Halle laughed. "Maybe we could date for a few months longer first."

"Hey, you brought it up."

"Only to test the waters. If we're giving this a go, Lyds, I want us to be on the same page."

"I know. I'm messing with you. Plus, we still have to experience the full honeymoon period."

"Ah, yes. Constant sex," Halle laughed. Lydia smiled, but it didn't quite reach her eyes. Halle sat up, pulling Lydia on to her lap. "I was joking, Lyds. You know I don't expect that."

"But you should. Expect that, I mean. That's what normal couples do, isn't it? Get together and have sex for weeks?"

There was that gnawing feeling again; the one that made Lydia feel she was going to hold Halle back if they continued down this road.

"Stop it. I know what you're thinking and you're wrong. Lydia, I don't give a shit what 'normal' couples do. I want you. Not just your body. I want your time."

"But what about sex?"

"We've literally just had it, Lyds," Halle laughed. "I'm perfectly happy with you taking the lead. There will be times I'm not in the mood, or just worn out. This isn't just on you, honey. That's what it means, to me, anyway, to be in a partnership."

"Will you promise to tell me if it becomes a problem?"

"I promise."

Lydia searched Halle's face. She only saw honesty. "Okay. Can we get back to what we were doing now?"

"Aunty Lydia?"

Lydia shot up from the bed, sprinting to the door, which was ajar, just in time to stop Jenny from catching an eyeful of something she was far too young to witness.

"Wait downstairs, Jenny, I'll be down in a minute."

"Okay. Mummy says Aunty Halle can buy us a pizza. Is she in there?"

"Um..."

"Yeah, I'm in here, Jen. We'll be down in a second."

They waited until Jenny's tiny footsteps disappeared. Lydia whirled round, panicked. "Why the bloody hell is Fe here? It's nearly seven."

"Why does Fe do anything? Let's go and find out, shall we?" Halle placed a kiss on Lydia's neck before throwing on her clothes. Thank God they'd waited until getting to the bedroom before stripping each other.

Downstairs, Fe was just about to shove a fork into the cooling moussaka. "Hey, that's our dinner," Lydia shot.

"It looked like you weren't planning on eating it anytime soon," Fe said with a grin.

"What are you doing here?" Halle asked, scruffing the triplets' hair as she went past.

"We had another bloody school meeting. Thought we'd swing by."

"The kids okay?" Lydia thought the triplets were settling down now Clark and Fe had spoken to them.

"Yeah, fine. We decided to have regular check-ins with the teachers."

"What time was the appointment?" Halle asked, eyebrow raised.

"Hm?" Fe pretending she hadn't heard a question was a typical avoidance behaviour, usually when she'd done something wrong.

"You heard me, Fe Archer."

"Oh, right, it was at half five."

Lydia stood with hands on hips. "It doesn't take nearly an hour and a half to get from the kids' school to here. So why are you really visiting?"

"Fine," Fe huffed. "Cathy called me and said you were in a weird mood. She was worried. I came to check up on you, but as soon as we came in, I noticed Halle's car keys. It didn't take much to put two and two together."

"So you sent Jenny upstairs?" Lydia screeched.

"I was fucking with you," Fe laughed. "She didn't see anything, did she?"

"Oh, now you're worried!" Lydia scoffed. "I don't want my niblings traumatised, Fe!"

"No, she didn't see anything. But maybe next time think it through, yeah?" Halle was always the calm one.

"Yeah. Sorry. So, does that mean?" Fe waved a finger between Halle and Lydia.

"Yeah, it does," Halle beamed, wrapping her arms around Lydia.

"Well, about bloody time."

Rolling her eyes, because Fe was ridiculous, Lydia made a mental note to chat to Cathy. She still felt bad for snapping, and once again, Cathy had proven herself a great friend by sending Fe over. Maybe she could get her a gift basket or something? Muffins? Sex toys, maybe? Lydia tittered to herself. Yeah, Cathy would love that.

❧

"What's this for?" Cathy asked, examining the spa day gift certificate. Lydia decided against the adult gift basket in the end.

"That's an apology for being an arse to you the other day. And a thank you for sending Fe to check on me."

"Oh, it's for two. Girls' spa day?"

"Only if you want. You can take Harrison."

"Sweetie, no. I love Harrison, but spending the day at a spa where he explains the different minerals in the mud treatment isn't conducive to my relaxation."

Chuckling, Lydia nodded in understanding. "Fair enough. Make the reservations and let me know."

"Will do. Now, you want to fill me in on the Halle situation?"

"We're doing it."

"About time. Toys or no toys?"

"No, not that! I mean, we are doing that, but I meant we're dating. Officially."

"Does that mean you told her how you were feeling the other day?"

"Yeah. She was in my kitchen when I got home, even though I said I didn't want to meet up."

Cathy's eyebrows reached her hairline. "So, she just showed up?"

"Not for the reason you think. She wasn't planning on still being there when I got home."

"I'm confused."

"Remember, I told you she made us breakfast that morning? Well, Halle being Halle, noticed I didn't have any

403

food in. She spent the day stressing I wasn't eating, so she came round and cooked me homemade meals to freeze. She was just finishing a moussaka when I arrived home."

"Christ, that woman is in love with you, Lydia Archer!"

"In love? You think so?"

"I know so. She's a smitten kitten."

"She's perfect, and gorgeous, and perfect."

"You said perfect twice."

"Because that's how perfect she is."

"Did you tell *her* that?"

"We had a conversation," Lydia smiled. "I think it's the first time I've really opened up."

"And she said?"

"So many things, Cathy. And I know you're right. I know she's in love with me, even if she hasn't said the words. She shows me."

Taking a sip of coffee, Cathy took a few seconds to watch Lydia. "Why do you think she hasn't said it?"

"Easy. She doesn't want to freak me out. But that's the thing: Now we've spoken, and laid it all out there, I'm not scared in the least."

"So maybe it's your turn to take a risk. Show her you feel just as strongly."

Lydia nodded. It was something she'd been thinking about ever since they became a couple. Halle would defer to Lydia, not wanting to push. But that meant Halle would hold back, and that wasn't okay. Lydia didn't want to be the reason Halle felt like she had to censor her feelings; not when Lydia felt the same way.

"I'm cooking dinner tonight as a surprise. Halle's always taking care of me, and I want her to know I've got her back, too. I think I can make an acceptable spag bol."

"Parmesan, sweetie. If in doubt, drown it in Parmesan."

Smiling, Lydia hugged Cathy goodbye, happy she'd taken the time to apologise. "Roger that. Okay, I'm off. I'll see you tomorrow."

Lydia had an hour to make her way to Elise Maynard's office. Even though it hadn't been three months since starting her new pill, Lydia needed some reassurance. And some advice.

The conversation between her and Halle in bed, regarding marriage and kids, was constantly at the forefront of Lydia's mind.

"Afternoon, Jean," Lydia said, greeting Elise's receptionist. They'd spoken several times over the past few weeks. Elise was becoming a part of their little friendship group, and Lydia happily met up for a coffee with the good doctor. *Being* a good doctor meant Elise didn't have a lot of time to spare, so Lydia would visit her at the hospital with a Starbucks. Jean was always so happy and friendly, Lydia began bringing her a coffee too.

"Lydia, hello, love. I see you've got a two o'clock appointment. She's running about ten minutes late."

"No problem. How's Diane?" Diane was Jean's neighbour who had taken a tumble not too long ago.

"Oh, she's fine. Already back in the garden."

"It's winter!"

"That's Diane. She has to be outside doing something. She's started collecting gnomes."

"Oh, wow."

"You're telling me. It's the stuff of bloody nightmares," Jean chuckled. "Oh, Elise just buzzed through. You can go in."

"Great. Thanks, Jean."

Lydia chuckled to herself as she crossed the waiting room to Elise's office.

What would Monty think of gnomes?

"Lydia, how are you?" Elise stood, offering a hand. Even though they were friends, whenever Lydia saw her in an official capacity, Elise was the consummate professional.

"Good. I just wanted to check in. Everything's fine, but I'm still bleeding regularly."

"Okay. Heavy?"

"Nope. Very light, it's just the amount of days."

"Let's double the dosage, then. Take two pills a day from tomorrow."

"And that's safe?"

"Absolutely. Some people need an extra dose to bring the bleeding under control."

"Thank you. Um...there is something else I want to discuss."

"Okay."

"Babies."

"Okay, let's look at options."

"Before that, I'd like your thoughts."

"As your doctor?"

"Yes."

Elise sat straighter in her chair. "You are in your thirties, which means your fertility will start to decline. Adding that to the endometriosis diagnosis and possible scarring, I'd say you would need to look at fertility treatment soon."

"So, if I want a baby, I need to start now?"

"The sooner the better. I know after your operation you were keen to get started, but I think it was important to get your body back in balance. If you're still determined to get pregnant, my advice is to take action."

"Wow, okay."

"Let me give you some information to start off with. Give it a thorough read and when you're certain, book an appointment."

"Okay, thanks, Elise."

"As your friend, Lydia. I'm excited, and I'm here for you. It could be rough, but I will do everything in my power to help you have a baby if that's what you want."

"Mince onions? How the fuck do you mince an onion?"

Maybe spag bol wasn't a safe bet after all. Lydia had fought the urge to gag when handling raw meat. She'd almost cut a finger off when chopping the carrots, and now she was supposed to figure out how to mince an onion?

The onion ended up being chopped into small bits because Lydia refused to lose her shit over a vegetable. With the table set and soft music playing, everything was ready.

Halle strolled in ten minutes later, her eyes scanning the dining room table. "What's all this?"

"It's me making you a home-cooked dinner that I'm eighty percent sure won't poison you," Lydia smiled.

"Wow, eighty percent sure. Who could say no to that? It smells great, Lyds. Thank you."

They spent several minutes kissing. Lydia had to drag herself away before another meal went uneaten.

"Sit down, I'll plate up."

"How was your day?" Halle asked.

Lydia had to smile as Halle tucked into the food, yet still gave her full attention to the conversation. "It was good. I had my follow-up with Elise."

"I know. You wouldn't let me come with you."

"Because it was just a quick checkup, babe."

"Still."

"She's put me on a double dose of the pill. It's supposed to help curb the bleeding."

"Great."

"Hmmm."

"Not great?" Halle put her fork down and took Lydia's hand.

"I need to talk to you about something important."

"Okay."

"It's about kids."

Easing into things didn't seem to be Lydia's forte.

"I've been thinking about it more and more. I wanted some advice. Elise explained I might need to start sooner rather than later. It could take months or even years. The endometriosis left scarring and has possibly affected my eggs."

Halle still hadn't said anything. Her eyes were wide. Shit, had Lydia broken her girlfriend? Of course she had; Lydia was discussing babies, for God's sake.

"Um...thoughts?"

"We've only been together for a few days. That's fast even by lesbian standards, Lyds." Halle's laugh was stilted.

"I know this is way too much pressure to put on a new relationship. But I feel I need to think about it, seriously. I don't want you to feel trapped or forced into even discussing this. We said we wanted to date before doing the big things, but I'm not sure I have the time to wait and see."

"Do you want a family with me?"

"Considering I'm completely in love with you, yes."

Halle's sharp intake of breath could've been heard in the heart of London. It was that loud. "You love me? As in *love* me, love me?"

"Um, I'm not sure what the difference is," Lydia laughed.

"Lydia!"

"Yes, I'm in love with you, Halle. It's fast and scary, but it's true."

"I..." Halle didn't finish her thought. Instead, she scooped Lydia from her chair. The soft brush of lips on Lydia's neck was followed by wetness. Pulling back, Lydia noted tears slowly sliding down Halle's perfect face.

"Please don't cry," Lydia whispered.

"You've just made me the happiest person, Lydia Archer."

"Even though I've just told you, I want to talk about babies."

"We need to think about it, obviously. But I'm here. And I want that discussion."

"I'm worried people are going to think I'm acting irrationally."

Lowering Lydia so her feet now touched the ground, Halle leaned back slightly. "It doesn't matter what anyone thinks. If this is what you want, that's all that matters. Only you know what's right for your mind and body."

"Do you think I'm trying to sabotage us?" Lydia had spent the rest of the afternoon reading the literature and analysing her feelings.

"Do *you*?"

Shaking her head, Lydia kissed Halle soundly. "I've thought about it. I know I have a habit of doing it sometimes, but not now. If I were certain I wouldn't have problems conceiving, I wouldn't even be bringing the subject up for a long time. I'm so happy my hormones are levelling out, and I don't want to mess with that, but I also know I want to be a mum."

"I completely understand that, honey. And you haven't got the certainty of getting pregnant, so it's only natural you want to look at conceiving. Or at least the idea of it."

Lydia nodded, resting her forehead on Halle's chin, taking in a breath before looking back up into Halle's eyes.

"And, I don't know, call me crazy, but this feels right: You and me. It took me way too long to come around, but now, as I'm standing here in your arms, it's perfect."

Halle brushed her lips against Lydia's humming in agreement.

Lydia pushed on. "I can see us in the future, with one or two kids. Monty with a playmate. Us eating a lazy breakfast on the weekend. I've never been able to picture that before. Not with anyone."

Leading Lydia back to her chair, Halle sat. "And if you can't get pregnant?"

Closing her eyes, Lydia took in a deep, cleansing breath. "I've thought about that, too. I know it could be tough. Not just on me, but on *us*. If I can't fall pregnant, I hope we would look at other methods."

"I'm okay with that, Lyds. But... I think in our discussion, we need to talk about limits."

"What do you mean?"

"How many times do we try to get you knocked up?"

"Oh, before we stop, you mean?"

"Yeah. And I promise I'm not trying to be negative, but I know what toll this will take, and I love you too much to see you hurting."

"That's something we'd need to talk to Elise about when we decide to go forward."

"True. Would you want to tell Fe?"

"No, not until we were certain."

"That's fine by me, honey."

"Have we just decided to maybe have a baby over a plate of subpar spaghetti bolognese?"

"It's not subpar."

"I didn't mince the onions."

"I don't think that's obligatory, babe."

"Are we really doing this?"

Scooting her chair closer, Halle took Lydia's hands. "We are. And we have from now until we decide to get a baby inside you, to date. But I already know you're it for me, Lydia. I knew it at eighteen, and I know it now. You're perfect."

Dropping her gaze, Lydia blushed. "I'm not."

"You are for me."

Epilogue

Halle saw her wife's changing mood in an instant. She saw Lydia's thoughts taking a dark turn as her eyes flickered from the young, thin server who had been openly flirting with Halle, to her own stomach. The way Lydia began wrapping her arms around herself in a bid to make herself feel more secure.

"Can I get you anything else?" the perky server asked, only looking at Halle.

"Just the bill, please." Halle refused to look anywhere but at her wife, who, in turn, looked anywhere but at Halle. As much as Halle wanted to reassure Lydia, she knew better. Anything Halle said wouldn't be taken to heart, not while Lydia was feeling like this.

Learning how to help Lydia through times of insecurity hadn't been easy, especially lately. But Halle wasn't a quitter, and she certainly wasn't going to allow her wife to feel bad about herself.

Opening the car door, Halle helped Lydia inside. It still felt strange driving a big car. Lydia had finally convinced Halle to buy a second vehicle, knowing full well she'd never get rid of Nora—who was now stored in the garage. Nora was Halle's weekend car. Unsurprisingly, Lydia was more than happy for Halle to go on jaunts by herself or with Fe.

The drive home was silent. Lydia kept her gaze out the passenger window. Halle bit her lip to keep quiet. The storm inside Lydia was still brewing and Halle had to wait for it to break before her help would be accepted.

Monty barked excitedly as soon as they stepped through the door. Halle moved in with Lydia three months after their baby-making talk. The transition had been easy, just like their relationship, ninety percent of the time. Things got dicey when Lydia came off the pill.

The moment they started the baby process, Lydia was overly sensitive. Halle knew why. It was born from fear; fear that Lydia wouldn't be able to conceive.

Halle only made the mistake, once, of trying to make a joke out of something Lydia said that was self-deprecating.

The devastation she'd witnessed slide onto her girlfriend's face was gut-wrenching, and from that day on, Halle never made light of Lydia's feelings.

She was a practised hand now. Halle knew Lydia would slink off upstairs for half an hour. She didn't like it, but she knew better than to follow. Lydia needed time to cry without a witness. Halle knew her wife would also self-deprecate in the bathroom as she tortured herself, looking into the mirror. Thankfully, times like this were getting further apart.

Still, tonight, Halle had some work to do. As predicted, Lydia ascended to their bedroom silently. Halle watched, her heart breaking.

How could she think she is anything but perfect?

Given the chance, Halle would have liked to ream out the server for being so disrespectful, and frankly, unprofessional. She might have been younger and skinnier, but that held no appeal to Halle—not when she had a stunning, curvaceous woman to call her own.

Getting angry wouldn't help. Calm and steady was the way forward. It was twenty minutes later, Halle heard Lydia come downstairs. "Halle, can you sit for a minute, please?"

And here it came. The eye of the storm.

"Sure, babe."

Halle sat back on the sofa watching her wife pace. Lydia was nodding to herself, obviously bolstering whatever decision she'd decided was the best one.

"I think…I think we should look at having an open marriage."

Well, that was a new one.

"And why's that?"

It's just her fears.

"I…I think it would do you good."

"It would do me good?"

God, how does her brain come to these conclusions?

"Yes. I'm aware that I look like a whale. We can't have sex, and that's my fault. You're young, and should be able to have your needs met, Halle."

"Honey, can you sit?" Lydia reluctantly stopped pacing and sat down. "Wait there one second, okay?"

"Okay."

Halle noted Lydia's hands went straight to her stomach. Happy that Lydia wouldn't disappear back upstairs, she slipped out to the garage. She'd been preparing for this. At some point, Halle knew Lydia would have an epiphany that Halle would be better with someone else. She hadn't seen the open marriage angle coming.

Reaching to the top shelf, Halle brought down the glass Mason jar she'd been hiding. Taking the decorated notepad, she jotted down her thoughts and popped it in the jar.

Okay, here goes!

"So, I want you to know, I heard you about the open marriage idea. But I'm going to decline."

"Halle, I'm not—"

"Can I talk? Please?"

Lydia nodded, wiping a tear from under her eye. Settling next to her wife, Halle placed the Mason jar on the coffee table.

"What's that?" Lydia's voice was husky and raw. Halle hated the fact she'd got herself into such a state.

"This is for you. Will you open it?"

Looking unsure, Lydia regarded Halle, and then, for several seconds, the jar. Eventually, curiosity won out. **"Perfectly imperfect, broken parts included!"** she mumbled, reading the label on the jar.

"You always tell me you are flawed and broken, Lyds. Every time I tell you, you're perfect to me, that's been your answer. So, I made you this."

"What is it?"

"Take a look."

With a shaky hand, Lydia grasped the lid on the jar and unscrewed it. Pulling out the first piece of paper her fingers touched, she gently unfolded it. Tears sprung unshed as she read what was on the paper. Dropping the note, she reached for another; then another.

"Halle," she breathed through a sob.

"This is the latest one." Halle slipped the note she'd written in the garage into Lydia's hand.

You tell me your belly is fat. That you're the size of a whale. I'm telling you it's perfect. Your so-called imperfect tummy is holding our children, keeping them safe and warm until they are ready to come into the world.

"I'll have ugly stretch marks," Lydia sob-chuckled as she gripped the note.

"And I'll remind you, those marks you see as another flaw, are a reminder of the wonderful thing you did. The lives you created and housed."

"Oh Halle, I'm sorry."

"Sooo, the open marriage is off the table, yeah?" It was safe to joke now. The storm had passed. Lydia's eyes were clearer.

"I'll kick your arse if you go near another woman."

"Thought as much," Halle laughed, taking Lydia into her arms.

"When did you do all this?" Lydia asked, picking up the discarded notes, putting them carefully back in the jar.

"I started six months ago when you were really struggling emotionally. I knew it was baby hormones, but that didn't take away from the fact you saw, or should I say, see yourself, in such a negative light. I wanted you to know, for every imperfection you see, I witness the opposite."

"Like my laugh lines," Lydia smiled, holding up a note.

"Exactly. You see wrinkled eyes. I see memories of all our fun together. You have a wonderful laugh, and I love it when it reaches your eyes."

"And my hips?" Lydia caressed the note gently.

"Those are my favourite! You see 'muffin tops,'" Halle rolled her eyes playfully. "I see womanly curves that are so sexy I can hardly speak when I see you naked."

"Oh, you big charmer." Lydia nuzzled into Halle's neck, laughing through a hiccup.

"Only for you, honey."

"You got this, babe!"

"Oh, fuck off, Halle, this is your fault!" Lydia was puce and currently grinding Halle's metacarpals to dust.

"All my fault, honey, got it! Now push."

"You push!" Lydia growled.

"I would if I could, sweetheart."

"I can't do this, Halle." Tears streamed down Lydia's face.

"Yes, you can. You're almost there."

The wailing cries of their third baby echoed through the delivery suite. Lydia fell back, exhausted, crying, and happy.

"And here's baby number three," Elise laughed, handing the infant over to a nurse. "Let's get you cleaned up, Lydia."

Halle stood staring at her wriggling kids. It had shocked both of them to learn Lydia followed in Fe's footsteps and conceived triplets. They'd been warned that multiple babies were a possibility, but they'd never really worried about it. Until Elise had showed them three heartbeats, of course, and Halle nearly passed out.

"Are they okay?" Lydia asked, exhausted.

"They're perfect. Oh, honey, you did so good."

"Ready for some skin-on-skin?" One of the four nurses asked. Lydia nodded, beaming as their first girl was laid on her chest. Girl number two was shortly put on the other side.

Shedding her t-shirt, Halle happily accepted their little boy onto her body. "Oh, wow. You are the cutest thing, little man."

"He looks like you. They all do." Lydia kissed the top of her daughters' heads. They'd decided to ask one of Halle's family members for help in the donation department. Harrison didn't mind at all. He was still happy to be an uncle.

"They have your eyes, babe, and your lips," Halle answered. The triplets had Halle's bronze skin, but there was no doubt in her mind who they looked like. "They're gorgeous."

"Mmm," Lydia mumbled, already close to sleep.

"They look like squished pigs," Joey commented, peering down into the triplets' cot.

"Smell like them, too," Jenny replied.

"You guys were the same when you were babies," Lydia laughed quietly.

"And you were super stinky," Halle added, making them laugh.

"Come on you three, let's leave the little ones to sleep," Lydia whispered.

Joey, Jenny, and Jack ran out of the room, already over the excitement of having new cousins. Halle and Lydia chuckled when they heard Fe trying to wrangle her kids. It was getting late in the day and everyone was ready for some sleep. Lydia had been home for a week and she was knackered. Three babies were a lot!

"Grab a shower, babe. I'll make you a cup of tea." Halle kissed Lydia's temple, ushering her out of the kids' room.

Lydia couldn't believe how hard it was to leave her children, even just to go shower. Halle was just as bad. They'd caught one another several times, sneaking into the triplets' room when they were supposed to be doing something else.

Shedding her clothes, Lydia happily stood under the shower spray for ten minutes. It was only when she started falling asleep and her head butted the wall; she knew it was time to get out.

Drying off, Lydia's eyes caught her reflection. Instead of lingering, she lifted her gaze to the framed note above the mirror Halle had given to her on that night she'd stupidly suggested an open marriage.

Looking back at herself, she studied her stomach, letting her hands drift over her still swollen belly and stretch marks.

"Perfectly imperfect," she whispered to herself, smiling.

"Perfect," Halle echoed from the door.

Lydia met her wife's eyes in the mirror. "Broken parts included," Lydia smiled.

Afterword

Thank you for reading Broken Parts Included.
Please spare a few more minutes of your time by heading
over to Amazon and Goodreads to leave a review.

Other Titles By Alyson Root

A Dance Towards Forever

Diving Into Her

Always Emilie

The Misadventures of Callie Compton

Broken Parts Included

Love & Other Wild Things

Finding Molly Parsons

Keeping Carmen Ruiz

The Wisdom of Bug

Sleigh Bells Ring

Risking Immortality
Waiting for Eternity
Fighting for Infinity

Acknowledgements

All I can say is thank you to the team of wonderful women who support me. Not just in my writing, but in life.

About the author

Alyson was born and raised in the heart of England. She moved to Paris in 2015 when she met her wife. Together they moved to the west of France, where they now live with their two dogs. Alyson spends her time reading sapphic fiction books, writing and Scuba Diving.

Alyson discovered her love of writing in her mid-thirties. Her debut book, *A Dance Towards Forever,* was inspired by her wife and their very own love story. Alyson wrote *Diving Into Her* and award-winning *Always Emilie,* which added with her first book, created The French Connection series.

www.alysonroot.com

a.rootauthor@alysonroot.com

HUMAN
AUTHORED™

THE
Authors Guild®

6296767